SUSAN

Born in the London slums, her mother dead
in childbirth, her father in and out of prison,
Susan, at twelve, is placed in an orphanage.
Rebelling against the strict discipline, she
runs away to Soho and becomes involved in
the sordid world of prostitution. Life looks
up when she meets a tough Cockney criminal
with a heart of gold. She swears to become an
honest woman but is forced to break her
promise when Billy is jailed. A lucky encoun-
ter sends her to Devon and a respectable job,
but her past catches up with her and threatens
her new-found happiness.

A MESSAGE
TO THE CHARNWOOD READER
FROM THE PUBLISHER

Since the introduction of Ulverscroft Large Print Books, countless readers around the world have confirmed that the larger and clearer print has brought back the pleasure of reading to an ever-widening audience, thus enabling readers to once again enjoy the companionship of books which had previously been denied to them due to their inability to read normal small print.

It is obvious that to cater for this ever-widening audience of readers a new series was necessary. The Charnwood Series embraces the widest possible variety of literature from the traditional classics to the most recently published bestsellers, and includes many authors considered too contemporary both in subject and style to be suitable for the many elderly readers for whom the original Ulverscroft Large Print Books were designed.

The newly developed typeface of the Charnwood Series has been subjected to extensive and exhaustive tests amongst the international family of large print readers, and unanimously acclaimed and preferred as a smoother and easier read. Another benefit of this new typeface is that it allows the publication in one volume of longer novels which previously could only be published in two large print volumes: a constant source of frustration for readers when one volume is not available for one reason or another.

The Charnwood Series is designed to increase the titles available to those readers in this ever-widening audience who are unable to read and enjoy the range of popular titles at present only available in normal small print.

LENA KENNEDY

SUSAN

Complete and Unabridged

CHARNWOOD
Leicester

First published in Great Britain in 1984 by
Macdonald & Co. (Publishers) Ltd.
London

First Charnwood Edition
published March 1985
by arrangement with
Macdonald & Co. (Publishers) Ltd.
London

British Library CIP Data

Kennedy, Lena
    Susan.—Large print ed.
    Charnwood library series
    I. Title
    823'.914[F]   PR6061.E597

    ISBN 0-7089-8248-4

Published by
F. A. Thorpe (Publishing) Ltd.
Anstey, Leicestershire
Set by Rowland Phototypesetting Ltd.
Bury St. Edmunds, Suffolk
Printed and bound in Great Britain by
T. J. Press (Padstow) Ltd., Padstow, Cornwall

To Margaret, my typist,
who stood by me in times of adversity.

1

A Bad Start

SUE'S thoughts drifted back to the earliest days of her childhood, when she played barefooted in the slum back streets, and pushed a shabby old pram full of babies to the park during the school holidays. She vividly recalled the squabbles and fights with the other kids, and particularly the bigger boys who swore every other word, told filthy jokes and exposed themselves behind the bushes, beckoning the girls to come and have a look at them. Yes, she could remember all that very well. But most of all she could remember a particular day, which came back to her now like a bad dream, when the police came charging through the house after her lively Cockney father who tried desperately to escape from them by scrambling over the roof tops. Young Sue had watched the chase in bewilderment but then she knew that an accident had followed, because of the commotion—the crowds milling about, the white ambulance that came and went and, most of all, her little mother screaming hysterically. No one bothered to explain to that skinny little girl what had happened, but she, quietly minding her twin brothers in the kitchen, knew that it was something bad.

The following day, her grief-stricken mother had collapsed down on the bare floor-boards, gasping and clutching her swollen belly. "Get the midwife, Sue!" she cried.

On long thin legs Sue had run down the street to fetch the old crone who returned with her, shuffling in old carpet slippers and carrying a large straw shopping bag.

Later that day, the ambulance came to the street once again, and her mother, covered with a red blanket, disappeared to hospital. For some hours afterwards, the neighbours stood about gossiping; some wept.

So then it was goodbye to the drab slum house with its dirty linen and faded wallpaper. How often since, she wondered, had her heart ached for that squalid room, where she used to sit up in bed surrounded by her grubby brothers and sisters, and share a sticky piece of nougat with them while she told them fairy tales? But it was no more. The back street home was replaced by a hard white bed, painted walls and three substantial meals a day, with a prayer before and after.

Nine years old, with her dark hair hanging on two long pigtails, Sue had stared insolently at the matron of the children's home, and carefully sized up the situation. Her cheeks had been so well scrubbed that they tingled, and rebellion seethed in her young breast. Let them start, she thought angrily; she was ready for them. They had taken the twins away from her earlier, without even letting her see them. Tears welled up in her eyes but she forced them back. She was not going to cry, she would not let them see how much they had hurt her. She hated these Nosey Parkers, and they were not going to keep her in this rotten school, she vowed, no matter how hard they tried.

"She's quite intelligent," explained Miss Woodcote, the welfare officer, to the matron. "It's a pity she came from such a bad home, with the father in and out of prison."

"Well, we get all kinds here," the matron replied placidly. "She'll soon settle down."

Sue spent three years at Barham House. She absconded twice and was brought back by the police on both occasions. How she hated the place! It never changed. Every day was dreary and monotonous. They did the same things at the same times in the same places. They ate the same old food, read the same old books and played with the same old jigsaw puzzles. Sue grew big and very tall, and her dark eyes became angry and brooding. It was not that anyone was unkind to her, it was just that she was starved of affection when her young heart was crying out to be loved and to give love.

Nearly twelve and her figure had begun to fill out. She had long, perfectly formed legs, and her small breasts were like spring buds as they pushed

3

shape into the sack-like gingham dress she had to wear. Her dresses always had the same faded light-blue checks. Sometimes they were too long, sometimes they were too short but always they were too tight around the bust for Sue. But Sue had seldom seen herself in a full-length mirror, and was quite unconcerned about her shape. When she walked, she leaned forwards slightly and took long, boyish strides. And her face always had a surly, hang-dog expression.

"Sue has settled nicely," remarked Miss Woodcote on one of her infrequent visits.

"Yes," replied the new young matron. "The staff all agree that she has changed considerably since I came." She beamed.

Miss Woodcote sipped her tea in an absent-minded manner. "I'm pleased to get a good report of Sue. She was a big problem here at first."

"She likes to see you," said Matron. "No one else has ever visited her."

"I'm afraid that this is my last visit," replied Miss Woodcote. "I'm leaving the service, and going to Africa on mission work, something I have always fancied."

"How nice," replied Matron, "but Sue will really miss you." She paused. "I must say, she is very handy with the small children."

"That's just as well," replied Miss Woodcote. "If she hadn't settled down here it would have been reform school for her, after the trouble she has caused." She placed her tea cup carefully on

4

the table beside her. "A slight hazard has cropped up concerning Sue," she said. "Her father will shortly be paroled. He is a very embittered man and permanently crippled by the fall he had while being arrested."

Matron nodded and sighed. "Oh dear," she said, "what troubles lie ahead for Sue, then? If her father claims her, I'll be forced to let her go."

"Yes," replied Miss Woodcote, "and most of our hard work will have been for nothing." She picked up her gloves. "I have to admit that I won't be sorry to leave the welfare service. Will you say goodbye to Sue for me? I don't think I can face it."

Thus Sue's only friend from the outside world was preparing to abandon her. Miss Woodcote had been the one who brought sweets and talked to her about that little back street called home. At first Sue had been waiting anxiously in the corridor for her, but then she had gone outside to listen to the women's conversation at the half-open window. Now she had heard enough. Sullenly, she hugged her long arms tight about her. Tucked under the faded cardigan, her nails bit viciously into her skin. She kicked her heels against the wall and her dark eyes squinted. "Beasts!" she muttered. "Mean, evil beasts!" She seethed at the fact that they were making plans and talking about her like that after all the work she had done for them, each morning sitting the little kids on pots which she then had the dirty job of emptying. Blast them! Who wanted to see the old man anyway? Hadn't he been the cause of her getting shut up in here in the first place?

Several girls wandered past, talking and giggling with each other. As Sue stared scornfully at them, her angry scowl centred on one child in particular, a dainty, pretty girl with long flaxen curls. "That stuck-up Lily Davies, I'll give her a bashing," muttered Sue. And without warning, she pounced, grabbing those silken tresses and viciously punching the other child. The two girls rolled over and over on the green lawn scratching and biting between shrill screaming. Other children ran quickly to the house. "Miss! Miss!" they called. "Come quick, Sue's hurting Lily Davies again."

A few minutes later, Sue stood defiantly before the shocked matron. And as Miss Woodcote's car left the drive, Sue was marched off for punishment.

At the age of thirteen, Sue was still living at Barham House. The head girl in a posh private school could not hold more sway than did Sue in this house for under-privileged children. After the departure of Miss Woodcote and the affair of Lily Davies, the sweet but firm matron, whose pink-and-white complexion could get extremely mottled in agitation, spoke kindly to this confused child and seemed to inspire her confidence. "Promise me, dear," she begged, "you will never eavesdrop again. If there is anything that you want to know, come to me and we will discuss it together."

Untouched, Sue had weighed her up. She was soft this one, she reflected. It wouldn't be hard to kid her. And with this thought, she appeared to give in gracefully.

Matron was sadly understaffed at the home. Sue was a strong girl, so it made good sense to give her some responsibility which would keep her occupied and out of trouble. "I'll make you a monitor, Sue," coaxed Matron. "But you must promise that you will never again be violent as you were to Lily Davies."

"Never liked her," Sue replied flatly, sucking on the boiled sweet that Matron had given her.

"Well, Lily's gone home now, so that's the end of that," sighed Matron, "but please try and control your temper, Sue, or it will be the undoing of you."

At night, Sue was dormitory monitor, mornings, she was baby minder and in between she was Matron's pet. Naughty children were smacked or fussed as required. With her dark eyes always on the alert, Sue kept order and made herself very useful. She grew big and strong and very capable. That last year at Barham House proved to be the happiest of her youth. In spite of the monotony, the dreary, unchanging meals and long prayers, the baby washing and ironing, it had become part of her life. At last, Sue was completely institutionalized.

7

One sunny afternoon, as Sue sat in a window-seat munching an apple and gazing towards the main gate, the ramshackle taxi from the station pulled up in the drive. There was something vaguely familiar about the man who got out. He walked slowly as if in pain, and grasped a walking-stick to support him. Behind him emerged a plump peroxide blonde.

As she ate her apple, Sue surveyed them dreamily. She was quite unconcerned. They are probably some kid's parents coming to take her home, she decided, and she dismissed them from her mind.

Not long after, Matron hurried down the corridor with a flushed and anxious face. "Sue!" she called, "I'd like to talk to you."

Casually, Sue got up from her seat and went into Matron's office. Just inside the door the cripple who had arrived in the taxi came towards her, hands outstretched. "Sue! My dear little Sue!" he cried.

Sue looked down in horror at this shrivelled little man whom she recognized now as her own father. But he was not the tall good-looking father she had always remembered; instead, he was an aged and wrinkled wreck of a man. Matron put a steady arm about her as she backed away. "These are your parents, Sue," she explained gently. "They've come to visit you."

"We ain't come on no visit," the blonde

woman's loud grating voice broke in. "We've come to take 'er 'ome."

"Take me home?" gasped Sue. "I live here. Anyway," she added, giving an aggressive stare at the woman, "who's she?"

"She's your new mother, Sue," her father wheezed.

"I'm not going," she declared obstinately, tossing back her head. "I'm all right here."

"But we've made a nice comfortable 'ome for yer," her father begged. "I want to make up for all the years you've 'ad to spend in this place."

Matron had become slightly annoyed. She straightened her back even more than usual. "I hope you have the necessary papers to take her away," she said tersely. "I will not let Sue go without the correct authorization."

"Let's get it over," said Sue's new stepmother, Lil, briskly. "Here are the papers." She thrust them in front of Matron. "We can't afford to make this journey twice."

In a flash, Sue made for the door. Matron did not try to stop her. She wanted time to try and reason with this dogmatic woman and her sick-looking husband. But it was hopeless. They were determined. "Sue's a big girl, her father is sick and needs her," insisted Lil. "We'll take her home today. Get her things ready. We'll wait."

Unable to do more, Matron packed Sue's few belongings in a plastic bag, consoling the girl with promises that she would do her best to get her back. Matron then accompanied them to the station to say goodbye. There were tears in her eyes. She had come to love this wayward child, and so the parting between them was not easy.

Wearing a long tweed coat, and a red ribbon in her hair, Sue sat in the corner of the train compartment scowling at her stepmother who nagged continuously. "Think yourself lucky, my girl," she said. "There's plenty in that place would like to have a good home."

Her father spoke seldom, but his face twisted constantly in pain. Sue sat motionless, her dark eyes gleaming such hatred that Lil began to get worried. She had not minded taking on an invalid husband, but she had not bargained for his difficult daughter as well. As the two surveyed each other, Sue wondered what had induced this cold, common woman to marry the hunched-up shell her father was. No doubt a fair nest-egg— the proceeds of the robbery that had destroyed his home and family—had been the bait.

Lil's home was in Camden Town. It was a small flat in a depressed area where a quarter of the population were immigrants. Sue's first impressions of her new home were lace curtains, paper roses, a plastic mat outside the door and the smell of furniture polish. And the moment she entered she felt depressed. When she met Lil's son, Tommy, a goofy, bespectacled boy of about twelve who stared mockingly at her old-fashioned coat and the red ribbon bow on her hair, she disliked him on sight, and felt even gloomier. How was she going to survive here?

Sue tried desperately hard to acclimatize herself to her new family but she found that she hated Lil and Tommy increasingly each day, particularly since they did not bother to hide their own feelings about her. To her father she was kind and considerate. She took off his shoes for him at night and put them back on in the morning. With his dead weight on her arm, she escorted him to the paper shop every morning and to Mass on Sundays. While in prison, her father had taken up again with his religion, and since the onset of his illness, he had spent many hours on his knees with his rosary beads. Now Sue would kneel stolidly beside him in the church. The stained-glass windows and flickering candles cast golden light on the beautiful statues around them, and the atmosphere was one of peace and tranquillity. But none of this made any impression on Sue. Her mind would tick over as she made plans to escape from the domestic web she was caught in.

At her new school she was a problem. Sue had received very little education at Barham House. All the years of baby-minding and washing, added to the fact that she was word blind, made her unable to compete with children of her own age. So in the overcrowded secondary modern school where she had been sent, she was the tallest girl and the biggest dunce. It was not long

11

before she had earned herself the nickname of "Soppy Sue" from the other pupils because she was so slow to learn anything. Friendless and bored, Sue would sit at the back of the class casting malevolent glances about her at anyone who dared look at her. The teaching staff also disliked her, for she was always violent and every breaktime there was invariably a fight to break up which involved Soppy Sue.

Life had become a little better at home. Lil worked all day in a factory. Mondays, Wednesdays and Fridays were bingo nights when she would go out straight from work. On Tuesdays she would gather up a big bag of washing and dash out of the flat on the pretext of going down to the launderette. Then she would return after ten o'clock, always smelling of port wine. On Thursdays she did stay at home in the evenings. With her platinum hair-do bound up in a turban and her large frame covered with a spotted nylon overall, she would systematically clean the flat. She swept, dusted and polished every corner and woe betide anyone who got in her way. Red-faced, bad-tempered and perspiring Lil was always to be avoided on Thursdays. On these days, Sue wandered the streets and hung about at the corner of the streets or in the playground. The playground was a concrete square which swarmed with kids of every colour and creed. They all congregated there each evening, fighting to get places on the swings and roundabouts. "Give us a push, Sue!" the younger children would cry out to her as she watched them from her position by the flower-beds. And because she had nothing else to do, she would obligingly push them high in the swing, ignoring the jeers from the girls of her own age who loudly chanted a street song, "Look at Soppy Sue". They stood in groups smoking cigarettes, wearing lipstick and high-heeled shoes as they chatted about sex and dating boys. But whenever Sue approached, all conversation ceased. "Have to be careful of her," they would murmur as they drifted off, "she's not quite the ticket."

Now nearly fourteen, Sue was a lonely and strangely naive girl, a square peg in a round hole in this working-class community. Her life was not made any easier by the persistent persecution of Tommy, her stepbrother, who, with his gang of mates, would follow her about calling, "Ol' Soppy Sue! Ol' Soppy Sue!" Sue would turn on them and chase them so that they fled in all directions but she could never catch them. She was nearly always the last to leave the park before it closed because she was searching to get Tommy. With her hands in the pockets of her old-fashioned coat, and her dark hair hanging wildly, she did not make a pretty picture as she hid near the park keeper's hut hoping to pounce on that nasty boy.

The old park keeper had recently been replaced by a younger, ruddy-faced man in his thirties.

13

This particular evening, Sue's dark eyes watched him as he stood in the doorway in his peaked cap and uniform munching a bar of chocolate. Sue was very fond of chocolate; few bars had ever found their way to Barham House. The park keeper noticed her looking hungrily at him. "Want a piece?" he asked.

"Oh! yes please," Sue replied, moving towards him. As he halved the bar, his bright blue eyes scrutinized her tight dress and the shape of her bud-like breasts. "Better cut along home, your ma will be looking for you," he said.

"I'll be lucky," she said. "She doesn't care."

The young man moved closer to her, all sympathy as Sue told him of Barham House. He too had spent his youth locked away, so he knew what it was like. Sue was very happy to be able to talk to somebody else about her problems.

Next evening, the park keeper beckoned her to wait until all the kids had left the park. "Got a big bar of Milk Tray in my hut," he said casually.

The thought of this mouth-watering delicacy induced Sue to help him chase all the other kids out of the park, including Tommy, before joining her new-found friend in his little wooden hut.

She sat on the table with her legs wide apart as he shut the door. "Come on, part up," she said eagerly. She held out her hand expectantly, unperturbed by the fact that he had taken off his peaked cap, to reveal a semi-bald pate, or that his eyes shone with extraordinary brilliance or that his breathing was short and heavy. All she thought about was that much-fancied bar of chocolate. He approached her, holding the packet up high. "Here you are, Sue, see if you can reach it," he said coaxingly. And as she leaned back, reaching out for that prize, he pressed himself close to her.

Eagerly she grabbed the sweet, tearing off the tin-foil wrapping, and biting into the soft brown bar. "Want some?" she asked, her mouth full.

"No," he said. His voice was thick and muffled as he fiddled with his clothes. "Shall I tickle you, Sue?" he muttered as his hand crept up her skirt. Sue hardly heard him as she munched her feast of chocolate. "Like this . . ." he gasped, his hand fondling her soft flesh.

"Scrumptious," nodded Sue, relishing the sweet flavour of the bar. She had now realized that he was lying almost on top of her and was quite agitated but she was not sure that she minded or was bothered. "Come on, Sue," he urged. "Lift up your skirt. You show me and I'll show you." He exposed himself to her and for a few moments she gazed dispassionately at this display of hair and flesh.

Suddenly, over the top of the door, Tommy's grubby face appeared. "Yah!" he yelled. "I can see yer." Then he dropped out of sight and fled.

Immediately, the keeper leapt back and grabbed his trousers. "Get out of here, you little slut!" he yelled at Sue. "Get out!"

15

"Don't do your nut," returned Sue calmly, and, cool as cucumber, she slid off the table.

"Get out of here!" he screeched, "and if you tell anyone, I'll slit your throat, you dirty bitch!" Nonchalantly, Sue drifted out the door, licking the final traces of chocolate from her lips. She took her time walking home, and was surprised to be met by an irate band of local residents led by Lil who was brandishing a poker.

"You ain't 'alf gonna cop it," yelled Tommy as he dashed past.

Lil caught Sue firmly by the arm. "Come on, my girl, we'll deal with that dirty bugger first, and then I'll settle with you."

The angry crowd moved on down to the park where the keeper was duly beaten up and only saved from a worse fate by being arrested by the police. Sue herself was soon placed under the care and protection of the state once more.

There followed the trial in the magistrate's court during which the nice young probation officer had described those sordid moments in the hut in such a nice manner. Sue had almost laughed aloud to hear the words, uttered so precisely: "He said that if she would show her private parts he would show his private parts . . ."

The old magistrate had stared at the prisoner in disgust.

"The defendant is suffering from diminished responsibility," pleaded his counsel. "He has been in the care of the state for many years. This child is very precocious, and she clearly encouraged him."

So it went on, like a game of tennis, with volley after volley of disgusting evidence. And Sue did not strengthen her case by telling the court that she did not mind being tickled.

At the end of it all, the park keeper was sent to a mental institution for treatment, and Sue, whose interests were taken up by the Roman Catholic priest who argued that an approved school would do her more harm than good, was to be sent to the convent where a watchful eye would be kept on her until she reached a more sensible age.

Thus our erring young delinquent was to find herself at St. Augustine's Convent. When Sister Agnes came to collect her, her mild manner and sweet gentle face had not the slightest effect on Sue. The harassed nun had not relished the task of separating a young girl from her family and had been expecting a scene. She was surprised. With a white face and hard eyes Sue stood by the door waiting for her. She was still wearing the old tweed coat that Barham House had furnished her with, and a small suitcase lay at her feet. "Come on, Sister, let's get it over with," Sue said abruptly as the nun arrived. "I'm ready."

The gentle sister looked for signs of tears, but the dark, inscrutable eyes stared back at her with no display of emotion at all. In the armchair by the fire, her father wept copious tears of self-pity, while behind him, with arms akimbo, his large spouse waited for Sue to leave. "Sexy bitch," she had declared earlier. "Never will be any good, and I've my Tommy to think of."

"Goodbye, Susan," she now said firmly and with no warmth in her voice.

"Why don't you say what you mean?" sneered Sue. "Good riddance would be more like it."

As Lil paled and Tommy sniggered, the sister hurriedly drew her cloak about her. "Come along, my dear," she said kindly and ushered Sue away.

Even from the beginning, the convent was a let-down to Sue. She had eagerly left the unsympathetic atmosphere of Lil's poky flat, dreaming of warmth and affection, and the green fields and good, if dreary, food of Barham House. The convent, she thought, would be like that. But as they entered the iron gates of St. Augustine's, her heart gave a leap and she had an almost overpowering desire to turn and run out again. It was too late. The gates closed with an ominous clang which made her shudder. But she kept on walking, keeping in step with the sprightly Sister Agnes in her long flowing robes.

She followed the nun through long cold corridors, past dark alcoves from which small statues peered, and the huge pictures of the blood-streaked face of Our Lord, which adorned the walls. They meant nothing to her; the disturbed mind of this child was not to find the

18

peace and sanctity that the other inhabitants shared within these pious walls.

They entered the great dining hall as tea was being eaten. Sue was sat on a bench where she gulped down weak tea and ate bread and jam while she surveyed those around her who were to be her companions for the next two years. They were mostly Mongol children whom no one had wanted, and who had now grown old. With their little short bodies and fuzzy heads, they were unwanted humans, pushed out of sight by families who were ashamed of them.

Sue looked fearfully at them as they stared inquisitively at her. Her tall, well-proportioned body, seemed completely out of place amid this flotsam and jetsam of humanity who acted still as if they were little children. Sue recoiled in horror at the sight around her; it was almost too much to bear. But Sister Agnes placed a cool hand in hers. "Come now, Sue, come and meet our girls. And don't look like that. They're not monsters, you know. You will find them all intelligent, warm and very loving."

But Sue could not move. She remained rooted to the spot, staring still in shock, so the kind nun left her alone and went off laughing with her little people as they left the dining hall.

Sue sat on a seat in the empty hall, feeling very alone and very forlorn and wondering how she might escape this terrible place.

It was at that moment that Gladys appeared.

Very self-important, she came into the hall pushing along a large bath chair which contained a pale, shrivelled shape of a fair young girl. Gladys stopped directly level with Sue. "Brought any goodies in with you?" she enquired.

"If you mean sweets, no, I did not," replied Sue with open hostility.

"All right," said Gladys, "keep your shirt on, I only asked. It's not so bad in here, you know," she said conversationally. Sue did not reply.

"Oh," said Gladys wisely, "I know what you're thinking, but I'll tell you, we ain't all as potty as we look."

This comical remark suddenly made Sue relax. She laughed and Gladys laughed, so they both laughed until tears ran down their faces. And so began the precious, life-long friendship between Gladys and Sue.

2

Convent Girls

SLOWLY but surely the convent disciplined Sue as no place had ever been able to do before. At first there were periods of disobedience and the aftermath of punishment. A wet towel was bound over her face to prevent her blaspheming; she was subjected to a solitary cell and a diet of bread and water for refusing to complete her chores; and she spent many hours of penance, kneeling beside stout Sister Winifred until her knees were stiff and sore. But she was young and hardy, and she survived, especially since she had her new friend Gladys there to share her sorrow or joy.

It did not take long for Sue and Gladys to become a team; they were hand in glove in all the little conspiracies that took place in the convent. For although Gladys always managed to keep out of trouble, craftily and steadfastly, she had broken every rule in that tightly run establishment. They shared a dormitory with several epileptic girls who occasionally brought added excitement to the nights by throwing fits, as did two little midget sisters who constantly fought each other tooth and nail. Gladys and Sue would urge them on to fight and then sit back to watch them struggling with each other stripped to the waist, their dried-up breasts swinging from their brown-skinned bodies. The sisters would wrestle and fight, kicking each other with little bandy legs, until they had become so excited that Sue and Gladys would smother them with pillows and sit on them until they had cooled down again. After a morning filled with prayer and schooling, and an afternoon spent standing in the steaming laundry washing clothes, this macabre fun provided relief for the girls. And so they managed to create a fairly reasonable existence for themselves.

Time rolled by, and soon Sue was sixteen. She had a tall and upright figure and in a loud and vibrant voice, she bullied her less capable inmates into shape. As in the children's home, Sue had established herself in a position of trust. The nuns had soon discovered that she was willing and very hard working, but part of her popularity came from her strong, pure singing voice. Sue could not read a word of Latin—it was unintelligible language to her—but the words she learnt by ear came from her long white throat in sweet, clear notes that were greatly appreciated by the nuns and priests of St. Augustine's.

Every morning at nine o'clock, Sue marshalled her squad of inmates, all dressed in striped cotton frocks, into the front row of the church. The children who attended the day school would laugh at the sight, and sit whispering and giggling at this queer assortment of females, whose heads were too large, and whose bodies were warped and misshapen. Some would not sit still, some twisted and turned uncontrollably, some rolled their eyes to Heaven. But on the first note of the organ their silver voices were raised up in praise of the Lord and rang through the church. All who heard them were spellbound. The Silly Girls Choir, as the congregation called it, had become the most magnificent in the district. They received invitations to sing in other places of worship, and once they even went to perform in Westminster Cathedral. As leader of the choir, Sue enjoyed this notoriety and the extra luxuries it brought—sweets and fruit, occasionally even cinema tickets.

That Sue was very capable there was no doubt. And some were misled by her apparent good behaviour. "You can never tell," remarked Mother Theresa to Sister Winifred, "Sue may even get a vocation to stay within the Church before she is eighteen."

Slightly more worldly, Sister Winifred only sniffed and ran her beads through her fingers as she muttered a prayer.

"Yes, Sue has settled in nicely," continued Mother Superior. "And no one seems to want her. I heard from Father Paul that her father has entered the hospital for the dying, poor man. Yes,

I shall definitely ask for Sue to stay on. I'll write to her probation officer today . . ."

As her future was being discussed, Sue had other things on her mind. She was in the hot, steamy laundry with her pal Gladys, sorting through a basket of old clothes the nuns had collected. Everything in it had to be repaired, washed and ironed, and then distributed to charity. With her head bent, she whispered down to the sphinx-like Gladys beside her, "I'm going to get myself a fella," she said in a mysterious tone.

Unmoved, Gladys held up an old dress for inspection. "How're you going to manage that?" she whispered in reply.

"On Saturday, when we go to the pictures," returned Sue. "I've seen one I fancy."

Now Gladys looked slightly astonished but went on rummaging through the clothes basket. If Sue said something was so, it was no use arguing.

Every Saturday afternoon, Sister Agnes escorted a small party of girls to the corner of the road where the cinema was situated. Sue was in charge of this favoured group and, of course, it always included her friend Gladys and various inmates who happened to be in her good books that week. The local people out shopping often stopped to stare as they passed by. They did make quite a sight, with Sue striding along in front, her long, shapeless cotton dress billowing out behind her like a ship in full sail, followed by the crippled ones who were helped on by Gladys. "She looks sane enough," people would remark, looking at Sue. "But she would not be in there if she was all right, I suppose," they would add. And Sue would pass them by after giving them a long, enigmatic look from those compelling dark eyes that were reminiscent of the Mona Lisa.

Three doors from the cinema was a musical instrument shop. Highly coloured posters and odd instruments adorned the windows but outside the door, always in the same spot, lounged a young man. He wore a dull red shirt and had long flowing hair. Tiny wisps stuck out on his cheeks as he tried in vain to grow a beard. He would puff surreptitiously on a strangely shaped cigarette, holding it behind his back as people passed by, and stare nonchalantly at the Saturday shopping throng in the street. He never noticed the convent girls go by because his mind was on another plan.

"That's me fella," whispered Sue to Gladys. "Ain't he smashing?"

Gladys squinted in his direction but said nothing. She seldom agreed or disagreed with Sue.

"Once we get in the cinema, I'm bunking out again," Sue continued. "I'll leave you in charge and I'll bring you back a comic," she promised.

Gladys' deep-set eyes gleamed. "Make it a horror comic—*Spiderman* or *Batman*," she said excitedly. If there was one dark obsession in her life, it was for horror comics. Gladys could not read but she would sit staring wide-eyed at the lurid pictures, usually in the privacy of the toilet.

"Right, then," said Sue, "I'll pretend to go to the lav. Don't make no fuss, and I'll meet you outside if I can't get back in."

Once all the girls were settled down and engrossed in the film, Sue sneaked out. But once she was outside, all alone in the bright sunlight, her boldness momentarily left her. Pulling herself up sharply she plucked up her courage and walked with her hips swinging to where the young man stood propped up against the doorway. Although she was trembling a little, as she got near, she gave him a provocative smile.

The young man did not seem to notice her. He continued to stare at the passing traffic as though she were not there. She turned and came back, trying the same approach once more with a sweet smile on her lips. But still there was no response. Finally, she stopped right next to him and pretended to look in the shop window, and in a last desperate effort, she smiled right into his face.

The effect was startling. "Scram, floozie!" he snarled. "Get going!"

When Sue did not move, he rushed inside the shop and slammed the door.

With tear-filled eyes, Sue wandered off down the street and went in through the glazed swing doors of Woolworths. There she went slowly around the counters, admiring all the pretty things on display. And before she left, she managed to purloin a brightly coloured slide for her hair and a very horrid comic for Gladys.

After taking a good look at herself in a full-length mirror as she came out of the shop, she returned forlornly to the cinema.

It was not until the girls had all rejoined Sister Agnes on the corner and were returning to the convent that Gladys hung behind to talk to Sue. "How did you get on?" she asked anxiously.

Sue shook her head sadly. "He wouldn't even look at me," she said. Gladys' dark, parchment-like face screwed up in grief. "It's all right, I got your comic, if that is what's bothering you," Sue retorted angrily. She deftly passed the stolen comic to her pal who immediately shoved it down her neck. "He is so lovely," sighed Sue. "I'm mad about him, but have you seen what we look like in these frumpy old dresses? I can't blame him not talking to me, a smart fella like that. I look about forty in this outfit. I'm going to get myself some good gear from somewhere—he might fancy me then."

Gladys squeezed Sue's hand sympathetically. "Hope you get a fella, Sue," she said.

After that disappointing adventure out into the world, Sue was determined to try once more. She had to get herself a fella at all cost. Had she not boasted to the other girls that she would? The

27

following evening she sat up in bed chewing her fingernails. All day she had been moody, and overwhelmed by a kind of melancholy that often obsessed her. She had viciously pinched the arm of one of the midgets until it was black and blue, and she had even struck out at Gladys, who fortunately seemed to be made of wood and was never hurt by blows. Besides, she was too intent at goggling at her comic under the bedclothes, while the little midget cuddled up to her, whimpering pathetically and cried herself to sleep.

Immune from all this, Sue leaned against her pillow, carefully planning how to obtain a wardrobe of with-it gear—a bright tight jumper and a mini skirt. "I've got it!" she suddenly yelled. "I'll pinch some of the clothes from the stuff Sister Agnes collects on her scrounging afternoons."

"But that's all so old-fashioned," declared Gladys momentarily looking up from her comic.

"That don't matter," replied Sue, leaping to her feet. "We'll alter them. The midgets can sew."

A long plaid skirt was quickly filched from the jumble basket and soon much shortened by the midgets whose keen eyes and nimble fingers could do wonders with a needle and thread. And then the sleeves were removed from a white silk jumper that Sue had also pinched from the laundry. At last, on Friday night, Sue paraded up and down the dormitory wearing her new outfit. No high-class Parisian model had ever moved more gracefully than she nor delighted her audience more. And what a sight she was, with a tall, willowy figure, dark hair to her waist, long slim legs that tapered from the short, tight skirt, and her two pointed breasts sticking out stiffly from under the skimpy white jumper. The midgets, Tilly and Milly, jumped up and down with glee but Gladys looked slightly sceptical.

"What's up with you? Don't you like it?" demanded Sue.

Gladys looked down critically at the white ankle socks the convent had provided and the baggy washed-out bloomers that hung two inches below the skirt. "It's all right, Sue," she replied timidly, "but I don't like them drawers hanging down and you ain't got no stockings."

Tears of mortification filled Sue's eyes. Gladys was right. You can't wear a mini skirt with baggy bloomers.

"Cut them short," suggested Milly, eager to help in spite of the way Sue bullied them all.

"I got a piece of lace to sew on them," cried Tilly.

So the bags were cut short and trimmed with lace, and the decision was made not to wear socks. "You've got such lovely legs, Sue," the midget said looking up admiringly from their four feet height to Sue's five feet ten. At last next Saturday's going-out attire was complete. And although the bloomers did not fit exactly underneath, Sue was not worried as long as they did not show.

Saturday was a hot, sunny day. As the convent girls lined up ready for their outing to the cinema, Sister Agnes' face was hot and flushed. It was hard work assembling these afflicted young women, for the least bit of excitement triggered off fits and bursts of disobedience. And Sue, who was usually so dependable, seemed preoccupied today. Tucked into the girl's bodice was a paper parcel and over her arm she carried a raincoat. "That raincoat won't be needed, Sue," the harassed sister told her.

"It might rain," Sue muttered sullenly.

"Nonsense, with all God's beautiful sunshine out there? Take the coat back!" urged the nun. But Sue stuck out her chin in her obstinate manner. Sister Agnes sighed. It was hopeless to argue with Sue. At last she gave the sign for the procession to move out.

Soon the girls were all seated in the second row of the flicks, having left Sister Agnes at the bus-stop, from where she went about her charity work until they came out of the cinema. Sue retired to the Ladies to dress up in her new clothes, and then walked out of the front entrance towards the busy shopping centre. As she approached the music shop, her heart missed a beat. He was not there! Her lovely young man with the red shirt and curly side whiskers had disappeared. Tears came into her eyes. She was so disappointed; all this finery was wasted.

Slowly she trailed down the road in the direction of Woolworths, admiring herself in the shop windows as she passed. Once inside the store, she went from counter to counter, turning over the merchandise. It was the make-up that attracted her most, for she felt a deep envy towards all those teenagers who wore owl-like expressions on their faces, their eyes weighed down with false eyelashes, shadow and mascara. To use make-up was her next ambition. Swiftly, she picked up a small box of eye make-up and slipped it into the pocket of the raincoat she carried over her arm. Then she leaned forward to examine more closely the long sticks of eye-liner. Her tall shape bent like a tree in the wind, exposing long bare legs and pink baggy bloomers.

A young man was wandering nonchalantly around the store, his hands in the pockets of stained painted jeans, a grubby red shirt open at the neck. When he was level with Sue he suddenly stopped and stared with horror at the long bare legs and baggy pants before him. And then the sleepy eyes showed an added glimmer of interest as Sue expertly passed the long stick of eyeliner into the raincoat pocket to join the other articles she had pinched. He shuffled up close to her. "Hi, droopy drawers," he hissed. "I saw you nick that."

Sue stiffened in fear but did not panic.

31

Drawing herself up to her full height she turned to face him. "What are you going to do about it?" she demanded. As the words left her mouth, she saw that confronting her was the lovely young man who usually held up the music shop window. She swallowed hard and her breath came in little gasps as she looked down at him.

The youth stared back at her and grinned appreciatively at the pointed breasts sticking out so defiantly from under the jumper. After a moment of tension, he winked and nudged her with his elbow. "Come on, kid," he said casually, "walk about a bit, yer never know who's watching."

Obediently, she stepped out beside him and they walked round the store. He was called Roger, he told her, and he seemed to be in a chatty mood this afternoon. "Cripes," he said, "you don't 'alf look quaint with those bags hanging down."

"Don't be so cheeky," replied Sue, blushing scarlet with shame.

"Better go over there and nick a pair of tights," he suggested. "Might make yer look a bit more presentable."

Sue stared back at him in astonishment, dumbfounded by this immoral young man who not only made rude comments about her mode of dress but also encouraged her to steal. Whatever would Sister Agnes think of him? But having acquired a fella at last, she was not going to argue with him. "Will a pair of stockings do just as well?" she asked timidly.

"Gawd, gel!" he scoffed. "Where have you been? None of the birds wear stockings now. It's all tights."

Sue remained silent. No one was going to know that she came from that crummy convent. Swiftly she pocketed some black silk tights.

"Got me own group," boasted Roger. Then he added, "Come round to me pad and I'll help you put on them tights." He raised his eyebrows and sniggered but Sue did not notice. So she went with him like a lamb to the slaughter. Having worked so hard to acquire him, this smart young lad, she did not want to upset him.

Roger's pad proved to be rather like himself—dingy and slightly mucky. It was a small dusty room over a shop and contained an old piano and a battered camp bed. Records littered the floor and lurid pop posters adorned the wall.

Sue and Roger sat side by side on the sagging bed. Each time they moved, the smell of stale body odour rose from the bedclothes. Sue sniffed and rubbed her nose disdainfully but kept her mind fixed on pasty-faced Roger who was now lolling back on the bed smoking one of those long cigarettes. "Got to have a couple of puffs to get me going," he explained.

Knowing nothing of the intricacies of pot smoking, Sue did not know what he was talking about. All she wanted was to kiss and cuddle this gorgeous young man, which she then proceeded to do.

Roger was astounded at the warmth and ardour of her embrace. "Here, cool it," he protested. "Wait till I've finished me joint." But Sue pressed him down tight, put hot lips on his and held him down with the weight of her strong body. What happened next was to be expected, but in the middle of it Sue suddenly caught a glimpse of his watch. In horror, she leaped off the bed and charged towards the door clutching those precious tights, still unopened, in her hand. "I've gotta go," she yelled, and then she disappeared, leaving Roger lying on the bed with his trousers down and his mouth wide open.

Back at the cinema, Sue just managed to get into the Ladies to change her clothes and emerge as the bewildered Gladys came out into the foyer with the other convent girls. Gladys was looking worried. "Oh Sue! There you are. I was getting scared," she gasped with relief.

"What of?" shrugged Sue with a prodigious wink. "I was only in the lav."

And Gladys knew that Sue had at last got a fella. But later that night in the dorm, she sat in bed and howled because in all the excitement Sue had forgotten to bring her a comic. However, she was soon consoled by hearing the long and vivid story of Sue's romance with Roger. With her eyes goggling with pleasure she listened to all the lurid details. "Didn't ought to have done that, Sue," she said. "If you get a baby they won't keep you here."

"Oh, well," retorted Sue defiantly, "that's one way of getting out of this gloomy hole."

3

The Pedlar

ALL the next week, although the cold grey walls of the convent school closed her in, in her heart Sue was free. She felt as light as air and bounded about the place like a young deer. She was in such an obliging mood and was so unusually pleasant to the other inmates that Sister Winifred watched her with the utmost suspicion. And there was a moment during choir practice, when Sister Agnes' neat eyebrows shot up in astonishment as Sue's loud sweet voice trilled high during a litany. Instead of three *Ave Marias*, the words that came from Sue's throat as she sang solo, were: "I love you, I love you dear Roger."

Soon Saturday came round again and the little crocodile of girls wended its way past the music shop. Not wanting Roger to see her with this bunch of idiots, Sue hung her head and turned away. But from the corner of her eye, she saw that he seemed preoccupied, his face pale and twitching, as he stood biting his fingers, and she wondered what was wrong.

It was not long before Sue emerged again from the Ladies in the cinema all dressed up in her short plaid skirt and very becoming black silk tights. Her dark hair, shining with brilliantine, hung free down her back, pulled away behind her ear by a little slide. Her eyes were enhanced by shadow and mascara and a line of lipstick coloured her lips. There was little now to link Sue with the convent. She just looked like a typical teenager out on a Saturday afternoon spree. Only her long strides and awkward boyish gait were likely to betray her.

"Buzz off!" snarled Roger as she approached.

Sue frowned in puzzlement. "But, Roger, darling, I'm your girlfriend," she pleaded.

"Some girlfriend," he sneered, "running off and leaving me like that."

But Sue moved closer and put her arms about him. "I'm sorry about that," she lied. "But I had to get back to work."

"Work? What work?" Roger stared suspiciously at her.

"I'm up at the hospital," she continued in a very convincing tone. "They're very strict if you go late on duty." She had acquired this information from a novice nun who had once been a nurse, and it seemed to satisfy Roger.

They walked to Roger's place in silence; he still seemed to be a trifle on edge. And something about his pad was different this week, Sue noticed: suitcases and musical instruments lay all around.

"The boys are back from Spain," explained Roger.

Sue had removed her precious tights and was now looking up at him amorously.

"Turn it up," he said. "We ain't got time now. I've got to go out." But Sue's kisses overwhelmed him. "Okay," he sighed. "I'll do you a favour if you do me one. You let me down last week," he grumbled. "You said you had had a lot of fellas —I didn't know you was a rooky. I mighta got you in the club."

But Sue was not even listening. "Love me, Roger," she whispered romantically, and in a passive sort of manner, he obliged.

"Hurry up," he said afterwards as she slowly replaced her tights. "I told you I gotta go out, didn't I?" From the end of the bed he had taken a bag. It had a long leather strap and was trimmed with a fringe. "Come on, doll, move!" he said in an exasperated fashion, "the boys will be back in a minute."

"All right," Sue replied sullenly, "but I ain't got to go to work yet for another hour."

Roger bit his lip and looked at her thoughtfully with half-shut eyes. "You can come with me if you like," he said finally. "Up London on the tube."

"Will it take long?" she asked with much interest. She had never been to the West End or on a tube.

"Twenty minutes, that's all," replied Roger.

And so, an eager Sue went with Roger on that exciting ride up town on the tube with dodgy Roger, the drug pusher.

At the end of the cinema programme, Gladys came out of the cinema with the girls in her charge and waited anxiously for Sue. She was determined to get her comic this time and had warned Sue not to forget. As the girls waited outside the cinema, Sister Agnes waited anxiously for them at the bus stop. Soon some of the younger girls became frightened and began to cry. Gladys raved at them impatiently and punched them in the way Sue usually did. Then the manager of the cinema came out to quell the disturbance, and rang Mother Superior, at the convent. Eventually, the little group had been reunited with Sister Agnes and returned to the sanctity of their home once more. Once Sue's absence had been noticed, the police were immediately notified.

While all the commotion went on back at the convent, Sue sat proudly beside her fella in the tube as it sped to the centre of London. Excitedly, she looked all around her—up at the coloured advertisements on the walls, across at the other passengers and down at her long, slim legs. She was having a whale of a time! The recurring dream she had had for so long, of being all dressed up in modern gear and out with a smart young man, was all happening. To hell with the convent! Time was passing on golden wings . . .

Beside her, Roger sat silent and upright, clutching his shoulder bag. He chewed his fingernails nervously and seemed to have little to say. But Sue was too happy to mind.

At Oxford Circus they got off the tube and stepped out into the back streets of Soho. Their first stop was a dimly lit coffee bar where crowds of young people sat about listening to loud pop music. Sue could hardly contain herself; her head spun, it was all so exciting.

They ordered two coffees and sat down. Another young man joined them, and Roger removed a small silver packet from his shoulder bag and passed it under the table. Some crisp bank notes were passed back in exchange. Without a word, the strange young man then left.

Sue sipped the milky coffee and tapped her feet to the rhythm of the music. The transactions going on at the table were incomprehensible to her. Next, they moved outside to meet two women standing on a corner. Each of these took a silver packet, and more pound notes were stuffed into the bag. After a while, Roger seemed to get very edgy. "Listen, doll," he said. "Take this bag and go and sit down in the tube station. Don't move, I'll send some people who will say, 'Got the stuff Roger sent me?'"

Sue listened, wide-eyed. "I ought to go to work," she murmured.

"Never mind that rotten job," snapped Roger.

"Help me get rid of this cabbage and we'll have a good time."

Sue did not want to argue, so she took the bag obediently, went into the station and seated herself down on a platform bench. Soon a thin, weedy-looking man whose face was all twisted on one side, approached her. "Got the stuff?" he hissed. "Roger sent me."

Sue handed him a silver packet, took the fiver he gave her and put it in the bag.

Next came a blonde woman with a hard, haggard face. "Okay, duck," she said, "Roger sent me."

Sue handed out the last packet to her and put the money in the bag. Then she sat waiting for Roger to appear. There was still no sign of him. Then, just as a train came swishing in to the station, Roger came rushing down the stairs. His face was deathly white as he snatched the shoulder bag from Sue's arm and jumped aboard the train as the doors were closing. "Scram, you silly cow!" he called to her. "Old Bill's after us."

Sue stood on the platform looking puzzled for a moment, and then she let out a heart-broken wail. "Roger, wait for me!"

As the train started to move out of the station, two broad-shouldered men ran down the stairs and shouted to the guard to stop the train. But it was too late. The guard did not hear, and the train was soon gone.

Sue suddenly felt a cold clammy feeling of fear

creep through her. She had never experienced it before, and she shuddered. The police were after her! With a swift movement she turned and dashed into the ladies' cloakroom, her face ashen, her dark eyes wide with fear. Inside she found the hard-faced blonde, who was just rolling down her sleeve and was about to wash her hands. "Christ, I needed that fix," the woman said on seeing Sue. "I was all in." She stared at Sue for a moment and immediately recognized the look on the girl's face. Without a moment's hesitation, she grabbed Sue by the elbow. "Keep calm, kid!" she hissed, handing Sue her coat and a flowered scarf. "Run in the lav, quick, and pop these on. Then walk out of here coolly and calmly. Don't matter what's going on, take no notice. I'll meet you round the back of the station."

As Sue took the clothes, Elsie turned back to the mirror and slowly put on a layer of scarlet lipstick over the loose-lipped mouth. "Bet yer life they sent for the blue-bottles. But don't you worry," she reassured the terrified girl, "I'll handle them, I'm used to it."

Inside the toilet, Sue squeezed into the tight coat and tied the scarf over her hair. Her hands were shaking and she could hardly stand up because her knees were trembling so much. She emerged from the cubicle and made for the door. Elsie was still at the mirror and winked as she passed by.

42

Sue walked out of the cloakroom, along the platform and then slowly up the stairs to freedom.

Two young policewomen ran past without giving her a glance, hurrying to apprehend Dodgy Roger's female accomplice. But they were to be disappointed, finding only a screeching, swearing prostitute in the ladies' cloakroom. "I'm no bloody pusher," Elsie shouted at them. "If you want any information, you'll have to take me in!" The policewoman did not bother to arrest her. Elsie was too well known to them, but she managed to hold their attention until Sue was safely out of the station.

Sue stood shivering in the doorway of the shop that Elsie told her to go to for what seemed ages. Next door to a dingy bookshop there was an antique stall with a display of all sorts of bric-à-brac. The fat, sweaty man in charge of the stall stared at her suspiciously, but then he said, "Waiting for Elsie?" Sue nodded. "Pop inside, then," he said, pointing to another doorway under a porch. "I'll nark out, and tell yer when I see her coming."

Standing out of sight from the street, Sue looked at the various postcards pinned on the door. One of them informed her that Elsie lived on the third floor and was a model. The first and second floors seemed to be inhabited by models, one of whom was French. Sue surveyed the notices with interest. It must be nice to be a model, she reflected . . .

At last Elsie came tripping along with a sheepish-looking young man. "Thanks, Sam," she said to the stallkeeper when she saw Sue waiting in the porch. "Come on, love, let's go up."

They climbed the stairs to the third floor, and Sue was thrilled to see Elsie's cosy flat with its pink divan and frilly curtains. She had never seen anything so beautiful.

"Pop in there and make a cup of tea, love," said Elsie pointing to a small kitchen. "I won't be long." She unzipped her dress as she spoke. "Won't be a tick," she said pleasantly, closing the bedroom door on herself and her melancholy manfriend.

In the neat tiny kitchen, Sue began to make the tea. The kettle had just boiled and tea leaves were in the pot when Elsie reappeared from the bedroom, now wearing a long housecoat. Sue heard the front door slam as the visitor left.

"That was a bit of luck," remarked Elsie, slipping a pound note into the top of her bra. "Now, let's have a cuppa."

Sue sat silently sipping her hot mug of tea and watching Elsie deftly butter the bread, put thin slices of luncheon meat between them and cut them into neat triangles. Elsie's square white hands were loaded with cheap rings which hovered like butterflies as she arranged the sandwiches on to a plate. She chattered all the time. "I'm on the game, love," she said, "but I expect you've already sussed that." She gave Sue a cheeky grin from her lopsided mouth.

Sue stared at her and thought vaguely that Elsie was not such a bad-looking woman. With her brassy blonde hair and neat shape, it did not seem possible that she was a street woman—one that took money for sex. She knew about that sort of thing; she had often talked it over with Gladys.

Elsie screwed up her eyes and peered straight into Sue's face. "You all right, love?" she asked. "On the stuff, are you?"

"No I'm all right," said Sue quickly, without understanding what Elsie had said. "I was just thinking about Roger."

"Oh, Dodgy Roger," Elsie laughed. "Well, don't love, because he'll soon forget you, I can tell you that now. He only used you, you know. I've seen plenty of his girlfriends come and go, I have." She passed the plate. "Here you are, love. Have a sandwich."

As Sue took a sandwich and nibbled at it greedily, Elsie's shrewd gaze surveyed her. "In spite of your size, you seem very green," she commented. "Where did Roger find you?"

"From the convent," replied Sue without thinking, relishing her sandwich.

"Oh, dear," giggled Elsie. "You must be joking . . . Fancy getting mixed up with that little swine."

Sue frowned at her, offended. "He's my

boyfriend," she insisted. "I'm very much in love with him."

This last remark seemed to annoy Elsie who suddenly became extremely aggressive. Banging her plate down hard on the table, she shouted, "Don't give me that! I'm a whore and I know exactly how much a man is prepared to pay for it and how bloody easy they get over it."

Sue's sandwich stopped half-way to her mouth and she looked at her, horrified. Elsie stamped her feet and yelled, pointing to the scar on her face, "Look at me! See my bloody face? Chivved me, he did. Me own old man did that. Oh, yes, I could tell you a thing or two, ducky." Then suddenly, Elsie put her head down on the table and wept noisily.

Sue moved over to her and touched her arm. "I'm sorry I upset you," she said gently. "I'll go now."

But Elsie caught hold of her hand. "No, don't go, love, it's me, not you. I'm a bleeding junkie, and that stuff don't seem to do much good lately. It wears off too quick." She pointed to the cupboard. "There's a bottle of gin over there, love, get it and we'll have a drink."

And so, for a solid hour, Sue, who had never drunk or smoked before, imbibed gin and tonics and puffed cheap fags with Elsie the prostitute who, with hardly a pause, related the trials and errors of her life.

Sue was feeling very woozy and her head was

nodding drowsily when Elsie finally said, "Well, I'd better take a bath and get off. Got to get on me rounds. There's a camp bed in the cupboard," she said. "Get it out and kip down in the kitchen. The coppers might be around in this area looking for you tomorrow, and I'll be busy all night."

It did not take long for Sue to stretch her long weary body on the camp bed. She slept like a log and did not hear a single sound as Elsie's customers went up and down the stairs all night.

4

A Street in Soho

WHEN Sue woke up the next morning, she sat up and looked around her. The surroundings were strange and unfamiliar. There was no fat nun ringing the bell to wake everybody up, no narrow white bed beside her with Gladys snoring like an old badger. No, she was in a modern, well-equipped kitchen and her feet were sticking out at the bottom of a small camp bed. She lay there for a while thinking over the events of the previous day, and then got up, found the tiny bathroom, washed and dressed and then returned to the kitchen where she made coffee. Carrying a cup to Elsie's bedroom, she tapped on the door.

"Who's that?" came a muffled voice from inside.

"It's me, Sue, I've brought you some coffee."

"Come on in, love," called Elsie. Sue entered the room which was dark because the curtains were still drawn. The air smelt of alcohol and stale cigarette smoke, and Elsie lay back on her large bed looking extremely dishevelled. "Just what I could do with," she sighed gratefully as she sipped the coffee. "But I don't get up very

48

early, love, so amuse yourself as you like. But be careful if you go out," she warned. "The cops are still looking for you." She giggled. "I expect they're digging up Epping Forest by now. They probably think you must have been done in."

When Sue looked disturbed by her words, Elsie grinned. "Don't worry, kid," she said, "they'll pick you up in the end so you might as well have a few days of freedom. Done a stretch in Holloway meself, I have—ain't got the heart to turn anyone in." She handed Sue the empty coffee cup and turned over to sleep again. "There's money in the kitchen cabinet," she grunted. "Get some fresh rolls. The other girls might want some jobs done, too. Keep busy, love, and give us a call about half two."

Used to obeying commands, Sue washed the cups in the kitchen sink and found the silver coins hidden in an old teacup in the cabinet. Then she went downstairs, still undecided about whether to stay put or get the tube back to the convent.

The deserted early morning streets of Soho were heaven on earth to Sue, who had known so little freedom—even to walk about on her own. Clean morning air, sunshine and leisure. What else did anyone want? There was no fat nun to chase her down to the hot steamy laundry, no stinking kids to wash, no dirty jumble to sort out . . .

It was bliss. With Elsie's old-fashioned basket on her arm, she strolled slowly along the street.

49

In her hand she clutched a big red purse that belonged to the Anglo-Indian prostitute who lived in the flat on the first floor. She was called Ida and had been very pleased when Sue offered to do some shopping for her, giving her a list and some money and instructing her to keep the change. Then there was money for whisky from fat Florrie upstairs. "Enjoy yourself," she had declared. "And don't hurry back, we like a good kip in the mornings."

Sue strolled nonchalantly from baker shop to off-licence, eating a bar of chocolate here, a cream cake there. Then she bought a packet of her favourite chewing gum, her large red mouth now moved rhythmically as she chewed steadily and watched the streets filling up with life. Office workers dashed briskly from the tube station to disappear into the maze of back streets; flower stalls and newspaper stands appeared, their owners chatting noisily to each other on the street corners. Sue's dark eyes caught every detail, she was interested in everything as she dawdled along. Once, two women constables eyed her suspiciously causing a little tremor of fear to go through her as she thought of being hooked back to that gloomy convent. But to her relief, nothing happened.

After a few hours, she returned safely to the doorway of Elsie's building. The antique stall was now open with all the bric-à-brac laid out for inspection. Sam recognized her from the day before. He nodded his ugly mottled face and unsmilingly grunted a good morning to her as he polished a heavy Victorian vase. In the shop behind the stall, a shrivelled hook-nosed old crone pottered about. She wore a woolly hat and a long, rusty coloured cape. "Hey!" she called to Sue, who hesitated in the doorway. "You there, new gel. Mind you clean those bloody stairs— filthy they are!" she grumbled. Sue took one look at the witch-like creature and fled up the stairs to safety.

The women all were still fast asleep but there was a plastic bag full of dirty washing outside fat Florrie's door. Pinned to the bag was a note telling Sue to leave the whisky and fags there and asking her to take the washing to the launderette when she had time. Sue sniffed. "Can't ever seem to get away from bloody dirty washing," she grumbled to herself.

The weeks passed quickly as Sue shopped and fetched and carried for the ladies of the house. She scrubbed the rickety old stairs and polished the knocker and bell push until they shone like glass. And she was quite content to open and close for customers who came and went. The ladies had bought her a new green pinafore dress which made her feel very smart. Fat Florrie had also given her a whole caseful of jumpers that had got too small for her, and Ida had provided her with plenty of frilly underwear. Sue felt very pleased with herself. Even gruff old Sam and his

51

grotesque mother had been kind to her—some old fashioned beads and a copper bracelet had come her way for little favours she did them. She would buy thick cough linctus from a special chemist for the old crone who was addicted to the stuff, or give an eye to the stall while Joe went off to put a bet on. All these tasks, Sue did with a willing obedience. "She ain't saucy," growled Sam approvingly to his old mother. "Don't argue, neither, not like some of those bleeding kids we've had here."

Institutional life had certainly made Sue disciplined, but a crafty shrewdness, probably inherited from her Cockney father, enabled her to agree with them all and take everything they offered her. For Sue had that inborn gift of being well able to feather her own nest.

The establishment did not always run smoothly. There was often trouble and then the East End boys who decorated the street corner had to be called in to sort it out. They were known as Sam's Boys and spent their days playing cards in the pub or cafe, or lolling on the street corner. But they were always handy. And thus this little community of vice somehow survived, progressed and lived comfortably.

It was not usually until about three o'clock that the first meal of the day was eaten. Elsie always emerged from her bed decidedly jaded and ill-tempered, but once she had had her fix and sipped a hot cup of tea, she would recover and entertain

Sue with lively gossip about the night life of swinging London Town whose streets she roamed until dawn. "The heat's off," she declared one day to Sue. "Been nothing about you this week in the paper or on the telly. They've put you down as missing. Forget all about you now, they will."

Sue stopped pouring tea and looked surprised. "Do you mean the police?" she asked hesitantly. "That the police are no longer looking for me?"

"Oh, they're still looking for you all right," replied Elsie, "but they probably think you've been done in and are just waiting for your body to turn up."

Sue was puzzled, and not at all sure that she liked the idea of being murdered. "Does that mean I can go where I wish?" she asked.

"Well, I expect it'll be quite safe to move about a bit more, Sue," said Elsie. "But don't go too far, just down Oxford Street. And be wary, always remain stum, my love," she placed her finger to the side of her nose.

With a long slim finger, Sue repeated the gesture, "Stum," she said, "that's the word."

The faded, sickly looking Elsie giggled and began to roll up her sleeve ready to inject the needle to give herself that ever-necessary fix. As always, Sue looked on in amazement. "Run out now, I have," Elsie said despondently as she withdrew the needle. "I'll have to get some more from somewhere soon. It's a great pity that Dodgy Roger got nicked."

"Can I go and get it for you?" asked Sue, anxious to help her friend.

"No, ducky," replied Elsie. "You got yourself in enough trouble getting mixed up with that bloody dope pedlar. You stay out of it now. Only wish I could meself," she muttered gloomily.

That night Elsie was not her usual amiable self at all, and she fought and screamed with a drunken man she brought home, who called her a dirty whore and blacked her eye. Then Sam's Boys were quickly called. Sue got up from her camp bed in the kitchen to watch the rough and tumble on the stairs—three men rolling down them, swearing and fighting, while the women looked on screeching foul oaths. Sue watched it all dispassionately as if it were on a television screen.

Soon order had been restored. The man had been ejected into the street, Sam's Boys had returned to their haunts, and Elsie lay sobbing on her pink divan. Fat Florrie hovered over her, telling her in no uncertain terms of what she thought. "If you don't lay off that bloody junk," she castigated her, "you'll land us all in Holloway . . ."

Long before dawn, Elsie pulled herself together and was out on the prowl again. She returned to the flat in the morning, jubilant and starry-eyed having managed to obtain a fix. "Got a new contact," she told Sue. "Pity it's down in dockland, as I like to stay in me own district, now I ain't got Alfie to protect me."

"Who's Alfie?" Sue enquired.

"He's me fella, used to live with him I did," said Elsie with pride.

"Where did he go?" Sue persisted.

"Got his collar felt, poor old Alfie," Elsie replied mournfully.

Sue's pencilled brows shot up in surprise. "Got what?" she laughed.

"Got collared, nicked, you silly cow!" cried Elsie irritably. "Christ, you're proper green as bloody grass, you are, Sue. Don't know Stork from butter," she grumbled.

Sue was anxious not to fall out with Elsie, so for once she backed down. "I'm sorry," she apologized. "I only asked."

"All right, love, take no notice of me," said Elsie. "I've got a lot on my mind just worrying about getting the stuff. Can't get on without it."

"I'll come with you," volunteered Sue. "I'll protect you—look how strong I am." She flexed her arm muscles.

Elsie hugged her kindly. "You're a great kid," she said. "You never make a fuss and are afraid of no one. I'm getting real fond of you. Tell you what, we'll take a chance tonight. You can come down the Isle of Dogs with me."

Sue was delighted. "Oh, thanks, Elsie," she cried. If she had been offered a free trip to the

55

Riviera she could not have been more grateful—
it was all one to her. The South of France or a
dreary East End tavern, it made no difference,
she had seen so little of the world outside.

Towards evening that day, Elsie seemed to
become more agitated, and she wandered about
the flat smoking incessantly. Her eyes had sunk
into her head and the floppy white puffs of skin
underneath them stood out more prominently
than usual. Quietly observing Elsie's anguish, Sue
wondered how old she was. She only confessed
to being twenty-five but without makeup she
looked at least thirty-five. In fact, Elsie's real age
was twenty-eight but the hard drugs and corrupt
life had already begun to take their toll.

Without comment, Sue continued with her
chores in her calm efficient way. She ran a bubble
bath for the distracted Elsie, and plied her with
hot sweet tea.

"Crikey!" ejaculated Elsie as she sat in her
bathrobe, her hands trembling as they clung to
the mug of hot tea. "I ain't 'alf got the shakes.
Hope the fella turns up with the stuff tonight,
otherwise I'm lumbered."

Sue shrugged impatiently. "Why do you have
to take drugs!" she asked. "Why can't you stop
now?" Her dark eyes surveyed Elsie with a kind
of sympathetic scorn.

"Oh, my God," wailed Elsie. "I wish I could
kick it, Sue, but while I'm on the game it's
impossible."

"Sit still," Sue told her contemptuously. "I'll make up your eyes for you and do your hair." She set at her tasks in a very skilled manner. Her cool firm hands held Elsie by the scraggy chin while she put on the bright eye-shadow, painted long black lines and applied false eyelashes. Then she took out the hair rollers and brushed the stiff pale-gold hair into position. Stepping back to survey her handiwork, she remarked, "Ah, that's better. You look more like a human being now."

"You're a smashing kid." Elsie clutched Sue's hands impulsively but Sue pulled away quickly. Unused to such affection, it embarrassed her.

"I'll get myself ready now," she said quickly. "I managed to nick a smart skirt from that boutique up the road yesterday, and I'll wear that Lurex jumper that fat Florrie gave me. Like my new shoes? I got them from one of Sam's Boys for ten bob—wasn't that cheap?"

Elsie heaved a deep sigh.

"You ought to be more careful, Sue," she warned. "Lifting gear from shops and buying stolen property, that's going to get you in a lot of trouble if you get caught."

"They've got to catch me first," jeered Sue.

Elsie resumed her worried expression and lay back in her chair puffing at her fag while Sue adorned herself in her new finery. She wore a white, pleated mini-skirt and a black silk jumper with silver thread in the material. The jumper fitted tightly over her full bust and had a deep, heart-shaped neckline. It was old-fashioned because it had belonged to fat Florrie but it suited Sue, accentuating her broad shoulders and showing up her white skin to perfection. Her long legs were clad in black silk tights and on her feet she wore very smart high-wedged shoes. Her long dark hair, gleaming from constant brushing, hung smoothly down her back, and her face made up to perfection—she had on eye-shadow, liner, lashes, the lot, all acquired surreptitiously on her trips around the big stores. "How do I look?" she finally demanded of Elsie.

Elsie had closed her weary eyes but now opened them wide in astonishment as she gazed at Sue. "Well, I'll be blowed!" she exclaimed. "You look about twenty, Sue."

"But do I look all right." Sue's voice quivered for a moment and there was uncertainty in her tone.

"You look lovely," cried Elsie. "Why, all the blokes will fancy you tonight. I'll lose all me customers."

Sue made no comment. This business of Elsie's with men bored her. All she cared about was looking modern and smart after years of faded cotton dresses and clumsy shoes.

5

The Prostitute

TRAVELLING in a cab through the moonlit streets towards the seamier side of London—the notorious docklands—Sue's heart beat quickly with sudden excitement. At long last, she was entering the glamorous night life of this famous swinging city. She had gleaned so much information about it from the highly coloured paperbacks that were so disapproved of at the convent. At last, she was going to see the real thing!

A strange feeling came over her as she realized that they had just passed the mean slum street where she had been born. She made no comment then, but a forlorn look came into her eyes as she saw the small park where she used to take the twins for their constitutional, the ride in the battered old pram. Instantly, one traumatic thought flashed through her mind: how had they fared? Did they still remember her?

The sound of Elsie's cracked voice brought her down to earth. "Taking his blinking time," she said, referring to the cab driver. "Ain't satisfied till they get the last lousy penny out of you," she groused.

Soon the taxi was swinging in and out of the heavy traffic, and then suddenly left it all behind as they carried on down a narrow lane with high walls either side.

"The docks are over there," said Elsie, pointing over to the right. "Used to be pretty lively down here, but most of the Cockneys got bombed out in the Blitz."

The cab had pulled up outside a brightly lit bar. Posters of half-nude women decorated the window. "At last, we made it," said Elsie.

"Three quid," said the cabby holding out a podgy hand.

"Robbery, with bloody violence," protested Elsie with disgust. But she reluctantly handed over the fare. The cabby stared insolently at her. "Ain't going to do a lot of good down here, Ma," he cackled. "Like them young down here."

"Balls!" called Elsie after him as he drove off with a silly grin. "Now, love," she said, patting her curls and nervously grasping Sue's hand in a clammy grip. "When we go in, stand up at the bar like you are used to it. Don't talk. I'll do that in case there's trouble."

Sue was amazed that everything was so complicated, but she was quite happy to do as Elsie told her. As they entered the bar, the noise and bright lights confused her for a moment, but she stood very upright, with a calm, collected expression on her face. Many eyes turned to look at her, but then, catching sight of her companion, turned away. One young Australian sailor gazed on in ardent admiration. "That's nice," he remarked to his friend, nodding in Sue's direction.

"No good, mate," the more knowledgeable one informed him. "She's just sex bait. The young one pulls 'em in and you end up with the old brass."

"I can't believe that," said the green young man unable to take his eyes off the tall willowy girl standing by the bar.

Sue was basking in the warmth of those dark blue eyes like a pussy cat in front of a fire. "Keep your eyes skinned," croaked Elsie as she twitched and fidgeted beside her, searching frantically around the room for a sight of that dope pedlar. "He's a big fella," she whispered. "West Indian. He wears those mod specs. Nudge me with your elbow if you spot him first." As Elsie carried on in her most agitated manner, Sue ignored her. Her head was spinning with joy. Here was life, music and male adoration—all the things she had been deprived of in her life. Elsie's problems were her own business. Warm and confident, Sue sipped gin and tonic and stared superciliously about the crowded bar. She looked enviously at the young girls in their mini-skirts laughing gaily with their companions; and she looked in fascination at the heavily made-up middle-aged women with their long dangling ear-rings and high hair-do's. It was all new to her but one

61

thing was for sure—so much living time had been wasted in that crummy convent.

On the ornate steps, the musicians blew, strummed and thumped with ferocity. A rotund woman in a short cerise dress and hideous wig was the star turn. To Sue the woman looked like mutton done up as lamb and her lewd antics sickened her.

"Stay put, Sue," whispered Elsie as she spied her contact at last. "I'll be back." She trotted off quickly, leaving Sue sitting up at the bar.

The excited and admiring young man was now only two feet away from her, caressing her with his gaze. The moment Elsie had vanished into the crowd, he was beside Sue. "Where's your ma?" he joked. "Gone home to bed?" Sue did not reply. She turned her head gracefully and showed her neat white teeth in a welcoming grin.

"What's your poison?" he asked eagerly. "Gin?" Sue nodded. "Come on," he said. "Let's go sit somewhere quiet."

So in a dimly lit corner they sat together. The man cuddled her and whispered words of love in her ear. "Where have you been hiding, beautiful?" he murmured.

Sue did not say a word. Elsie had instructed her to remain stum and she had every intention of doing so. She flicked back her false eyelashes and stared inscrutably at him.

"Wow!" he cried, all the more excited. "Just like the old Mona Lisa. Come on, baby, put me out of my misery. Just tell me your name." He grasped her hand.

The corners of her mouth twitched but she did not smile this time. "I'm called Sue," she said softly. The man jumped to his feet and began to pull her up. "Come, Sue, let's leave this hell hole and go somewhere and have a meal."

"No," replied Sue, pulling away. "I must wait for Elsie."

"What, that old floozie?" he exclaimed in disgust. "Whatever for?"

But again Sue remained dumb and refused to budge. The man sat down again and began swallowing his pints of beer in a sulky manner. He was nice, Sue thought, and she liked that excited feeling inside her. When he pressed close to her and his hand fondled her knee, little tremors shot up her thighs.

It was not long before Elsie had returned, bright and starry-eyed again having got her fix and found a new supplier of the drugs she needed. She looked appreciatively at Sue's companion but he stared back at her with hostility.

"She's not on the game," Elsie informed him, "but I'll give you a good time for a tenner." She winked knowingly and her lopsided mouth pouted in an absurd manner as she plied the wiles of her trade.

The man had leaped to his feet and was backing away. "Christ!" he cried. "I don't want to buy it. I only want to hire it for the night. And I want the kid, not you. You're too old for me."

Elsie ignored the insult. "What about a drink?" she asked pleasantly.

The Australian produced a wallet stuffed with notes and swayed to the counter to order drinks. Elsie's eyes gleamed greedily. "Hang on to him, Sue," she whispered. "He's loaded." Then she added, "That black git rooked me for that fix," she complained bitterly.

Sue scarcely heard her. Her head began to spin and she had to get outside in the smoke-free air. She got up and went out. Once outside, she breathed in the clean air that blew up the Thames and immediately felt revived. Her young admirer had followed her out and still clung to her, saying he wanted to dawdle awhile and look at the river. Elsie also came out and became very domineering and business-like. Within minutes she had called a taxi. In the taxi, Sue enjoyed the passionate kisses of that drunken youth, while Elsie sat watching them with a pale, angry face.

They arrived back at Elsie's flat and climbed the rickety wooden stairs. The man, blind drunk, was escorted into Elsie's bedroom. Elsie gave Sue a determined push. "Get to bed!" she cried. "I don't like whore robbers. And lock the bloody door!"

For the first time since they had met, Sue stood up to Elsie. Drawing herself up to her full height, she sneered at her. "I won't," she said. "He's mine. I found him."

The change in Elsie was remarkable. Showing her teeth like a mad dog and with eyes blazing, she flew at Sue, caught her by the hair and dragged her into the kitchen. Caught off guard, Sue was too surprised to defend herself and Elsie pushed her inside and locked her in. "You can get back to that bleeding convent if you defy me," she yelled through the keyhole.

Sue stretched out on her narrow bed and wept tears of frustration. Her young man was so nice. How she would have enjoyed making love to that sun-tanned body! What a spiteful bitch that Elsie was. Seething with resentment at that old junkie, she eventually fell asleep, but only to be aroused later by a shocking shindy.

The young man had woken from his drunken stupor to find himself in bed with Elsie. Furious, he yelled at the top of his voice. "God darn you, bloody old strumpet! Where's that young bird I paid you twenty quid for?"

With her ear to the door, Sue listened feeling very shocked. Had Elsie actually sold her to this man and then swindled him out of her? Getting down on her knees, she peered through the keyhole to be met by a strange sight of the young man prowling about the hallway of the flat dressed only in a short shirt. An odd tent erection stuck out of it. Then Elsie dashed out of the bedroom, struggling and screaming and yelling for Sam's Boys to come to her aid. Within minutes, they had come bounding up the stairs but the sailor was a powerful lad with a flaming temper, and he put up quite a fight. The struggle went on for some time until he was eventually overwhelmed, and dragged, unconscious, down the stairs. Screaming filthy words at him, Elsie threw his jacket and trousers after him.

Sue watched all this with fascination, and then quietly crept back to bed. A strange thrill ran through her, and she felt as though she had just watched an exciting television play. Feeling no sympathy whatsoever for the unfortunate youth, that violent scene had excited her. She had actually enjoyed the spectacle. She lay awake on her narrow bed for a long time afterwards, pondering on what she had just seen. Feeling so keyed-up with emotion, she hugged herself tight under the blankets until at last she fell asleep again.

At ten o'clock the next morning, as Sue made her usual pot of tea and the ladies of the house were still snoring, she heard an unusually heavy tread upon the stairs. For a moment, she froze, standing wide-eyed and scared, the hot teapot still in her hand. But then she breathed a deep sigh of relief at the sight of Sam's grizzled head. Sam rarely climbed the stairs to the flats above, but did so this morning puffing and blowing. His rugged face was almost blue from the exertion.

"Where's Elsie?" he growled.

"In bed, Sam," replied Sue. "What's up?"

"Never you mind. Get her up!" he snapped.

Elsie was looking very dishevelled and rather worried as she let Sam into her bedroom. The moment the bedroom door had closed, Sue pressed her ear to it and listened to the conversation going on in that room. "Been and done it this time, Elsie," Sam growled.

"Why? What's wrong?" asked the anxious Elsie.

"Wrong?" he uttered in disgust. "My life, it's all gone wrong. You're likely to get us all nicked, bringing that kid in here. And that ain't all, the boys croaked that geezer last night and lifted his wallet. He had close to a hundred quid on him —he'd just been paid off his ship."

"You mean they killed him?" Elsie croaked.

"No, but they knocked him abaht. The point is, he sung like a dickie bird, he did, when he came round in the hospital. That this should happen to me," wailed Sam. "Been a good friend to you gels, I have."

"Oh, my gawd," said Elsie in disbelief, "but he was as drunk as a fiddler's bitch when I brought him home. How'd he remembered anything?"

"Well, he knows your name and the kid's. It's all on the news. They've connected that girl is the one who escaped from the convent. They're going to comb the back streets of Soho, they said."

"Oh, dear!" gasped Elsie. "I warned her not to talk. She must have told him."

"Well, it's done now," said Sam. "Bet your life they'll be here soon. I'm hopping off down the country with the old gal till it blows over, but you mind what you are about," he threatened. "Likely to get the other side of your face shived if the boys get done."

These last words really upset Elsie and she began to weep very loudly. "I ain't frightened of them," she squalled. "I'll be glad when my Alfie gets out. Clumsy lot of sods your boys are."

"That may be," growled Sam. "But don't say I didn't warn yer, and don't let them get hold of that kid—sing like a bleeding canary, she will." Having said his piece Sam lumbered through the flat and disappeared down the stairs.

Within seconds, fat Florrie arrived on the scene followed by Ida and her coloured boyfriend. They talked excitedly, all at once and the din was deafening. Florrie's deep voice boomed out above all the rest. "Better hide the kid," she said. "She knows too much."

Sue glided in amongst them. "Hide me? What for? I haven't done anything!"

"No, ducks," said Ida gently. With her bronze skin and short hair, she was the most attractive of the prostitutes. "But we can't afford to let them catch you. Come with me! Old Bill will be here soon." With a firm hand she grabbed Sue by the arm and guided her down the back stairs, leading through Sam's shop into the back yard which was overgrown with weeds. At the back, by the wall, a thick creeper covered a small door. "Here we are," said Ida. "Hop in there and lock yourself in. It's Sam's old toilet. It don't get used now. Not many know it's there."

Sue stood looking at the dirty, unused lavatory but Ida gave her a sharp shove. "Don't make a sound or come out till we call you," she ordered.

So Sue sat on the edge of that evil-smelling seat for a long time. She felt miserable. Cobwebs massed the walls and the stench in the tiny room was unbearable. But Sue did not dare move. Soon she could hear muffled voices, the wail of the police sirens and the tramping of feet as the police searched the premises. Cold, sick and unhappy, she sat and waited for four hours until Ida came to fetch her. Once the all-clear signal had been given, they all sat in Elsie's kitchen, the prostitutes were laughing and giggling over a bottle of wine, and feeling very pleased that they had fooled old Bill.

But Sue did not smile. She felt disturbed and somewhat queasy. "I feel sick," she moaned.

"It must have been that dirty lavatory," said fat Florrie. "Cheer up, we've saved your bacon."

"Give her a glass of wine," urged Ida.

Elsie took a wad of notes from her bra and waved them about in the air. "That's a bit they never found," she cried jubilantly. "Took that

Aussie for thirty quid, and then he never got nothing."

They all began to laugh uproariously, but Sue found little to laugh about. She got to her feet and ran to the bathroom just in time.

"I've been thinking," said Elsie the next day, "that fella probably gave a good description of you. They might still be watching outside for you."

Sue did not reply. She still felt off-colour. Elsie eyed her in a speculative manner. "No reason why you can't come out with me," she said. "The blokes seem to like you, and I've got to work hard the next few weeks to pay that swine for my grass."

Sue took no notice. She just sat staring out of the window. She had something on her mind and an awful sick feeling at the pit of her stomach.

Elsie rummaged in the kitchen drawer. "I've got a home perm in here, and an auburn rinse. Let's change your image—short hair makes a world of difference."

"Cut off my hair?" Sue gasped in horror. "Oh, no, Elsie, I couldn't. My long hair is the best thing I've got."

"Well, it's up to you," snapped Elsie. "Old Bill's still prowling about out there. You might have to stay cooped up a long time. If you change your appearance you can come out with me. But its up to you." Sue pondered for a while. "Might get a job in a club if you look older," continued Elsie. "Ten pounds a night, they get."

The idea of working in a night-club interested Sue. That world of neon lights and vice sounded very inviting. "All right," she said finally. "Get the shears, Elsie." Bending her head, she threw her lovely long tresses forward ready for the scissors.

Elsie made short work of Sue's hair. In no time at all, the long silken lengths fell to the floor. Then came the tedious and unpleasant application of the home perm. Twice during the long procedure, Sue pulled away and escaped to the bathroom. "It's the smell of that stuff that's making me feel sick," she complained.

Elsie had begun to look shrewdly at her as she brushed out the frizzy auburn mop which gave Sue a strangely erotic appearance. "Your hair will be all right when it settles down," she muttered, frantically trying to brush it into shape.

But Sue took one look at herself in the mirror, uttered a loud cry, and dashed off to the bathroom once more.

Listening to Sue sobbing and occasionally retching, Elsie began to feel worried about the kid. She made some coffee and at last persuaded Sue to come out of the bathroom. Sue looked ghastly. With that odd frizzy head and her weeping red eyes, she was certainly no longer a beauty. The short hair emphasized the strong jaw line, and her neck looked longer and her

71

shoulders broader than usual. In fact, she looked longer and lankier than ever.

Elsie's lips twitched in a smile as she looked at her. "Come on, Sue," she cajoled. "Your hair will look smart when it's set. Your mother would never recognize you then."

Very much the worse for wear, Sue sank into the armchair and gratefully sipped the hot coffee.

"Been here about six weeks, haven't you, love?" ruminated Elsie.

"I think so," replied Sue.

"I heard you being sick in the bathroom," continued Elsie. "So I was wondering if you're overdue. You did tell me that Dodgy Roger took advantage of you."

"I know," wept Sue. "That's why I'm getting so worried."

"Poor little cow," said Elsie kindly. "Must have clicked first go."

"Do you think I'm in the family way?" Sue almost screamed out the words in terror.

"No good kicking up a fuss," said Elsie calmly. "But you've certainly queered your pitch. I'll get some pills and if they don't work, you'll have to start earning. It's a hundred and fifty quid for a quick abortion."

6

Approved School

THE news that the kid had clicked travelled fast among the ladies of the house.

"Damned shame," said Ida, who had paid for Sue to go to a local hairdresser to have her woolly auburn frizz cut, trimmed and set into a smart shape. Despite her earlier misgivings, the new boyish look suited Sue.

Fat Florrie kept producing concoctions that were supposed to "bring it orf", as she told Sue, but they only had the effect of confining Sue to the lavatory and were a sheer waste of time.

Elsie was more helpful and practical. She got Sue two nights' work a week in a seedy club. "It's hostessing," she told Sue. "You don't have to do anything you don't want to, but if you do they pay for a hotel and you get extra. I'll save the money up for you and before you're three months, you can get an abortion."

Everything was decided for her so Sue cheered up a little. A few days later, she set out for Oxford Street. Again it was her kleptomaniac habits that trapped her. She had decided that she needed lighter make-up to go with her auburn hair. She was due to start her new job that night and she wanted to look the part for it. Wandering into a large department store, she picked up and examined various tubes of lipstick, before surreptitiously slipping one into her pocket. Then she moved on to the perfume counter. After an hour, she had quite a nice little haul. Then she suddenly spied a jewellery tray full of rings. They looked very nice—large and ornate and very modern. She carefully tried them on one by one, visualizing her slim hands loaded with posh rings. She spotted another tray with more expensive rings in a glass cabinet nearby. She swiftly put her hand over the counter, picked one of the rings and slipped it on her finger. Shoving her hand in her pocket, she nonchalantly walked towards the exit. She had only got as far as the swing doors when a rough hand grabbed her from behind. "Pardon me, madam," a stern voice boomed at her, "but I believe you have goods that have not been paid for. I'm afraid that you cannot leave the store."

Wide-eyed with terror, Sue spun round to stare into the cold face of the store detective. Without a moment's hesitation, she jerked her arm away and dashed through the shop to another exit, only to be confronted by a stalwart woman constable. As the policewoman lunged at her, Sue fought and screamed and fell to the floor kicking out her legs in all directions. Some shop staff ran to the aid of the policewoman and the store detective and in no time at all, Sue had been bundled into a Black Maria, where she sat handcuffed and very sullen.

And so, once more Sue was held in custody behind confining walls. The walls of Holloway Prison closed about her just as the convent walls had done. Elsie's words rang in her head: "Don't talk, Sue. Never tell the cops anything, they only come down harder on you if you do." So she remained stum. As a result, the prison authorities were unable to find out where Sue had been in the last two months, but it did not take them long to discover that she was six weeks pregnant.

Sue spent three weeks on remand in the prison while her future was decided upon. Sue soon learned that she was still a juvenile and would be dealt with accordingly, but by the end of the year, after her child had been born, she would be seventeen and out of their jurisdiction.

"Thank God for that," declared the visiting welfare officer who had spent a particularly exhausting morning trying to get on the right side of Sue. "Honestly, I think she has a mental kink somewhere," she informed her colleagues. "She doesn't show the slightest sign of any remorse, and her one ambition seems to be to get free and become a prostitute." She wiped her brow with a dainty handkerchief. "It's like hitting your head against a brick wall, trying to get through to that girl."

But the tall, robust matron of the remand centre was not so easily rattled. She had handled and conquered many an erring young woman. "A few weeks here of hard work and discipline, and she'll soon come round to a saner way of thinking," declared the Captain, as she liked to be called. It was a name that this white-haired virago had kept since her youth when she had been a Girl Guide captain. "I'll put the girl under the care of the consultant psychiatrist," she continued firmly. "If we can find any hereditary mental disorders, the child might not have to be born."

"It's a pity," said the young welfare officer, "she never seems to have had a chance in life. She's been in institutions, on and off, since she was nine years old. And Lord only knows what happened to her while she was adrift in London for two months." She sighed. "I give up. Do things your way, Captain, it might have the desired effect."

So the Captain took over and Sue was hooked out of her cell to work in the laundry where the wardress was given instructions to keep a strict watch over her. Immediately Sue's temper improved, for she was back in her old element in that hot, steamy washroom. She worked hard and willingly and seemed extraordinarily content to do work that others resented.

The Captain was slightly nonplussed to see how well Sue was behaving. She had been expecting her to react differently. She thought she would lose her temper and become so violent that it would have been the Captain's duty to recommend a mental institution, and a quick abortion. In her eyes, it would have been the right decision. Bad blood produced inferior stock, she reasoned, so why put another problem child on an already overburdened welfare state? Had Sue been a vicious dog or cat about to have kittens, the Captain would have given the creatures the greatest care, and understanding. But Sue was a dirty-minded, uneducated human being and the Captain despised such creatures. Now her steely blue eyes surveyed Sue who was marching nonchalantly along the corridor carrying a huge basket of dirty linen from the staff room to the laundry. "Susan Ward," she called sharply.

Sue stopped immediately, her dark eyes wary. She was as tall as the Captain and stood facing her now, quite unafraid.

"Carry that basket in a proper manner," the Captain ordered. "I don't want linen littered all over the corridor."

"Aye, aye, Captain." With an insolent grin on her face, Sue gave her an insolent salute.

The Captain only just stopped herself from hitting the girl, but she gave Sue a paralysing look and marched away.

"That took the mike out of the old cow," Sue proudly told her laundry companions afterwards. One of these was a faded alcoholic, called Jilly, loaned from the women's prison, and the other was a good-looking Maltese girl called Carmen who had knifed her lover. Carmen's English was somewhat limited but she had spent some time on the East End streets where she had learned a fine list of swear words with which she liberally peppered her conversation. Any that she was short of were quickly supplied by Jilly, so Sue learned plenty of new words which she used loudly and freely.

Eventually Sue came up before the juvenile court where it was decided that she should be treated leniently. The psychiatrist's report had recommended this action, pointing out that too much responsibility had been placed on her at too early an age. The girl needed gentle handling; time and a lot of care, it was believed, would effect a cure.

First Sue was to be put in a training centre until six weeks before her baby was due, and then she would be put in an unmarried mother's home, possibly with further training until she was eighteen.

With a pale face and hard eyes, Sue said goodbye to Carmen and Jilly, and was once more bound for an institution far up north, as far away from London as she could possibly be put. The Captain watched her leave with a big sigh of relief.

Out of the train windows, Sue looked at the fast-disappearing buildings of London and wondered how Elsie was and if she knew what had happened to her. Elsie had been a good friend to her for those weeks they spent together. She would miss her and the other ladies, she thought wistfully. And then she wondered with dread what this new institution she was going to would be like.

The new school, in fact, turned out to be a pleasant surprise for her. Situated high on a hill and surrounded by green parklands, it made a nice change from that old remand centre which had smelled of damp walls and carbolic soap. Surely the head one here would not be such an old cow as that Captain.

"I don't know about me being potty," said Sue scornfully to the young social worker who had travelled up from London with her. "She was a nut case if ever I saw one."

"You'll like it up here, Sue," the young lady informed her. "Most of the girls do."

"We'll wait and see," scowled Sue.

"It's like a big boarding school with properly qualified teachers. If you want to learn to type or do dressmaking, or anything like that, you'll be given plenty of opportunity to do so."

"I expect I'll end up in the bloody laundry," said Sue, "like I always do."

Her introduction to the training school was nice and informal. The petite blonde matron who had previously worked as a ward sister was clean and neat, smiling and alert. She had taken the trouble to find out about Sue and was determined to make the girl happy.

Sue was introduced to the other girls and, after a tasty high tea, they had games and watched television. There was not a lot of discipline in the school and the atmosphere was free and easy. Sue should have been grateful for all this but she was not. Within three weeks she had been nicknamed Surly Sue and had been in plenty of trouble for bullying the other girls or dodging classes.

The young, enthusiastic teachers spent many hours trying to coax Sue to read, knit or sew, but it was hopeless. She did not have the slightest interest in anything they suggested. She did, however, develop a very healthy appetite for food and spent most of her time lazing about.

The evenings were spent in the dormitory where the girls would tell each other rude jokes or have pillow fights.

There were several gymslip mums waiting their turn to go to the unmarried mother's home. They would constantly swap stories of how they went to all-night parties and got raped, or of their addiction to pep pills and how they never had a clue what happened to them on that particular Saturday night.

Sue decided that the whole lot of them were a silly bunch of nits and that it would serve them all right if they ended up in Holloway. "Silly lot of cows," she would mutter loudly. "I've been on the game, I have," she would boast. "No bleedin' man gets me for less than twenty quid."

Fascinated, the girls would gather about her to listen to her fantastic, lurid tales of her exploits as a Soho prostitute.

"I don't believe you, Sue," one brave girl protested one night. "You're not old enough to have done all these things."

"That's right," said another, "and, anyway, how come you got in the family way? Prostitutes are not like us—they know how to prevent it."

"Now don't you be so bloody cheeky, Irish Peg," scowled Sue. "Just because your black boy let you down . . . Me, I've had all kinds and all nationalities." Her audience listened, enthralled by her lies.

"At least I know who's the father of mine," flared out Irish Peg.

"She's right, Sue," said Pauline, a girl with a solemn face and large specs. "How can you know who the father is if you've had so many in one night?"

"Never you mind!" retorted Sue. "Experience teaches you that. I know who he is, he's a boy called Roger and at this moment he's in the nick."

"Sorry, Sue, I don't believe you either," said little Rosie who was reported to be carrying twins. "It's possible that your baby is just as likely to be black as Irish Peg's."

"Oh, nuts!" said Sue. "Wait till I get back to

Soho. I'll get the boys to carve you up if I catch any of you soppy lot hanging around."

There was a general scramble back to bed, they all began to laugh.

The months ticked by and Sue became very heavy. She was always eating and had become extraordinarily lazy.

"You must pull yourself together, Sue," the social worker warned her earnestly. "How are you going to take care of yourself and your baby? You really ought to learn a trade or at least take an interest in baby care."

But Sue only gazed silently and superciliously at her. What did she want to sit in a stuffy classroom for, watching a lot of giggling girls playing with a doll, washing it and dressing it? They could not teach her anything about babies; she had taken care of enough of them at Barham House.

When the baby classes were in progress, Sue would hide in the greenhouse and roll herself a cigarette with tobacco scrounged from the old gardener. She liked the greenhouse. It was warm and bright with hanging fuchsias and pots of red geraniums. It was also very peaceful in there, away from the screeching teenagers' voices. One morning she leaned against the bench and surveyed her large, swollen belly. To think that a smaller edition of Roger might be in there, she thought, and she had practically forgotten him already. That she could keep this child if she wanted to, she was perfectly aware, but what fun would it be to slave in some factory all day long and cope with a screaming kid all night? No thanks, she told herself, what a life; she had seen what childbearing had done to her mother. No, the baby would have to be adopted and then she would get back to Soho to the cosy flat and the lively chatter of Elsie and her cronies.

Within a few weeks, the four girls whose babies were nearly due, including Sue, were transferred to the unmarried mother's home run by the Salvation Army. Life was harder there: the discipline was much stricter, the food was poor and the Army sister believed very strongly that scrubbing was good for the stomach muscles. As a result, many hours were spent scrubbing the bare boards and large kitchen tables. This was not such hard graft to the institutionalized Sue, but it was for some of the young ones who considered it to be degrading. They often rebelled and wept, and there were many hysterical scenes which Sue ignored. There were some extremely young girls there—aged thirteen and even less. But they seemed a hard lot and more carefree than those from the approved school; they would spend their precious spare time dancing to pop music and holding their wobbly bellies.

On Sundays, worried and adoring parents arrived to bring sweets and flowers for their errant daughters. Small family groups would walk in the gardens laughing and looking happy, but Sue would sit on a bench with her long legs stuck out before her watching them all with a contemptuous smile on her face. No one ever came to visit her.

Whenever one of the girls awoke in the night yelling with their labour pains, it was Sue who hooked her out of bed and walked with her across the park to the hospital ward. She would hang about awhile to hear the girl yelling, getting tremendous sadistic satisfaction that something was hurting her.

Eventually it was her turn, but she gritted her teeth, did not scream and never complained. It was with comparative ease that she gave birth to a baby girl who was the spitting image of Dodgy Roger.

Much to the surprise of the staff and the other girls at the mother's home, the moody, taciturn Sue was very gentle with her baby and even proud of her. In fact, she plagued the other young mothers in the ward by always remarking upon how pretty her little Elaine was and how ugly the rest of the babies in the ward were. "My goodness, what an ugly little sod," she usually said as she inspected the latest baby. The teenage mums were incensed to have their babies criticized by Sue, and it reached climax point one day when Sue screwed her nose up at Irish Peg's little piccaninny. "Monkey face," Sue called him.

Peg leaped from her bed with her Irish temper blazing, and it took both the sister and nurse to hold her down and prevent her attacking Sue.

"It's not fair!" Peg wept. "She's a whore, a real prostitute, and look at the lovely baby she got and she don't want it. I want to keep mine," she wailed, "and can't because I can't go back home to Ireland if I do." As poor little Peg sung out her tale of woe Sue just sat on her bed with a smirk on her face and her arms akimbo. She made it obvious that she enjoyed the scene she had created.

"She's beyond me, that Sue," sighed the ward sister later. "But I can't have her upsetting the other mothers. We'll put her in a side ward."

And so Sue was left to recuperate in solitary and her baby was taken to the nursery as soon as it was fed, to prevent Sue from petting and fussing her.

There was one very conscientious nurse on the ward, called Eileen. Deeply religious, she had a pale, freckled face that always looked rather as if all the cares of the world rested on her own shoulders. "Why don't you try to be good, Sue," she begged. "I know you love your baby."

"What's the use?" sniffed Sue. "She's going to be adopted anyway."

"But she doesn't have to be," urged Eileen.

"I wish they'd take her now and get it over quick," complained Sue.

"But, Sue," protested the gentle salvationist, "you don't have to have your baby adopted—I know plenty of unmarried girls who have kept their babies. A lot of help and care is given to you these days, you know."

But Sue just scowled at her. "I got over it before," she said bitterly. "I expect I'll get over it again."

The young woman looked puzzled. "But you've never had a baby before," she said gently.

Sue immediately lost her temper. Putting her hands on her hips, she shouted down at the pale, freckled face, in a loud, dogmatic voice. "What about the twins, then? I wasn't consulted about them and they was like my very own babies!"

Eileen sighed patiently as she realized what Sue was referring to. "But they were your brother and sister," she said kindly. "This baby is your own flesh and blood—there's a lot of difference between them, dear."

"Shut yer face!" roared Sue. "Bloody lot of Nosey Parkers, you are! I'm bloody fed up with the lot of you."

"Hush, dear, don't swear," begged Eileen. "Come and help me on my rounds and tell me all about it, love."

To Eileen's surprise and relief, Sue responded to this gentle firmness and calmly followed her to attend to the newborn babies. Eileen was astounded by the girl's capability as Sue fed and changed the squalling babies with swift, cool efficiency. And she listened quietly while Sue told her story, of her much-admired father who had returned home a whining cripple, of her poor

86

mother who had died of TB, and of the baby brother and sister she had been so fond of. She listened in silence as Sue boasted of how she was going to get her own back on all the people who had kept her in care. Of how she was going up the West End to make a pile of money, of how she would show them that they could not do what they liked with her.

Gently Eileen tucked in the sleeping infants into the cribs. "Why don't you take up child nursing, Sue? I think you've got a vocation for it," she suggested.

"No thanks," said Sue dismissively. "I know exactly what I'm going to do when I get out of here."

"Oh Sue," pleaded Eileen tearfully. "Pray to Jesus to save you, love."

"Oh don't start all that," declared Sue impatiently. "I thought you were my friend."

"But I am your friend, I always will be, remember that," cried Eileen. But Sue was unimpressed. "Don't go much on all that hypocrisy," she cried. "Do more harm than bloody good, those do-gooders."

Knowing that there was no point in pursuing the matter further, Eileen just sighed and went on her way. Putting her small army bonnet on her head, she set off to spend her off duty hour delivering the *War Cry* to the sinners in the pubs.

Eileen's efforts all proved to have been in vain. Not long after, Sue signed the adoption papers without a moment's hesitation or the sign of a tear. Her little babe of six weeks old had a mop of dark curls and merry blue eyes. Her sunny temperament made her the most loved of all the unwanted babies. Sue kissed and loved her and took excellent care of her but she refused to take an interest in the baby's future.

"Sometimes I think that Sue has a mental kink," the harassed matron remarked one day. "And I'm rather worried about what her reaction will be when we take the child tomorrow."

"Let her go with Miss Jenkins," suggested the doctor. "It often helps when they see that the child has a good foster parent."

Miss Jenkins was tall, untidy and short-sighted but of a very sweet, obliging nature. She was working hard for her exams in order to become a probation officer and did these voluntary assignments with good will. Next morning, Sue, dressed in a neat school uniform and a white blouse accompanied Miss Jenkins into town. In her arms she carried that special little bundle of love, her own beautiful baby. The staff had expected a dramatic scene but there had been none. Sue's face was set like a cold white mask and she said very little as she cuddled her little one close.

At the local council offices they met a fresh-faced young woman in her thirties who was to foster the baby until an appropriate time had passed before legal adoption. Standing red-faced and hesitant in the doorway, she looked sympathetically at the young girl who still held the child in her arms. Suddenly Sue thrust the child at the woman and walked out of the room without a word. There was no sign of emotion on her face but tears poured down poor Miss Jenkins' face. She took off her spectacles to wipe her eyes. "It's all for the best, Sue," she ventured timidly.

Sue stared hard at her. "Got a fag?" she demanded.

Miss Jenkins looked slightly shocked. "You can't smoke going along the street, Sue," she said. "Let's go and have a cup of tea. I've got some cigarettes in my bag."

They walked a little way down the main street to a self-service teashop. As soon as they had found a window table, Miss Jenkins handed Sue the packet of cigarettes and then went to the counter to get some tea.

The cups were filled and on the tray and just as she paid the cashier, she glanced back at the table. Sue was gone. The seat by the window was empty. Miss Jenkins let out a cry, plonked the tray down on the side and rushed out into the street where she stared short-sightedly up and down.

But Sue was already half-way down the underpath that led to the motorway, her long legs carrying her swiftly to freedom.

7

Return to Soho

HIGH in the Yorkshire moors, the motorway winds towards the South. Sue walked rapidly along the hard shoulder feeling rather confused as a long line of traffic tore past her. The noise was deafening as lorries and heavy tankers roared past, side by side, striving to out-race each other. It was desolate and wild on the moors, a strange, lonely world up there beside the motorway.

She heard the siren of a police car and, scenting danger, quickly ducked behind a clump of blackberry bushes to hide. She lay very still, even though the blackberry bushes pricked her legs. Only the wild life around her stirred. A rabbit hopped out from behind another bush and a blackbird perched in the small tree above her head and sang his song of love. In a few minutes she was fast asleep, exhausted from her flight.

When she awoke, a cold mist had begun to rise. Stiff and damp, Sue began to wonder if her escape had been such a good idea. It might be a hundred miles to London and she was not even sure which direction it was. Feeling rather depressed, she sat hugging her knees as she peered through the bushes at the traffic that still rumbled past. Lights had begun to twinkle on the cars and the road looked damp and shiny. She had no money, she thought gloomily, and not even a warm coat. Perhaps she ought to go back the way she had come . . .

She got up stiffly, looked back down the road, and then, with a determined shrug, continued along the hard shoulder. "Must lead somewhere," she muttered. "And the further away I get from that rotten school, the better I shall like it."

Darkness had now fallen. Headlights shed a cold glare on to the road. At last, a bridge spanned the shadowy space and an illuminated sign read: London. It was straight ahead. Sue shivered and put her hands into her blazer pockets. "At least I know I'm going in the right direction," she said optimistically.

At a turnoff, there was a well-lit cafe and a fleet of lorries parked outside. Immediately Sue cheered up and headed for it. Finding the toilet, she tidied her hair. It was now a short bob with the auburn rinse fading. Her own coal-black hair was starting to show through once more. "Look a mess, don't I," she muttered to herself as she stared in the mirror. "And I'm hungry."

She followed the smell of cooking to the cafe window where she stood looking at folk eating inside. Then she wandered over to where the huge lorries were parked.

A short stout man was examining the ropes of his heavy load making sure that it was all secure before getting his supper. On the side of this lorry were painted the words: Ferry Road, London. Without hesitation, Sue went straight up and stood beside the man. He was busy inspecting the tyres of his lorry and did not look up when she came up and stood there waiting.

"Will you give me a lift to London?" she asked sweetly.

The man looked up with a red face. Surprise registered in his mild blue eyes when he saw how young she was.

"Well, will you?" Sue asked again as he said nothing.

"Well, it depends," he replied slowly, rubbing his oily hands together and shrewdly surveying the busty figure under the school uniform. "You're on the run, ain't you, chum?" he asked suddenly.

Sue nodded. "That's right," she said. "From an approved school."

His attitude suddenly seemed to change. "I bet you're hungry," he said. "Come on, kid, let's get some grub."

Sausage, egg and chips, had never never tasted so good before as Sue gobbled them down hungrily. And Bill was jolly company in spite of the fact that his eyes were tired and red-veined and his chin was bristly for want of a shave.

"They'll cop you," he informed her. "They

92

always do. Many times I hopped off when I was a lad at the naughty boys' home." He chuckled and rammed huge lumps of sausage into his mouth at the same time. Sue was too tired to answer. She ate her meal slowly and allowed the warmth of the cafe to soak into her cold wet body.

"Ended up in Borstal, I did," boasted Bill. "But I used to enjoy those few days on the run."

"I've got a friend in London," Sue said through mouthfuls. "They won't get me again."

"Okay, kid," said Bill. "I'll take you there but I have to put you down at Walthamstow. You can nip down the tube there. I can't take you right in, 'cos the cops might be on the look out and I can't afford no trouble. I've been going straight since I got spliced. You're only a bit of a kid, it's a bloody shame. But I'll do what I can and no strings attached." He gave another fruity chuckle.

And so soon Sue sat up in the cab beside Bill wrapped up warm and cosy in an old overcoat that smelled of diesel oil. As they sped down the M1, Bill sometimes whistled a cheery song or just chatted about his adventurous youth in reform schools. Sue dozed and lightly listened to the drone of his voice as they rode through the night. "Got to keep whistling or singing," he explained. "Gets monotonous on this part of the motorway. I'm likely to doze off and have a crack-up. I often pick up a passenger just for company but not always a nice girl like you. Some of them travellers make me feel cootey. Still, that's me, muggins, can't never say no to anyone in trouble." He gave another deep chuckle. But Sue was sound asleep. She had lost any fear she might have had, and felt safe and comfortable with Bill, the long-distance driver.

It was a cold, dark, misty morning as they entered the outskirts of London. At Walthamstow tube, Bill pulled up his lorry. "Here's five bob, luv, I can't spare no more. Pop down the tube and wait for the first train." He winked. "And good luck," he added. With a friendly wave and his tail lights flicking a farewell, Bill went on his way.

It was seven o'clock in the morning when Sue rang the bell of Elsie's flat. At first there was no reply, so she pressed the bell once more. Perhaps Elsie had gone to bed after a hard night, she thought. But then a frightened voice called out, "Who's there?"

"It's me, Elsie," Sue called back.

"Crikey!" exclaimed Elsie's cracked voice. "Open the door, Alfie, it's only Sue."

The door was opened by a big fat man with wide shoulders, an enormous belly and a thin straggly moustache that wandered over his upper lip. His hair was long at the sides, which gave him an odd sort of appearance, Sue thought. Two hard, brown eyes now surveyed her in a very hostile manner.

"Come in, Sue," called Elsie. "Meet Alfie, he's me fella. I told you about him, didn't I?"

Sue nodded and looked about the little flat. It was a mess. With her hair all awry, Elsie kept running about the room stuffing clothes into a suitcase and wrapping up all her little knick-knacks from the shelves. "Did they let you out, Sue? Or are you on the run?" she asked, still busily packing.

"I'm on the run," replied Sue flatly.

"Oh, dear!" sighed Elsie. "Did not ought to have come here, Sue. Got enough troubles of me own. We're hopping it, me and Alfie. Bleeding bookie's boys are after us. Just getting on all right I was, too." Her voice broke into a wail. "Been making a bomb, I have, since Alfie came out. And now this . . ." She sniffed and cuffed her eyes with her hand. "I warned him not to gamble, but he can't help it, he can't."

While Elsie nagged, her ponce sat stolid on the settee with his hands resting on his fat tummy. His dark, almost black, eyes assessed her, making her feel very uncomfortable, and giving her a prickly feeling at the back of her neck, as if they could bore right through her.

Frantically, Elsie rammed her belongings into the suitcase, moaning all the while. "Me, I flog meself to death for a few quid and he gives it all to the bookies. Now he's grassed on them and they're out to get him. I've been shived before, and I ain't staying here to get done up again."

Without a word, Sue stepped forward and closed the suitcase and locked it for the distraught Elsie. She zipped up her dress for her, then began to pick up the odds and ends that lay strewn about the floor.

"You ready?" grunted Alfie, taking hold of the luggage and opening the door. Elsie took one last look around her cosy flat and her eyes flooded with tears. "Oh, dear, Sue," she wailed. "What's going to become of us all?"

"Cheer up," said Sue casually. "You'll be all right." She did not hesitate to say what was on her mind. "Can I stay here?"

"It's twenty quid a week," replied Elsie. "But it's paid until the end of the month so you might as well park here, I suppose. You ain't got nowhere else, I don't expect. Ta-ta, love." Giving Sue a friendly peck on the cheek she dashed out after Alfie who was already climbing down the stairs.

With a deep sigh of satisfaction, Sue stretched out on the pink divan and looked around. Well, she thought, at least I have got a place to rest in. I don't suppose they'll find me yet.

The fact that she was penniless did not worry her at all. In Elsie's larder she soon found a few tins of soup and packets of food she could eat for at least a week. And it would be two weeks before old Nick the landlord would call to collect the rent. But twenty pounds . . . That was a lot of money. If she was going to stay here she would have to think about how to start earning it. Still, she thought, there's no sense in crossing my bridges till I come to them. She decided that she would have a good sleep and then go down and see Ida. Being so well versed in the art of prostitution, Ida could teach her the ropes. It never occurred to her that there might be easier ways of making a living; she was just determined to follow in Elsie's footsteps.

Stripping down to her bra and panties, she washed herself in the little bathroom and then lay full-length on the pink divan, delighted not to have to sleep on that narrow camp bed in the kitchen any more. As drowsiness crept over her, her mind drifted to an image of her baby's little soft head snuggling so close. For a fleeting moment, her face assumed a melancholy expression which she quickly changed. "Pull yourself together!" she scolded herself, reaching out for the small dog-end that Elsie had left in the ashtray. I must find out from Ida about those pills, she thought. Can't afford to get in the family way again. Finally, as she began to be a little more relaxed, she dropped off to sleep.

When she awoke, the room was in darkness. Switching on a lamp, she realized that she had slept away the whole day. She also realized that there was someone at the door. That was why she had woken. The door knob was rattling and someone was pushing against the door from the other side in a most alarming manner. Then she heard masculine voices. "Open up, Elsie. We know you're in there."

Sue leapt from the bed and frantically began to search for her skirt. A moment later, the door latch gave way and the door flew open to reveal three very belligerent young men.

With one leg in her skirt and trying desperately to pull it up, Sue stared at them with terror. It had to be a police raid, she thought. The men came lumbering across the room towards her as, terrified, she backed against the wall. The first was flat-nosed and hefty; the second, tall and red-cheeked, and behind them, she saw to her great relief, the small scrawny shape of Freddie the Sly. Sue's sense of relief almost overwhelmed her. She laughed. "Blimey, you didn't half scare me," she exclaimed, rapidly zipping up her skirt. "I thought it was the cops."

Freddie the Sly, his greasy blond hair hanging untidily over his shoulders, looked sheepishly at her. He had been one of Sam's Boys, and had been sweet on Sue. It had been he who had acquired those high-wedge shoes for her first night out. "What the hell did you want to come busting in like that for?" Sue asked as her courage returned to her. Freddie said nothing, standing with his mouth open as he goggled at her exposed white shoulder and her tight-fitting bra straining across her breasts.

The man with the broken nose leered at her in a greedy fashion, while the red-cheeked man demanded, in a gruff voice, "What's all this? Where's that bleeding ponce, Alfie?"

He stuck out his chin in a most aggressive way and Sue became annoyed. "Hop it!" she cried. "He's gone and so has Elsie. This is my flat now."

"What's the game?" the first man snarled, bringing his hand down heavy on her shoulder. "Don't try kidding me or you'll be sorry."

Sue wrenched her shoulder from his grasp and delivered him a swift punch on the nose. The blow was so unexpected that he almost laughed. "So we want to spar up, do we?" he challenged. Instantly, his big fist shot out and hit her full in the stomach. The blow winded her and caused her to double up just in time to catch another on the end of her chin. This time she could see stars. "Freddie!" she screamed. "Why don't you help me?"

"Sorry, Sue," said Freddie apologetically. "I don't work for Sam now, I'm with Apples."

"Had enough?" roared her attacker, dumping her on to the divan.

"She's only the skivvy," muttered Freddie feebly. "I don't think it's worth roughing her up."

"Mind your own business," said his boss, "and get on and search this place. Might find out where Alfie hopped off to."

Systematically, Freddie and the other man searched the flat, opening drawers and tossing everything out on to the floor. Meanwhile, Apples plonked himself heavily down beside the breathless and indignant Sue. "Have a fag," he said offering her the packet. She took a cigarette, and he lit it for her staring right into her face. "Not grizzling, are you?" he queried. "Mmm," he nodded approvingly, "tough little baby, ain't you?" His teeth showed pure white as he grinned at her.

Despite the bruises he had given her, Sue felt curiously drawn to this tough hoodlum. His eyes were grey-blue, long, and deep-set. When he smiled, laugh lines appeared about them and it was as if his whole rugged countenance lit up. She rubbed her shoulder ruefully. "I'm all bruised," she said.

"Teach you not to interfere in what's none of your business," Apples replied unsympathetically.

Sue noticed that Freddie was prowling about pocketing bits of brass while the other one searched all the shelves. "Don't make such a bloody mess," she shouted at them. "This is my flat now."

This seemed to amuse Apples who burst into roars of laughter. "Hear what the lady said?" he chuckled. "Beat it!" he insisted. "Get off down the café."

Once alone with Sue, that bombastic manner disappeared as Apples seemed to become shy. Sue got up from the divan and slipped on her blouse.

"What are you going to beat Elsie up for?" she inquired.

"It's not that old brass we want," replied Apples. "It's that fat Alfie. Welshed on us, he did."

"Well, I'm taking over this flat," she informed him once more.

"You don't need to keep telling me. I heard you the first time," he said rudely. "All I hope is that you got that twenty quid when old Nick calls. My boys are gentlemen compared with the Greekoes he's got working for him."

"You mean they'll come after me if I don't pay the rent?" She stared at him in disbelief.

"Come after you," jeered Apples, "with a razor, gel, and ready and willing to use it on yer pretty face."

Sue went pale. Her mouth opened but no words came. Apples reached out towards her and drew her gently on to his knee. "Come here, doll," he said quietly. "Don't look so scared. Apples won't let no one hurt you."

By some natural instinct, Sue snuggled close and his mouth covered hers in a long kiss. It was the most wonderful thing that ever happened to her. It was a beautiful kiss, so sweet and gentle.

"Listen, doll," said Apples as he stroked her hair. "Don't tell me that you're a prostitute, because I'll never believe it."

"No, not yet," said Sue very seriously. "But I intend to start soon."

Apples moved away warily. "Well, you ain't starting on me," he said. "I never did like whores and I ain't lumbering myself with one now."

Sue's eyes showed their disappointment. "Oh, I'm sorry, Apples, but how else will I live?" she asked.

Now Apples looked annoyed. "Live? You work, gel, that's what. Not on the game, like Elsie, shagging her arse off every night to keep a fat ponce like Alfie. What sort of life is that?"

"I know," she said woefully, getting closer to him, her hand caressing his face. "But I'm on the run from an approved school, so I can't get a regular job."

"There's plenty of ways to get a living," said Apples, "legally or otherwise. But all that filthy sex and porn, I got no time for it." Slowly her arms went round his neck and they closed together. A timid knock at the door made them start, and then Freddie's thin voice called for Apples.

"Fluff off," cried his boss. "And tell the old lady I'll be home in the morning." Turning his attention back to Sue, he said, "That's me mum."

Sue nodded as his kisses rained down on her passionately. Her heart was racing with excitement as she began her first real love affair. That she was shy and inexperienced he was about to discover, but that they appealed to each other, there was no denying.

8

Roast Beef on Sunday

AFTER several days and nights of love-making, Apples decided that he had better go home to his mum. "She's nearly eighty, you know, I'm still really scared of her," he confessed. "Every time I go home she gives me hell."

"Don't try and tell me a ruffian like you is still a mummy's boy," Sue mocked.

Apples' face flamed, as he blushed almost scarlet. "Turn it up, Sue," he begged. "It's just that I'm the last one left at home, and there used to be nine of us. What's more, all the five years I was in the nick, the old lady stuck by me, fought to get me a parole and never missed a visit. It's my duty to return her favour now that she's old and lonely. But I do admit she bullies me."

Sue had a rare smile on her lips as she pushed back a lock of brown hair from his brow and planted a soft kiss there. For some reason she was feeling good this morning. "It must be nice to have someone who really cares about you," she said wistfully. "It's a luxury I've never had."

Apples looked down at her with a gentle expression on his face. "I'm a real villain, Sue," he said, "a damned muscleman. But I make a good living, and enough to take care of you if you'll let me. Please give me a chance to take care of you," he pleaded.

Sue could not believe her ears. "You mean live with me?" she asked incredulously.

"Give me the opportunity, Sue. Don't let me lose you. I'll pay the rent here, but that means you play straight with me. I want no more talk about going on the game."

"You're kidding me" she replied. "I'll probably never even see you again." Life had made her wary.

Apples' big hands grasped her wrists so hard he was nearly crushing her bones.

"Don't!" she cried. "You're hurting me."

"I'll hurt you much more if you let me down," he threatened. "It's not often I take a fancy to a bird, so listen, dolly, be mine. Be mine and never, never let me down."

Sue had never had so much excitement and fun as she did for those first three months living as Apples' woman. There was the thrill in her blood whenever he arrived at the flat bringing lovely presents for her—gold rings to wear in her ears, bangles and beads for her slim wrists, and real diamond rings for her fingers. No longer an unwanted burden, under Apples' care and protection, Sue blossomed into womanhood like a peach tree in spring. She felt comfortable and happy, and had a sense of security at last. She no longer roamed the streets dodging every copper she saw. There were elegant clothes in the wardrobe and smart shoes in the cupboard. Everything had been bought and paid for; nothing was stolen.

"Look here, doll," Apples would say, as he sat playing endless games of cards with his pals. "Go get something nice to wear. And bring me back the receipt. I don't want you lifting anything. No bird of mine is going to end up in Holloway," he warned.

Although Sue would laugh at him, she did not disobey. She had learned her lesson during their first few weeks together when she had openly boasted of her exploits in the stores. One day, after she had restocked the larder from the supermarket, he had caught hold of her by the hair and banged her head hard against the wall. "Get it in your stupid noodle," he had yelled, "I'll have no petty thieving in my establishment."

"Look who's talking!" she had screeched back at him.

"Listen, doll," he replied grimly, still holding her hair tight. "I'm a crook, a real hoodlum, but I like my woman respectable. Stop this thieving or I'll personally cut your bleeding fingers off." And Sue knew that he meant it. And so, after half a dozen social workers, welfare officers and salvationists had failed to make her go straight, it was Apples who succeeded. He was her man. She really and truly loved him. And it was mutual. No one could separate them—not even that old mother he was so fond of. Sue obeyed him totally. She cooked him meals and washed his shirts and found supreme happiness.

Most days Apples just hung about the flat chatting to his pals who were always dropping in, often looking very tired and seedy. "Put the kettle on, doll," Apples would say to her. "Make some toast. Run and get some fags."

Always willing, Sue obeyed these commands and was very popular with the boys. And she would sit listening quietly as they planned various jobs. No one had any doubts about Sue's trust-worthiness. "Not like the majority of birds," Apples would boast. "She can keep her trap shut."

Under his care, Sue grew better looking, she lost her hard expression and became more soft and alluring. And she always took good care of her appearance. When she and Apples went out together at night—either to the dogs or on a pub crawl—he was proud of his beautiful doll, and she felt happy and carefree with him. But there were some nights when he would come back at dawn, and creep shivering into bed beside her. Then she would cuddle him tight, knowing that it had been a bad night and some job had gone wrong. They never spoke about his activities, but when his working clothes—dark shirt and rubber plimsolls—were laid out in readiness, Sue knew that he would be going out without her that evening. And on successful occasions Apples would sit and celebrate with his mates the next day, drinking the hours away while they shared out the loot. Sue would go down to the bakers and buy hot rolls for them and make black coffee. She fitted into this dangerous existence perfectly.

During Sue's first month living in Elsie's flat, Ida had visited her one morning. She did not look as smart and sophisticated as she usually did, her coffee-coloured skin looked rather sallow and there were dark rings under her lovely Asian eyes. "Oh, it *is* you, Sue," she exclaimed. "I wasn't sure. And when I saw those boys on the stairs, I knew they were after Alfie, so I lay low."

"Come in, Ida," Sue welcomed her.

"I must say you're looking extremely well," said Ida, looking her up and down. Sue was wearing the scarlet lounge suit that Apples had bought her. It fitted very well and suited her white skin and emphasized her dark hair. Sue laid out a couple of tea cups.

"How did you manage to get away from that school?" asked Ida.

"It wasn't hard," said Sue loftily. She poured the tea dreamily. "And I got myself a regular fella," she announced.

Ida did not look impressed. "What's the difference? They all do the dirty on you in the end," she said bitterly.

"No, not this one," Sue assured her. "My Apples loves me."

Ida looked incredulous. "You ain't got one of those tearaways have you? Crikey, Sue! You're a bigger mug than I thought."

"Do you mind," sniffed Sue, offended. "He wants to marry me."

"A lot of water will have gone under the bridge by then," muttered Ida. But then, seeing that Sue was rather crestfallen at her cynical response to her love affair, Ida felt a little ashamed. "Sorry, ducks," she apologized. "I'm being a little bitchy. It's not been the same since Johnny hopped it with all me dough."

"You mean your lover ran off?" asked Sue, scandalized. Everyone knew how much Ida had loved her coloured protector.

"Yes," Ida said sadly, "it's changed plenty since you got picked up, Sue. Fat Florrie snuffed it—was found dead in bed, and now Elsie's gone." She assumed a mournful expression as if pining for the good old days. Sue sipped her tea and listened quietly to Ida's gossip. So fat Florrie was dead, she pondered, so no more four-lettered words would come roaring down the stairs.

"Got a couple of queer boys up there now," continued Ida. "They make blue films for a living. Old Sam moved down to the seaside when it got too hot for him around here. He sold the shop to a bookseller, and crumbs! What books he sells! It's pornography in the raw." She giggled

108

as if the thought of the dirty books cheered her up.

"It seems very quiet downstairs," said Sue. "Have you been working, Ida?"

"I'm not doing much," said Ida, woefully. "As a matter of fact, I'm considering quitting and going to Tiger Bay. It really threw me when Johnny ditched me."

"I'm sorry," murmured Sue.

"Stripped me of every cent, the bastard," continued Ida, "so I got a job flogging fags at Wing Wong's Club to try to put a bit back in the kitty."

"So you're not on the game now . . ." Sue could not hide the note of disappointment in her voice. To her mind, there was still a lot of glamour attached to the profession.

"Not entirely, Sue," replied Ida. "I just hang on to those kinky old devils on afternoon sessions because they pay so well."

"Kinky old devils?" Sue repeated the phrase as if she failed to understand.

"Christ!" exclaimed Ida. "They wear me out, but as long as they part up, I can take it. Do you know they actually enjoy being whipped, and one silly old fool likes stinging nettles up his bum." Back to her own merry self, Ida began to laugh heartily.

It was contagious; Sue joined in. "It's not true," she choked, "you're kidding me."

"No, I'm not," laughed Ida, "I'm afraid you've

got a good deal to learn . . ." And she proceeded to go into more intimate details of her profession.

Eyes gleaming with interest, Sue lapped it all up. "I just find it beyond belief," she kept gasping.

"It's all true, honey, I can assure you," worldly Ida replied. "Why, some old geezers actually call out for their mummy . . ."

That was the first of several intimate gossips Sue and Ida had in the flat until one day Apples arrived home early and caught Ida there. He was not at all pleased. "Get that tart out of here!" he ordered. "And keep her out." So Ida and Sue's education in the ways of the world stopped for a while.

These were happy and contented days for Sue. The house was quiet as Ida slept most of the day and worked in Wing Wong's Club all night. The effeminate youths from upstairs crept furtively past her door every night. They had long, bleached hair and shoulder bags she noticed, but they did not bother her at all. She noticed that not so many old pals congregated at the flat nowadays.

"Where are all your mates?" she asked one day. She missed the jokes and friendly patter of the East End boys.

"All in the nick," said Apples despondently. "I suppose I can be grateful to you because if I had not been out with you celebrating your birthday last month, I'd have probably got me collar felt, too."

Thinking back to that night, Sue was reminded of something else. They had had a good meal in a restaurant and got back very drunk. They had started to make love as soon as they got home, and through her alcoholic haze she had remembered the pills that Ida had obtained for her. Stumbling and groping her way to the bathroom, she had swallowed the first pill she found and fell back into bed beside her man. It was only in the morning that she had realized that she had taken an aspirin by mistake. She had been very disconcerted, but Apples had just roared with laughter and then consoled her in that warm affectionate way he had. But a month had passed. Now, with a worried expression on her face, she told her lover of her fears.

"Don't worry, doll," Apples said confidently. "I've got a big job coming off soon. We're a little short on cash at the moment but this time I'm going to make it big so we can leave this bloody brothel, and buy a little pub in the country."

"I wouldn't go through all that again," she told him, "I still dream of little Elaine, my baby they took from me."

Apples cuddled her close. "Now, Sue," he said gently. "Don't look back. Look only forward to happiness. This kid is mine and he'll want for nothing as long as I can provide it."

She snuggled close, happy and content to hear

these words. Everything would be all right this time . . . It was almost too good to be true.

"When this big job is over," he said, "we might even get married, that is, if I can get my sister to take the old lady," he muttered rather doubtfully. He stuck out his chest. "That's it, Sue, we'll get hitched, that'll surprise 'em."

"It must be nice to belong to a big family," said Sue.

"I've got three brothers and four sisters, and they've all done well in life, except me. I'm the black sheep. Take after me father, I suppose," he added.

Every Sunday, Apples spent the day with his mother. "I can't get out of it," he complained to Sue. "She cooks a joint of beef on Sundays and nags for weeks if I miss one dinner." Apples tried to explain his attachment to his domineering mother. "She's used to having a family to cook for and simply can't break the habit on Sundays."

It did not bother Sue too much because she had the day to herself. She would stay late in bed, then wash her hair. Later, she would go down to the launderette to listen to the local gossip spread by the skivvies, the dreary old women who open and close doors for the prostitutes. But for Apples, Sundays became more and more frustrating. In the morning he would go down the Lane to buy a piece of china or a plant in a pot, "for muvver" and then go on to see her in his old home. In that small, bright living-room there was a fantastic array of pots all over the window sills, and shelves. Indoor plants trailed and climbed everywhere; glass and china bric-à-brac lined the mantelshelf; family photographs lined the walls. "Blimey, Muvver," Apples would always say, "why don't you get rid of some of this junk, it's like King's Road market in here."

His mother's wiry little figure would stiffen in wrath. "If you don't like it here, you can go where you've been all the week," she would declare. Her wrinkled face would be screwed up in anger, and her rosy cheeks would stand out.

"Don't know why you live in this dump," Apples remarked this particular Sunday. "Why don't you go and live with Lilly up in Epping?"

This suggestion really incensed her. She began to stamp about her kitchen. "Want to get rid of me, eh? Don't worry, I won't bother you much longer. I'll go, but in a box. Fifty years I've been in this house and no one is going to drive me out now."

"All right, Mum, don't get upset." Apples tried to calm her. "But I was thinking, suppose I got married?"

"Married!" his mother shouted in disgust. "Who's going to marry a layabout like you?"

With a frustrated sigh Apples got up. "Give over, old lady. I ain't going anywhere," he said, "unless it is over the pub to have a drink." A few minutes later he stood in the bar across the road and drained his pint to the dregs. Through the window he could see that tiny house with its starched lace curtains the hearth-stoned doorsteps in a perfect circle. He could almost smell the aroma of roast beef as Muvver basted the joint in the oven. How pleased he had been when he had finished that long prison sentence and come home to Muvver and the roast beef on Sunday. But since he had met Sue it had lost its appeal. Also, the old lady was just getting even more awkward . . .

That evening, he discussed the matter with Sue but she was noncommittal about his mother. "How can I advise you?" she said. "I never cared tuppence about anyone until I met you."

Apples hugged her. "Honest to God," he murmured, "I never ever thought of going straight before, but now I want our kid to have a good life, a posh home and birthday parties."

Sue sat on the bed, nonchalantly varnishing her nails a bright purple. "What's for us we'll get," she said philosophically. "At least I've learned that much," she said.

"I guess you're right, Sue, it's the luck of the draw."

"That's it, lover, let's live for today," she replied. "Where are we going tonight?"

"It's your choice, Sue," offered Apples. "Say where you like."

So, like brilliant moths about a candle, they fluttered around the bright lights of London from pub to club, until the early hours. At midday the

114

next day, they were still sleeping it off, lying close together. Suddenly, they were woken by a pounding on the door. Sue opened it to see the small Chinese boy who worked at Wing Wong's standing there. "Got a meesage for . . ." he announced to the sleepy-eyed Sue.

"Well, what is it?" she asked, very irritated at being roused.

But the boy shook his head. "Me onny to hem," he said defiantly. Apples had heard and was getting out of bed and pulling on his pants. "All right, Lu, I got the message," he called. And the boy scooted away.

"What on earth was all that about?" Sue asked as she poured the coffee.

"It's the big job," he replied, "the signal I've been waiting for." Swiftly, he packed his dark shirt, plimsolls and his shaving gear.

"Be gone long?" asked Sue placidly.

"I hope not, but don't try to contact me. Whatever happens, just go on as always. That'll keep you out of it. If it's impossible to come back here, someone will bring you a message."

Her dark eyes surveyed him in a deep sombre gaze, causing him to grab hold of her close to his heart. "Oh, my lovely Sue, you are the best thing that ever happened to me." He picked up his bags. "I'll be back and loaded. Then you'll have the best that this damned world can give."

The door closed and he was gone. An air of gloom slowly descended on the flat as she heard his footsteps down the stairs until there was silence. He was gone, never to return to that little love nest in the heart of Soho.

9

No Return

IT took a while before Sue realized that
something had happened. The first few days
after Apples had gone, she lazed around the
flat thinking about him and paying great attention
to her looks. She would carefully make up her
face, re-set her hair and gave a lot of thought to
what she should wear. In the evenings, she would
go out to eat in Wing Wong's expensive
restaurant. There she would take her time over a
good meal and ponder on her life before she had
met her lover. One evening her thoughts drifted
to Gladys, that little mongol who had been her
only close friend, she wondered if she was still
living in the convent. When I'm married and
settled down, I'll go and get her, Sue decided.
She'll be a great help if I have a big house. Thus
she wallowed in pipe dreams while savouring the
warmth and comfort of the restaurant where she
received special attention from the staff who knew
her man was a big spender.

After her meal she would cross the road to
Wing Wong's Club. It was there that Ida sold
cigarettes and other things from a tray. She would
always be dressed in a very short skirt from which

her slim coffee-coloured legs tapered and which had a very low neckline. It was so low that her bosom peeped out of the dress and almost rested on the tray of wares she carried about her neck. She always gave Sue a wink as she tripped by.

Sue would sit at a table and take in that revolting floor show and observe how the hostesses wiggled their hips provocatively as they persuaded the customers to buy more drinks. Wing Wong, the proprietor, was a very suave young man whose only Chinese features were those narrow slit eyes. In all other respects, he was almost a Cockney. He certainly sounded like one, having imbibed the language from the East End rogues he associated with. He always treated Sue very courteously and warded off any ardent males who wanted to get to know the lovely young woman who sat all alone perched on the bar stool night after night. After a while, Sue realized that no one ever mentioned her man, or even asked after him, and she began to have a feeling that down here in this dreary club that they knew a lot more about Apples than she did. And there was a feeling in the air of watching and waiting; it worried her.

After two weeks the money Apples had left her had dwindled to almost nothing and Sue felt very despondent. There was still no sign of her lover. On Sunday she went to the launderette. She liked going. It was bright and light in there, and people chatted to her and happily included her in their conversations. So when she entered that steamy atmosphere, clutching her plastic bag of smalls, ready to listen to the gossip of the turbanheaded woman, she was quite unprepared for what she heard. Two middle-aged women greeted Sue pleasantly, and then returned to their perusal of the Sunday paper.

"They caught that bloke," one remarked. Sue stuffed her washing into the machine.

"What, that bloke that shot the copper?" asked another.

"Yes, up North." She pointed to the article in the paper. "It says here. They've been trailing him for days. Never got a light from that bullion hold-up. Some say the coppers were tipped off."

"You don't say," whispered another.

"I know him well. Comes from around here, he does," said the reader of the paper.

Sue looked anxiously over her shoulder to look at the newspaper. There she saw a large photograph of a man with a coat over his head being escorted by two policemen. Only his two large feet were exposed to view, and Sue gave a cry of dismay. Those familiar legs were bent at the knees as if the weight of that tired body could not be supported by them. The caption confirmed her fear. It read: "Capture of Billy Rafferty, the armed bandit." Leaving her washing in the machine, Sue turned and ran out of the launderette. Billy Rafferty was Apples' real name. Tears poured down her face as she ran desperately

119

back to her little flat, where she threw herself down on the pink divan and gave vent to her grief. For a long time she cried and sobbed herself almost into hysterics, until Ida's gentle hands soothed her brow and fortified her with hot sweet tea.

"What's wrong with me, Ida?" she cried. "Why did I not try to stop him?"

Ida eyed Sue scornfully. "It's not your fault, love," she said. "You're as green as grass, you know very little about this stinking world we live in."

"You may be right, Ida, but I'm beginning to learn," she replied. "I love him, and I'll fight to keep him."

"Sue, darling," sighed Ida, "Apples plugged a copper. You have to resign yourself to the fact that he will go away for a long time."

"I must see him," wept Sue. "How can I find out where he is?"

"That won't be hard," replied Ida, in a softer tone. "I'll find out tonight, at Wing Wong's. That Chinese bastard is up to his eyes in it."

Ida's good-looking face looked more wan and sallow than ever when she returned from her night's work the next morning. Sue had been sitting by the window chain-smoking anxiously as she watched Ida cross the road and come wearily down the narrow street. As she heard the prostitute's footsteps on the stairs, she sprang eagerly to her feet. Ida was bringing news of her lover. "Heard anything?" she gasped excitedly as Ida came in.

"I did, Sue," she replied seriously, "and the message is that on no account are you to visit him."

Wide-eyed with disbelief, Sue stared back at her. "Why not, Ida," she said with a puzzled look on her face. "Please, for God's sake, what did he say?" She was panic-stricken at the thought he did not want her.

Ida looked depressed and shrugged her shoulders. "He's right, Sue," she said. "Once those newspaper hounds get a wheeze of you, they'll be here like bees round a honey pot, not to mention the cops that will come with them."

Sue stood by the window with her hands clasped in front of her. "How will I know? What shall I do?" she cried plaintively.

"He's going to smuggle out a letter later on," Ida assured her, "so relax, darling. Come on, let's go down to the pub. A stiff drink will buck you up."

A couple of weeks later, a crumpled badly spelled letter arrived home with Ida one morning. In agonized silence Sue read this battered missive from her lover who wrote that he truly loved her, but that she was not to think of waiting for him. Having messed up his own life, he said, he did not want to ruin hers, too. "They are going to do me, doll, good and proper this time. Get rid of that teapot lid. I won't feel so bad about us then.

Don't come near the court and don't write to me. They read all the mail," he warned.

Sue sat for a while in a daze, letter in hand. So it was the end of a wonderful dream. It was easy for him to tell her to get rid of their baby. Her fairy castle now lay in ruins. Fate had decided for her. She would probably end up like Ida, now, flogging fags at Wing Wong's . . .

After that there was a long period with no news. The days seemed long and endless as she waited to hear more. Wing Wong had discreetly disappeared and the staff at the Club were not so polite now to her anymore. Money had become a big problem, and she sold a piece of jewellery to make ends meet. A dark-skinned evil-looking character called for the rent and after that had been paid, there were only a few pounds left for food.

Ida was losing her patience. "Got to do something about that baby soon," she informed Sue. "Can't leave it too late."

"I'll wait till he's sentenced," declared Sue. "If he gets a light sentence I might go on and have it."

"God in heaven," wailed Ida. "Wake up, will you? He's already done five for grievous bodily harm. He'll get ten at least."

Sue shivered. "Please don't say that, Ida. Oh, whatever shall I do?"

"Same as others do," replied Ida. "Keep going.

But personally, I would not raise a kid whose old man was in the nick."

"Oh, I know you're wise and probably right, Ida," wept Sue. "But I honestly haven't a clue how to go about it."

"Just get the lolly, and I'll make all the arrangements," replied the resourceful prostitute. "Harry the cabby does all the business. He takes you there and brings you home. But it's for a price, a big price. Makes a good living, does Harry."

As Ida chattered on, Sue remained quiet. There was wild terror inside her at the thought of killing this life. It belonged to her and her true love, her true love who was shut up behind high walls, just as she had been not so long ago. Suddenly her mind was made up. "I must see him," she cried. "I want him to tell me to my face that he doesn't want our baby."

"Christ!" declared Ida. "Don't make an issue of it, Sue, it will only make it harder."

"No, I'm determined to hear it from his own lips." Sue's mouth assumed an obstinate line as she spoke.

"Well," shrugged Ida, who could see that Sue meant what she said, "I'll see what can be done. He'll be brought up to London for the sessions. He'll be in Brixton, no doubt."

"Thanks, Ida," Sue said gratefully, and in a rare show of affection, she put her arms about Ida's neck and kissed her.

"Don't know why I stick my bloody neck out for you," said Ida brusquely, but there was a hint of tears in the eyes of this battle-scarred prostitute to whom sentiment was a real luxury.

The next few weeks were very dreary, spent drinking with Ida in the saloon bar at the local. Each day Sue sat with her to pass the time away consuming many gin and tonics before going home in a befuddled state to sleep the night away. Then, at last, the long-awaited visiting order arrived after Apples had finally relented. How thrilled she was at the idea of seeing him once more. She could hardly wait for the day . . .

A week later, tall and majestic, and very solemn, she walked into that gloomy building. Her heart was beating fast, as she saw him behind a square window of wire and glass. For a moment she had an impulse to turn and run as a claustrophobic feeling gripped her but bravely, she resisted it and looked into the tired face of her man. Apples was smiling, and showing those fine teeth and those little creases about his eyes. She noticed faint blue bruises on his face and there was a fresh scar at the side of his mouth. "How are you, dear?" she whispered.

"Oh, I'm bloody fine. Don't I look it?" he grinned.

Sue relaxed, they had made contact once more.

"I warned you not to come here," he grumbled.

"But I had missed you so terribly," she muttered pathetically.

"Now look here, doll." His voice was low and tense. "I'm telling you to forget me. It'll be a long time before I get free."

"I'll wait for you," she said earnestly. "I'll work hard and look after our baby," she pleaded.

His hands clenched till the knuckles showed white. "Do as I say, doll," he commanded. "I'll write later on, but at the moment old Bill is listening to every word." As he looked away, she saw tears in those grey-blue eyes but then he turned back and hissed viciously, "Now scarper, doll, be a good girl and do as I say. Get going quick before anyone recognizes you."

Sue got up and left as slowly and majestically as she came. Although her cold, pale face showed no emotion, inside it felt as though her heart was breaking. Not a sound from the dense London traffic penetrated her ears; it was as if a cold melancholic silence had swept over her. She went straight back to Soho and joined Ida at the local pub where she downed a series of straight gins. Gradually the noise of the other customers in the bar ebbed through her stunned brain. The lunchtime crowd was noisy with its laughter and merry chatter. Slowly her mood turned into vicious, violent temper. With a sneering gaze and her mouth turned downwards she surveyed those smug, well-cared-for office workers out for a lunchtime drink with the boss. They all looked safe and comfortable, and middle class. Her fingers tightened round the stem of the glass, as she had an impulse to smash it into the face of the nearest respectable female, and then tear out her hair, and rip off her nice dress. Her dark eyes glowed with hatred, and her face stood out fierce and white as she looked for someone to attack.

Ida instantly scented danger. Leaving her escort's side, she gently took the glass from Sue's hand and placed it on the bar counter. "Come on, kid," she said. "Let's go home."

Once inside the flat, Sue burst into a shrill scream that echoed through the house, then she pulled all the bric-à-brac off the shelf and flung it to the floor. Sobbing and crying out, she trampled it all into the carpet. Next came the cups from the dresser. One by one they smashed as she aimed them against the wall.

Ida sat quietly outside on the stairs, watching through the open door. "That's it, kid," she commented cheerfully. "Let off steam." She nodded her appreciation as each piece of china smashed. "It's only a lot of bloody junk that Elsie collected, anyway," she said.

10

The Street Walker

ON a sunny morning in the sleepy back streets of Soho, life began to emerge. News vendors put up their stands; flower sellers arranged their wares; crowds tumbled out of the tubes to invade the office blocks. And the vice girls turned over in their tumbled beds—it was much too early for them to rise. Up in her flat, Sue wallowed in a luxurious bubble bath. The hot, scented water was so refreshing to her after a very sleepless night. She had been unable to sleep because there was so much on her mind. This was the last day of Apples' trial which she had followed diligently on the news and in the newspapers. But today she was determined to be at court to see and hear him for the last time.

All the arrangements for going to the abortion clinic had been finalized. Harry the cabby would pick her up at six o'clock that evening. The money had been raised by selling almost everything she possessed. And when it was all over, she would forget him just as he had advised her. She would make a living in some way—perhaps on the game—who cared? Passing the sponge over her body, she surveyed her tummy with its small hard lump. There was no feeling there yet. That small life that was part of them both was going to be disposed of, flushed down the toilet, like so much filth. She began to think of Elaine, that beautiful babe she had cuddled so close. She would be ten months old now . . . It was strange how prolific she was, she thought. She must take after her own mother. Her thoughts wandered back to a traumatic picture of a faded woman retching into a chamber pot each morning. Her face yellow with fatigue, and the room reeked of baby nappies and body smells. If Sue had been able to live a normal, happy life she would probably have raised a big family—at least she would have known how to care for them and keep them clean. That, at least, was something her life had taught her. But one thing was certain now, she thought, splashing water over her legs: she would never lead a life like that of her mother, who was sick and defeated at thirty, and died leaving a brood of children to the care of the state. She squeezed the water from the sponge with vicious intent. "They won't beat me," she muttered. "To hell with them! I'll live a life of my own." And she leaped from the bath and carefully prepared herself for the final visit to the courtroom to hear the father of her child being sentenced.

Inside, the court house was quiet. Newspapermen huddled expectantly at the door, pencils poised. In the front row sat a long line of

128

Apples' friends and relations. Sue, sitting half way down the room and next to Ida, could see their sober faces, and observed the mixed variety of hats and tammies, and thinning heads and long hair-dos. Her gaze travelled along the line with interest. His family seemed to be there in full force, she thought. Although she had never been introduced to any members of this much-talked-of family, she was infinitely curious about them. That must be his mum, she thought, looking at a wizened old woman who wore a funeral-black turban on her silver hair and sat bolt upright, her sharp eyes darting about the room. From the family likeness, Sue could count the nine brothers and sisters and God knows how many grand-children. For a fleeting moment she thought about rushing up to the front to tell them her secret. After all, one more little one added to that great brood would surely not make any difference. She did not, of course, and she felt her chest harden with bitterness. If they wanted her, they would have included her, she thought. Her road was already washed with bitter tears; she could not go back.

Suddenly the court clerk rose to his feet and called for everyone to be "upstanding". Then, from a door behind the bench, the great judge appeared and marched solemnly to the throne. Sue gave a gasp as she saw that the judge was a woman.

"That's Ena Rosenberg, the woman High Court judge," whispered Ida beside her.

"Then she'll probably be merciful," Sue whispered back.

"Not on your nelly," retorted Ida. "She's a hard cold bitch."

Now her man was standing in the dock, Sue tried hard to will his gaze in her direction but it did not work. Apples stood upright with a far-away expression on his face, as if to say, "let's get it over with".

The summing-up went on for hours, with long speeches from the lawyers from both sides, and the slow court procedure. At times it was very boring, and Sue lulled herself into complete oblivion with her gaze fixed on the judge. It was she, the expressionless, middle-aged woman in large spectacles and a grotesque wig, who held Sue's own life in bondage. Could it possibly help if she jumped to her feet and cried out: "Oh, don't take him from me, he's the father of my unborn child." But Sue knew that it would be useless; a woman like that had little compassion for the working classes.

At last it was time to pass judgement. Fixing the prisoner with an icy stare, Judge Rosenberg began. "You are a most fortunate young man," she said, "that the constable you attacked received only a minor injury. But you have continuously defied and broken the law and this last time was with the use of a firearm. Therefore,

I find it necessary to impose the maximum penalty. You will go to prison for fifteen years."

A murmur of dissent swept through the court room. There was a shrill scream and the sound of much sobbing. The prisoner himself covered his face with his hands as he was led away.

As everyone else left the room, Sue stayed put, dazed and numbed, with hardly any feeling at all.

Harry the cabby was very punctual. At ten minutes to six his fruity Cockney voice called upstairs: "Ida, is yer mate ready?"

Sue was having that last cuppa with Ida in the flat. Her suitcase, packed, was beside her. Her face looked pale and scared. "Oh, Ida," she whispered suddenly panicking. "I'd sooner have the kid than go through with this."

Slick and smart in a tailored suit and stiff white shirt, Ida laughed loudly. "Do me a favour, Sue, it's nothing. You'll be back tomorrow."

And so, screwing up her courage, Sue allowed Ida to take her suitcase and escort her to the waiting taxi. Harry greeted them as he squeezed his enormous bulk into the driving seat. "Come on, girls," he shouted. "Anchors away!"

Moments later, the taxi pulled out leaving Ida waving a cheerful goodbye to Sue, the very doleful figure in the back seat.

The journey to the nursing home was uneventful, except that during a traffic jam, they were stopped for some minutes right outside the convent where Sue had spent many of her teenage years. Peering out of the taxi's dark windows, she stared at the grey turrets, and tiny barred windows and at the blue plaque on the gatepost that informed passers-by that the Bishop of Westminster had once lived there. There was not a sign of life from the huge dwelling. It was six-thirty, so all the girls would probably be at prayers before going to bed. She thought of the little mongol, Gladys, and wondered what had become of her.

Soon they were driving along leafy lanes and then turned down the drive of an exclusive nursing home tucked away on the borders of Epping Forest. After a few discreet words with the receptionist, a bright little nurse conducted her up the wide oak stairway to the cold clinical atmosphere of the abortion clinic. Harry the cabby shouted after her, "Collect yer same time tomorrow. Good luck!"

Sue remembered very little about the next twenty-four hours, although she did recall a dark-skinned doctor with gold in his teeth and a grim-faced theatre sister. She remembered, too, waking from the anaesthetic feeling deeply depressed and unhappy. Now there was nothing left of that all-consuming love affair and nothing but emptiness in the cold dark world outside.

She heard Harry's gruff voice in the corridor, earlier than she had expected. He had brought in another customer and had arrived at four o'clock instead of six. But Sue was quite ready to get out of that place as quickly as possible. "Just as well you came early," she complained, "or I might have jumped out of the window."

"Got rid of yer bleedin' bundle, didn't yer," shouted Harry. "What are yer grousing abaht?"

Sitting in the back of the taxi, Sue had nothing to say, but Harry had plenty. "Christ!" he ejaculated. "A hundred and fifty nicker! Making a bleeding fortune. Wish I knew the ropes, I'd do it me bleeding self, I would."

Sue sneered, "You get your cut, you fat old ponce. What are you complaining about?"

"Well now, that's nice I must say," retorted Harry with a throaty chuckle, as if she had paid him a compliment. But suddenly Sue's attention was elsewhere as her gaze caught sight of a little group of girls outside the cinema. There was Gladys, as small and tough as ever, marshalling her squad of convent girls who still wore those short white socks and their hair in long plaits with bows tied on the ends. Still the same little crippled ones were helped along by the hideous ones, and they were still all in the charge of Gladys, who pushed and punched them into position. Sue opened the window. "Gladys!" she called, but the cab shot across the lights and passed them quickly. "Stop, Harry!" she cried. "I just saw someone I know."

"Sorry love," replied Harry. "My instructions

are to take you back to where I picked you up. From then on, it's your pigeon."

Tears pricked her eyes, and Sue felt even more depressed. Seeing Gladys had brought back forgotten memories. I'll go back and see her once I've rested up, she promised herself as the taxi pulled up in her Soho street.

Ida came down to welcome her. "Come on, honey, have a nice drop of hot gin and then it's beddy-byes," she said.

Sue was grateful to Ida for her kindness. She felt she needed some care and attention because she felt a peculiar kind of light-headedness. The weeks following the abortion were strange and hazy. Sue frequently felt faint and far away, and for the best part of the day, she would doze fitfully in a chair, only rising in the evening to go with Ida to the cafe for a meal. Gone were the days of expensive Chinese suppers and visits to the Club bar. Money was now very short. The last piece of jewellery had gone to pay the clinic, so she knew it was to be a hand-to-mouth existence until she found some means of supporting herself. Ida was very kind and always as generous as she could be. It was she who paid for those meagre meals of sausage, egg and chips at the Italian café. Tonight, over coffee, they discussed the future.

"Can't afford to go mad now," said Ida, thoughtfully, picking the food from her good teeth. "I've got used to living easy, but that Wing

Wong's a mean old git. Don't exactly overpay me."

Sue stared desolately at her friend with cow-like eyes. "I'll pay for the meal today," she said firmly. "I'm going to start work tomorrow."

"Work, Sue?" exclaimed her startled companion. "But where?"

"On the street," Sue replied flatly. "How else?"

Ida frowned. "Be careful, Sue," she warned, "there's a lot to learn. It's no picnic, you know —why do you think I'm wanting to quit?"

"Don't worry, Ida, I'm big enough and ugly enough to take care of myself," replied Sue with a trace of the old grin.

"Pity you still got that charge hanging over your head. You could get a nice shop job if you could acquire some National Insurance cards."

"Give over, Ida," scoffed Sue. "You're clucking and fussing like some old hen."

Ida shook her head. "I'm fond of you, kid, but I suppose we all have to learn the hard way." Then she changed the subject with a nonchalant shrug.

The next evening, after Ida had gone to work, Sue left the flat wearing long, black silk tights and a short leather skirt. Swinging her handbag to and fro, she walked to the corner of the street with a provocative swing to her hips. Then she hesitated. For on each of the four corners, stood the pimps. As the slant eyes surveyed her with knowing winks, sallow faces exchanged evil grins. She knew exactly what those men were thinking: "Here comes a rooky. Better watch it. Don't want her pinching our girls' clients." Gathering up her courage, she crossed the main road, walked the length of Oxford Street, and once around Piccadilly Circus. Every time a solitary man hurried past her, she would give him a meaningful look, but nothing happened. By now her legs had begun to ache and she was feeling thoroughly unhappy. Making her weary way back to Soho, she dived into the little bar where she and Ida often had a lunchtime drink. Ordering a gin and tonic, she sank, exhausted, into a red plush seat. Young couples cuddled in dim corners. Virile young men lined the brightly lit bar. But not once did a head turn in her direction. Sipping her drink, she pondered over the strange fact that men had fallen over themselves to flirt with her while she was with her lover, but now that she was on her own, they were not interested in her. However did one start? What were the magic words one spoke to differentiate oneself from a girl out on the town to a paid prostitute? She sighed and looked in her purse. She had four shillings left—just enough for another gin. She went to the bar, ordered her drink and put the money down, but a firm hand pushed it away and a voice said, "Make it a double."

Her heart leaped. She had made it at last! She had clicked, as Elsie used to say. The man was tall, fair and young—probably about twenty. His bright blue eyes were sleepy and streaked red by alcohol, and it was on slightly unsteady legs that he carried the drinks over to a quiet corner where they sat down.

"Cheers," he said raising his glass. "Drink up and cheer up," he said.

Sue smiled wanly. The warm liquid flowed down her throat and helped to restore her confidence. Soon she was able to chat with her pick-up, who said his name was Terry. He kissed her cheek, put his arm about her and in a very maudlin way told her of how his sweetheart had gone off with his best friend in his home town in the Midlands.

Sue was scarcely listening. As he came out with his sorry tale, she was busily working out what to charge him and how best to approach the subject. He had told her that he was a student, so he might be broke. If this was the case, she would have to tactfully back out of this situation. Then the tipsy young lad gazed wistfully at her. "Let me come home with you, Sue," he whispered.

She fixed him with her hard, dark eyes and was about to say, "Only if you pay me," but he rattled the loose change in his trouser pocket and then, reaching inside his jacket, took a five pound note from his wallet. "That's all I've got, Sue," he said, "but you're welcome to it. I need the company tonight."

With a swift movement, Sue took the note. "Come on, lad, let's go then," she said in the professional tone she had heard Elsie use. Terry looked a trifle surprised, but he took her arm and they walked to the flat.

Terry's lovemaking was rather like his person —clean, warm, sweet and generous. But at one time during the night he wept on her bosom, and cried, "Don't leave me, Sylvia." Sue suddenly felt very ashamed, and cuddled him close. Terry finally fell asleep but Sue lay awake for some time. This lovesick boy's ineffectual passion had stirred that animal desire in Sue, and she longed even more for her lovely strong man who was now shut up behind bars.

By the time dawn came, she had fallen asleep very heavily. She woke at nine o'clock to find that her customer had fled. On the mirror in the bathroom he had written in lipstick: "Bye Sue." Picking up a tissue, she wiped the lipstick away. That had been an easily earned fiver, she thought, but she wondered if it would always be so. At the thought of that crumpled fiver, she panicked. Dashing back to the bedroom, she looked in her handbag. It was still there, safely tucked into the corner where she had placed it the night before.

Contrary to Sue's expectations, Ida was not very impressed by her first exploit as a prostitute. When Sue visited her that afternoon, she was sitting cross-legged on her divan, clad only in a brief black bra and panties. She looked very tired.

"Thought I'd never get through that session," she declared having just disposed of one of her kinky regulars.

"I did it!" Sue informed her jubilantly, and proceeded to tell Ida all about it.

But Ida was quite scornful. "It's no good, Sue," she said. "A soft guy like that is likely to come back for more and without any dough. He'll pester the life out of you. And I know, I've been through it all."

"Not him, he's too nice a boy," Sue defended her youthful client.

"Get us a drink, Sue," said Ida. "I'm all in. Might take a holiday. Would you like to carry on here?" she asked.

Sue looked nervously at the formidable array of whips and dog leashes hanging up in the half-opened cupboard by the wall. "Oh, no," she gasped. "I couldn't. I'd be terrified."

"No more terrifying than being beaten up or getting a dose," said Ida bluntly. "And that's what is likely to happen to you, Sue, unless you find a protector. Not only that, but the cops are likely to run you in if they catch you prowling the streets."

"I don't care," cried Sue defiantly. "I don't want no ponce to run my life for me. I'll go it alone."

"Please yourself," replied Ida. "But don't say I didn't warn you."

Without any heed to her friend's warning, Sue

obstinately went out again on to the streets that night. It was a wet night. A cold wind drove clouds of fine rain along the damp, shiny pavements as the theatre crowds hurried home. With a provocative strut, she prowled the streets for several hours—up and down the road, and round and round the square. But her luck was out. Soon she was tired and fed up. Her shoes let in water and her grandly lacquered hair-do had collapsed into an untidy mess. Desperately, she stepped out in front of a gentleman wearing a white belted raincoat. "Would you like some love to warm you up this cold night?" she asked coyly.

The man looked astonished at first and then he smirked. "Not tonight, darlin'," he replied before hurrying across the road. Sue crept into a shop doorway out of the wind, and stood there thinking for a while. Then she saw that same man talking to a traffic cop at the junction where the lights flickered from red to yellow. As the red light flashed, Ida's warning went through her brain, and she knew that he was telling the police that she had accosted him. With her heart pounding against her ribs, she darted quickly through the back alleys, running, fleeing from that fear of the grey prison walls, of being caged like a wild bird . . . A police car went whizzing by, blue lights flashing and siren screaming. Wet and shivering, she pressed her body back into the dark recess of a doorway until she could hear the siren no longer. Suddenly she realized she had company.

In the opposite corner of the doorway, she now made out a shadowy shape who was distinguishable only by the light of a cigarette. She gasped fearfully.

"Who's old Bill after?" a thin, bitter voice asked. "Done a bunk or just soliciting?" As her eyes became more accustomed to the darkness, she could see a youngish man with long hair that flowed down to his shoulders. He was wearing a bright plaid shirt and old jeans. He came over to her side. "Christ!" he exclaimed. "You look all in. Have a fag." He passed her the packet and lit one for her. She puffed gratefully with shaking hands.

"What the cops after you for?" he asked, putting his hands in his pockets and eyeing her speculatively. "A brass ain't yer?" he decided. "Must be new at it—they don't often freak out like that."

"That's right," she answered. She could feel her courage returning; for some reason, this impudent young man irritated her.

"Got a pad, have you?" he asked.

"I've got my own flat, if that's what you mean," she replied airily.

"Good," he said, "then what are we waiting for?"

But as he took hold of her arm, she pulled away. "I'm not for free," she snapped. "It's my living."

"Okay I'll pay," he replied. "But don't get so shirty—its bleeding cold out here."

With the long-haired youth slouching beside her, Sue returned home. While she was removing her wet clothes, he had found a can of beer in the fridge and was guzzling it. Silently he surveyed the room with mean eyes. Spotting the biscuit tin, he opened it and grabbed a handful, munching the biscuits and spilling crumbs all over the carpet. In the bathroom, Sue rubbed her hair vigorously. For some reason, she was feeling very apprehensive about this wild-looking, grubby man. He definitely smelled of BO, there was some other, sweet, sickly smell that she could not recognize. The house was very quiet, and she wished Ida were home. Still, she told herself, she had chosen this way of life and had to take the rough with the smooth, as Elsie had frequently commented.

Emerging from the bathroom, wearing only a dressing gown, and with her hair hanging loose, she saw that he was leaning against the door with the beer can in his hand and a sneer on his face. She glanced at his long, dirty fingernails and was disgusted. "Well, let's get it over," she said sharply. "Money first." She held out her hand.

The man threw the beer can down on to the floor and lunged at her. He grasped her wrist so swiftly she was thrown off balance and went down on the floor with a crash. What followed was the most revolting experience of her life. The man straddled her and placed his filthy hand across her mouth. Sue was a strong girl but she did not stand a chance against this maniac who had the strength of ten men. For what seemed like hours, she fought like a tiger while he stuffed parts of his filthy body into her, tearing at her breasts with his teeth slobbering and grunting like an animal. At one time he held her down and beat her on the head with the empty beer can, until she was practically unconscious. But not so unconscious that she could not then see him standing over her and sending a stream of filthy smelling liquid into her face as he urinated over her. Then she passed out.

When Ida returned at dawn she was surprised to find the front door wide open, and running up the stairs, she found Sue a weeping, pathetic mess on the floor. Ida gently bathed the filth from Sue's young body and tried hard to comfort her, but she nagged her, too. "Oh, Sue, you little fool. I warned you. It's lucky he never done you in. Some damned junkie, I expect. Better come round to the quack's tomorrow. God only knows what condition his body was in. Oh, Sue, silly little Sue," she wailed. "Just give it up, love, you're too soft for all this."

Sue lay on the bed, too bruised to move. Her eyes were blackened and her lips were swollen. Each time she moved at all, she cried out in pain. "Men! I hate them!" she muttered.

"He was an animal, Sue, not a man," said Ida.

"But it doesn't do any harm to hate, not in our profession."

It was nearly a month before Sue had recovered. She had had to get medical treatment and the doctor was bound to send in a big bill. Ida was very kind but Sue had begun to feel obligated to her. Also, she looked so tired and Sue knew that she was not making life any easier for her. Ida had settled the month's rent and Sue had no funds for the next month. She just could not impose on Ida's generous nature any longer. Something had to be done. Staring out of the window, she would shiver at the idea of walking the streets again. She could not face it, her confidence had gone. No, she would have to leave Soho, she knew that, but where could she go? She could return to the convent and throw herself on the mercy of the nuns, but she shivered at the thought. And then suddenly, a brilliant idea flashed in her mind. Her old friend from the convent, that capable, strong, aggressive Gladys would be the ideal protector. If she had Gladys, perhaps she could stay in Soho . . .

Next Saturday, she crept quietly from the flat. Wearing a long mac, with her hair covered by a scarf and with her face devoid of make-up, she looked more like a maid on her day off than a prostitute from Soho. The bus deposited her outside the cinema where Sue waited patiently.

Punctually, at three o'clock the little procession from the convent arrived. There were the two bathchairs containing little twisted bodies—one pushed by Gladys and the other by stout Sister Winifred. Behind them trooped seven or eight girls. Sue recognized Milly and Tilly, walking hand in hand, as always. They seemed shorter than ever, and they laughed and giggled as they went by. For a moment Sue felt very sad. How dull and grey their lives were, yet these unwanted human beings retained so much humour and affection for others. They were so brave.

Sue waited while Sister Winifred had bought the tickets, and shepherded them all inside. From then on, the group was in the charge of Gladys because the sister went off to spend the afternoon shopping. Swiftly, Sue got her ticket and in no time she was seated behind Gladys and her squad. Gladys' charges whispered and rattled sweet bags noisily, thoroughly enjoying their Saturday treat. Sue did not make her presence known until the interval when she tapped Gladys on the shoulder. "It's Sue," she whispered in a low voice. "Don't turn round yet, Gladys." Gladys' large head turned slightly, and her small hand came out and gripped Sue tightly. "Come out, in the toilet," Sue whispered. "Don't let anyone see you."

In that small compartment between the sink and mirror, the two women met once more. Gladys flung her arms about Sue's neck, "Oh, Sue, I thought you'd been murdered," she cried.

"Don't be daft," joked Sue. "Who's going to do me in?" But she was as close to tears as Gladys from the emotion that their reunion had brought forth. "I'm doing fine," she told her friend. "And I've got my own flat. Want to come and live with me?"

Gladys looked shocked. "You mean, run away?" she whispered in awe. She had been in the convent since her teens. Now turned thirty, it seemed a terrible thing to even think about running away.

"Well, you will have to make up your mind quickly," Sue told her brutally. "I can't hang about here in case Sister Winifred recognizes me."

Gladys' parchment face was screwed up in emotion as she stared up at Sue's tall figure. "Will I live with you forever?" she asked eventually.

"Of course, darling," replied Sue, "you're my best friend." Sue went gently down on one knee and cuddled her.

"All right," decided Gladys, "but let's go now."

Out of the cinema, they ran hand in hand across the busy Saturday afternoon street where they boarded a bus back to Soho. Sue had found a protector.

Over ten years, under the dogged protection of Gladys, Sue flourished in her chosen trade. One satisfied client would pay her well and recommend her services to a friend. And so her business grew until she was an established

146

prostitute in Soho with regular clients, a large bank account, and a notice on the front door which read: "Sue, model. Knock twice". Sometimes she was depressed, especially when the occasional letter arrived for her from Apples in prison, and sometimes she drank too heavily and became aggressive but overall, Sue was happy with her life and her contentment showed in her glowing features and healthy body. Most of all, her happiness stemmed from her friendship with Gladys, the little mongol, the only person in the world who had always loved her and remained loyal. Although she would never admit it, Sue valued her funny-looking friend more than any of the comforts she had earned herself through her success. And Gladys, as always, was devoted to Sue.

11

An Old Client

THE last few years had not been unkind to Sue. Hers was a hard life and as always she was quite prepared to take the rough with the smooth. She got drunk very often, smoked incessantly and swore like a trooper, yet still her figure was perfect—her waist was slim and her limbs were well-shaped. Her velvety-brown eyes had hardened but the nonchalant expression with which she stared out into the world was no different from that she had had as a teenager. Now nearly thirty, she no longer prowled the streets looking for customers, nor did she sit in the night bars watching furtively for some man to look in her direction. She did not need to. She was well known and had the reputation of giving a fair deal. She was the tops of her profession. In fact, other ponces would often recommend her to particularly well-set-up young men looking for a good time. These were mostly young businessmen with expense accounts who would not touch the ponces' own tribe of doped-up young whores. And so, Sue made a good living, with little inconvenience. Best of all, she could pick and choose her clients and take time off, if she felt so inclined.

Gladys was still firmly entrenched in her position as Sue's protector and friend. She did not seem to have aged at all. Her flat brown face, with its sallow skin and slanted eyes, looked the same as ever. And she still clung to Sue with a passionate devotion for the person who had snatched her from a dreary convent. Her small squat shape could often be seen walking beside the tall, willowy Sue as they walked along Oxford Street on shopping trips. The two made a familiar sight, with a smartly dressed Sue swinging her hips sexily, while Gladys plodded alongside, a grim expression on her rugged features. And she was always dressed in a rusty brown dress and battered straw hat.

"Why do you have to wear that horrible brown shade?" Sue would frequently ask. "It only makes you look more sallow." Sue herself was always very careful about her appearance.

Then Gladys would look up at her with an irritated look and say gruffly, "I likes brown." Indeed, when she bought a new dress, it was always the same shape and colour.

From under her veil of false eyelashes, Sue would stare disdainfully down at Gladys' well-scrubbed face. "God knows why I put up with you," she would often remark.

Little Gladys would laugh out aloud but it was obvious that she was irritated. "I knows why," she would reply, "because yer don't want no dirty ponce bashin' yer abaht, that's why. Because of me, yer makes good money and I don't take 'alf of it orf yer."

For a few moments Sue would stare coldly at Gladys and then start to laugh. And Gladys would dash forward like a little child and put her arms about Sue's slim waist. "Oh don't let us have a row, Sue," she would beg.

Sue would stroke that fuzzy head and say, "All right, love. You're right, I know I couldn't get by without you."

Then peace would be restored for a while.

Elsie's old flat had now been modernized and two more rooms had been added. The landlord —the son of her old landlord, old Nick the Greek —had doubled the rent. But Sue did not mind since she was well able to pay. She had made a lot of money these past five years.

The majority of Sue's customers came regularly on business trips and left behind a hundred pounds or more. They always took her out to expensive dinners and were not ashamed at all to be seen escorting this tall, well-disposed model. Certainly the word "whore" was never used.

One bright day, as Sue and Gladys strolled along Oxford Street on a shopping trip, they met an old friend. It was Gladys who spotted him first. "Don't look now, Sue," she muttered, "but here comes one of those old kinky sods—you know, one of Ida's leftovers."

Sue was wearing dark glasses under a wide-brimmed straw hat, but taking off her specs, she looked in the direction that Gladys had indicated. "Why," she exclaimed, "it's old Claud. He looks a bit weatherbeaten. I wonder where he's been these last two years."

Gladys pulled a long face at her. "Come on, Sue," she said. "Don't stop. It don't look like he got a lot, so why bother with him?"

But Sue stood still and smiled directly into the old man's face. Claud walked with the aid of a stick and wore heavy tweeds. He had a red face and a bushy white walrus moustache. "Hello Claud," cried Sue. "Long time no see."

As he realized who was calling to him, Claud's face lit up with a smile which displayed large white false teeth and humorous blue eyes. "Well, I'll be jiggered!" he cried. "It's Sue." He held out his hand to her. "How's tricks, old gel?" he asked, poking Gladys playfully with his stick. "Ah, little donkey, still going strong, I see."

Gladys gave him an evil scowl as she recalled one of his kinky sessions when he had insisted on riding stark naked on Gladys' back and singing the "Donkey's Serenade". Sue had rolled about on the bed with hysterical laughter at the expression on poor Gladys' face. Gladys had not been at all amused.

"Well now, what about a drink, gels?" Claud suggested, and hailed a cab.

The three of them went off to "The Duke",

Claud's favourite pub in Soho. Sue was pleased to meet him again, for she had always had a soft spot for old Claud. She had inherited him from Ida, who had given up the game and gone home to Tiger Bay. Claud had not been around for a couple of years. His tastes were kinky but usually paid her well and he was no trouble. In fact, she had had many good laughs with old Claud.

Now they sat drinking gin-and-tonics and discussing old times. Gladys sat in the corner looking like a statue of Buddha, stolid and silent with disapproval written all over her face.

"I don't get up to town much these days," explained Claud. "Lost me wife, you know, and had a bit of a stroke last year. Ain't up to the old antics."

"Well, it's nice to see you again, Claud," said Sue pleasantly. "I often wondered what happened to you."

When Claud was in his prime his special act was to tie a blown-up balloon to his penis, chase Sue all over the flat and toss the balloon up in the air until it burst. Sometimes when it really got out of hand, he had chased Gladys as well. She had never forgiven him for that. Sue was always grateful to Claud, for he had given her a few good laughs, which not many of her clients did.

"I've packed it up now, old gel," admitted Claud. "Got too old for all that."

"Well, never mind, love," said Sue kindly. "But we did have fun, didn't we?"

"We sure did, Sue." Claud looked her up and down. "I must say you look well and prosperous."

A smile crossed Sue's face. "Things aren't bad, Claud. Made a few quid and don't have to slog now."

"Good, good, now look after it, there's a good gel. Put a bit of money away for that rainy day." He produced a card from his waistcoat pocket. "If you're interested—it's holiday flatlets, a new idea in self-catering holiday flats. Plenty of money in it, too. I'm on the board of directors." He handed her the card. "My address is on the back. Got a small hotel in Devon, in East Bay. You might like to come down there for a holiday. It'd do you the world of good."

"I'll think about it," said Sue. "You coming home for a coffee, Claud?"

Claud shook his head regretfully. "No, lovey, got to catch a train. Only up for the day. Don't forget, give me a ring and I'll be at the station to meet you. It's been lovely seeing you again. Good luck, old gel. Take care." And off he went to the station.

Back home, Sue took a bath and got ready for her next client. He was a young business executive she had not met before who was coming over from Holland that evening and staying for a few days. He would probably be very young and expect a lot of sex. And no doubt his conversation would be unintelligible and extremely boring. She lay in the perfumed water thinking. She could not complain, she told herself, the money was always very handy. And they did not bother her, these soft, stupid young men; she could eat them for breakfast. Her thoughts settled on her old lover, Apples, or Billy, as he was really called, locked up in jail. Now, he had been a *real* man. If she had kept him she would never have wanted to bed another man.

Rising languidly from her bath, she put on a gown and went over to her wardrobe and took out an old cash box. In it were all the souvenirs of her time with Billy. There was the little turquoise ring, the first he had ever given her. She had had to pawn that to pay for her abortion years ago but she had got it back the moment she had some money. It meant a lot to her. Then there were the two letters, both on blue, official notepaper and marked "OHMS—Prison Service". The first letter had been sent when Billy was on remand and had ordered her to get rid of the teapot lid —the baby she had been expecting. The second letter was posted only last year, when he was in an open prison up north, and it said that he might get parole in a year. He had explained that he was sending the letter to the old address hoping that someone would forward it to her. "I'm sure that you've left Soho behind," he had written. This, to Sue seemed like a veiled threat, for Billy detested whores. He had been a violent criminal but he hated loose women. So she had decided not to answer that letter but she put it with the other one and kept them both safe. They were very special to her and always brought back vivid memories of her true lover, Billy Rafferty, known to the underworld as Apples. Now he was about to end his long prison sentence. Sue longed to visit him or write to him, but much water had passed under the bridge since then, and if Apples found out about the life she lived he would certainly cut her throat without any qualms. Next to the letters in the cash box was a stack of bank notes, all earned the hard way, and some letters from clients making appointments or thanking her for a good time. Thoughtfully she examined them and then put them back. Searching in her handbag, she found the card that Claud had given her that very day. In big black letters it read: Maritime Investments, High Holborn. Perhaps she should put some money away for a rainy day, as Claud had advised. Then, if it paid up good dividends, she would give up prostitution and become a respectable citizen with a good residential address. Who would ever know how she had obtained her money? She was still in good health at the moment, but she might not always be so lucky. "Yes, that's it," she muttered to herself. "I'll kick the game and be there to meet Billy when he comes out." Her heart beat excitedly at the thought of seeing him again.

With a knowing smile she closed the box with a bang and put it back into the wardrobe. Then she heard three sharp rings on the front door bell. "Gladys!" she yelled. "That's that bloody cheesehead. Let him in!" And so business began again.

12

A New Way of Life

A WEEK later, on a bright sunny morning, Sue prepared to leave the flat on her own. Seeing Gladys' expression, she said, "I'm going out alone. Tidy up a bit. I don't want any more callers today. I've some business to attend to."

Gladys screwed up her face in dismay. During the day, she went most places with Sue.

"No, you can't come with me," shouted Sue, slipping on her smart, tailored jacket. But seeing how unhappy Gladys was, she softened. "You can go to the launderette if you like," she added.

A trip to the launderette was always a special treat for Gladys, particularly these days when she was not allowed to go there very often. It was at the launderette that she gathered up all the local gossip from the other maids who took care of the tomcats of Soho. For a long time it had been her main source of social life. But then over the years the Soho scene had changed dramatically. The Chinese had moved on and Commonwealth immigrants had moved in. Gladys was an aggressive racist and disliked them all. "Bloody niggers," she would say loudly. "Slimy Pakkies,

I hate the sodding lot of them." And, of course, her loud remarks in the launderette often landed her in trouble. There was one fight in particular which landed her in the local police station where Sue had to go to collect her and promise to keep her out of trouble in the future. After that, Gladys was barred from the local launderette but occasionally, as a special treat, Sue would allow her to go to the big new washerette on the main road, but with a stern warning: "I'll let you go but you behave yourself."

Having appeased Gladys with this olive branch, Sue strolled out into the street shortly after nine o'clock. The streets were almost deserted and quite silent—so different from what they were like at night. As usual, she was struck by how different the area was from what it was like when she first moved in. Wing Wong's Club was now a hamburger bar and a souvenir shop combined. Wong himself had left in a hurry for Hong Kong a few years back. Now the surrounding streets made up a hive of beer cellars, strip joints, blue film shows and porn shops, which only seemed to exist when their blazing neon lights were turned on after six o'clock. Now in the cold light of day Soho had a dreary face. A few junkies were hanging about on the corners, coming down to a shivering miserable existence after a night on drugs. Ignoring them, Sue recalled bright sunny days before she was even on the game, when she had gone shopping for the prostitutes, Fat

Florrie, Ida and poor Elsie. The wide boys had stood on the corners then and given her shrill wolf whistles as she passed. She could remember the lovely smell of freshly baked bread that wafted from the small delicatessen and the fat man laying the checked tablecloths on the little tables outside. In those days, strings of onions hung in the shop windows and the shelves were laden with the bottles of foreign wines. It was all gone now, that small Continental community. The modern world of vice and violence had driven it out.

Still in a nostalgic mood, Sue boarded the bus to the City. Perhaps it was time she opted out of this world, she thought. Next year if Billy came looking for her, it would be a disaster if he discovered she was on the game.

Getting off the bus at Holborn, she wandered past the tall finance buildings until she reached her destination—the offices of Maritime Holdings. She went up in the lift, and, as Claud had instructed her, requested to see a certain Mr. Henderson. After several minutes waiting, she was ushered into a large office and was soon sitting opposite the managing director, who was a bright young executive and typical of her business expense customers.

"I came here on the recommendation of Mr. Claud Ames," she said, handing the young man the card Claud had given her. "I want you to explain to me how to make an investment in this Maritime Holdings."

The managing director was very pleased to explain it to her. "We have holiday homes all along the coast and now we're about to expand to the Continent. It's a new venture in self-catering chalets. We let them and keep them in good repair and there is a good dividend each year. Many professional people have found it a very good way to invest profitably. I can also assure you it is completely honest and above board, as your Mr. Ames has probably told you."

Sue sat very still in her chair. Her long legs clad in sheer nylon stockings, were crossed and she looked very cool and calm in her neat black suit and white blouse.

Surveying her, the managing director wondered who she was. She was certainly rather attractive. "Is there a sum you had in mind that you wish to invest?" he asked.

"Yes," Sue replied coolly. "Five hundred pounds."

His eyebrows shot up over his specs in surprise. "Well, that's a good sum," he said. "If you will kindly sign these documents, I'll expect your cheque in about a week's time."

"I've brought the money with me," said Sue, opening her handbag and handing him a bundle of notes.

This sight gave the clever young man another rude shock. The pen was quivering in his hand as he wrote down her name and address. His eyes furtively glanced at her long legs. The address she gave was a shady one and he thought it had a familiar ring about it.

"Is Mr. Ames an old friend of yours?" he asked casually.

"No," said Sue without blinking. "Just an old customer."

The man saw her out of his office and very politely said, "Read those papers carefully. They'll give you all the information you need." Once Sue had gone, he darted back into the office to inform his secretary. "Guess what," he said proudly. "I've just signed up a prostitute from Soho. Five hundred pounds in notes she brought with her."

"Don't know what I am wasting my time at this bloody typewriter for," the secretary returned acidly.

When Sue returned to the flat, she wrote a letter to Claud in Devon telling him of her investment. Within a couple of days she received a letter from him in return. "Great guns, old gel," he wrote. "Now take a holiday. I shall be expecting you. Come now while the weather is still fine."

So it was that in September Sue cancelled all her engagements and went on a holiday. It was something she had never done before.

Gladys did not like the idea of a holiday at all. "Why," she exclaimed, "you've got some regulars due this month, and good payers they are too."

"Let 'em sweat," announced Sue breezily. "I've always longed to go to the seaside. All my life I've wanted to, so I'm going now." She had been thinking a lot lately about her poverty-stricken childhood and was quite determined. "Down our street they all used to go hop-picking about this time of year," she said. "I used to watch them put everything except the kitchen sink into an old van, then load it with the kids, aunties, dads and even grannies, and off they'd go to the Kent hop fields. I always thought it was the seaside they were going to, and I'd feel very deprived."

Gladys did not reply, and just gave a dis-approving grunt. Her childhood and youth had been spent in that dreary convent. She had never seen the sea and had no desire to do so now.

"Now, pack up the glad rags, Gladys, and we'll 'gang awaw'," Sue said cheerfully, using a phrase she'd picked up from a Scottish client.

Gladys did as she was told but very un-graciously, slamming doors and crashing open wardrobes to show her disapproval of Susan's latest folly.

The following Monday morning, they travelled from Waterloo Station, first class. Sue looked particularly smart in a well-cut cotton suit and a white blouse. Her dark hair was plaited and bound around her head, and small pearl earrings dangled from her dainty ears. She looked, smelled and felt very expensive.

Leaving Gladys to take care of the luggage, Sue lunched in the dining-car where some of the comfortable-looking gentlemen at other tables gave her admiring glances. She ignored them all. She was going to have a break from that world of sex and vice, she told herself. She was now just a well-dressed lady travelling with her maid.

As they passed Southampton Waters she peered out of the window to stare at the long silver strip of the Solent as it flowed out to sea, and the huge liner in the docks. "That's the sea, Gladys," she whispered. "Isn't it exciting?"

Hours later, the train came to a halt at the quiet little station in Devon. As he had promised, Claud was on the platform waiting to greet them and, to Sue's surprise, outside in the car park stood a smart pony and trap he had brought to collect them.

Gladys was very nervous about climbing aboard. "Mind 'e don't run away," she cried anxiously. " 'old 'im."

Sue made no fuss. She climbed into the trap and sat upright like a queen. Surveying the distant white cliffs and the vast expanse of blue sea, she murmured, "So much space. It's amazing." Almost overcome with a strong sense of freedom, she wanted to stretch out her hands towards the sun. But she restrained the impulse, and just sat very still with a secret smile on her face.

Claud was a little boozy but as gracious as ever. He held the reins gently as the little pony trap rattled along the steep cliff road. The strong sea breeze ruffled the pony's mane. "I like this form of transport," he said. "I lost my licence to drive a car last year—had one too many—but this little chap is marvellous, always knows his way home."

The East Bay Hotel was situated high upon the cliff tops. The only nearby buildings were a few modern bungalows, and the view from the hotel over the bay was stupendous. In awe, Sue gazed down at the sea beating against the huge rocks below. "Oh, it's just as I thought it would look like," she cried.

"It's a wild, rocky bay," replied Claud, "but I like it. It does get a bit lonely during the winter months, though. It's all right this time of year. Still got a few guests—shark fishermen. Don't go in for a lot of visitors since I lost my wife. Used to at one time, though."

But Sue was hardly listening, so thrilled was she at the view from the garden. As they entered the small hotel, she noticed that it had a quiet air about it, and the smell of furniture polish and spicy food helped to make her feel at home. Claud showed them their rooms, which were clean and very comfortable. But Gladys, still in a very bad mood, complained about the cold.

"Oh, do shut up complaining!" Sue told her after Claud had left them to settle in. "I'm here on holiday and that's what I intend to have."

After dinner, Sue went to the bar and drank with Claud who introduced her to some of the shark fishermen. These were husky, sun-tanned men who went out to sea fishing each day, but at night drank themselves silly and sang songs in raucous voices. Sue enjoyed their company and a good time was had by all.

The next day, she explored the small village and climbed down to the rocky shore where the huge gulls screeched overhead. She felt ecstatically happy. All her life there had been someone making demands on her, using up her energy, dulling her mind. She had always been tormented by a nagging feeling that there was something else to be done. Now this was really freedom! She was as free as those gulls circling overhead . . . In the children's home and the various other institutions where she had lived, the days had been divided into time. Every night in Soho someone needed her body. There had never been time to do all the things she wanted to do. Now, on this wild, rocky shore she was alone and completely free. It was a strange and wonderful feeling. She found herself thinking of Billy and wishing that she could share this moment with him. She wondered if he would appreciate it as much as she did.

Gladys would never go very far from the hotel.

She would occasionally go out into the garden but never for long. The sight of the high cliffs and the narrow path down to the sea really scared her. And there was too much expanse of blue sky and sea.

"No, fanks," she said when Sue first asked her to accompany her. "One false step and you could break your neck. I'll sit in the garden."

Sue spent her days alone, feeling free and completely captivated by this rocky cove on the Devon shore and she began to entertain thoughts about leaving London and settling down in this peaceful haven. But when she mentioned this idea to Gladys, her poor friend immediately became very alarmed.

"Sue," she cried. "Have you gone raving mad? This 'ere place will be deserted in the winter. It'll be a wild and windy place, and with that terrible rough sea, and nuffing else to look at."

This was a long speech from Gladys, but she was outraged that Sue could even consider giving up her way of life in Soho.

"Don't worry, Gladys," Sue tried to appease her. "You'll still be taken care of. You know you have a home with me as long as you need it."

"It wouldn't be the same, Sue, if you came 'ere," Gladys tearfully explained. "You wouldn't be independent no more."

But now Sue lost her temper. Flying into one of her terrible rages, she slapped Gladys across the face and shouted and raved at her. "Don't be so bloody stupid! Who's independent? I let some bastard do anything he likes with my body just because he pays me a few quid. So how independent is that?"

Afraid of Sue's temper and unable to stand up to her, Gladys wept and then went into a sulky silence.

Feeling very angry, Sue went down into the bar and, for the first time since her holiday had begun, had too much to drink.

After a while Claud joined her and then they retired to Sue's bedroom. But Claud was well past sex nowadays and his efforts to achieve it made Sue want to vomit. "Better tie a bloody balloon on it, like you used to," she said nastily. "That's the only way it's going to rise up."

Claud was sitting on the edge of the bed completely naked. He had a sad look of dejection on his face, but his old wrinkled body and his wispy grey hair repulsed her.

"Sorry, Sue," he apologized. "I wanted to try and please you. I'm fond of you, you know that, but with me it's all over—there's no use in me trying any more. But if you want to come down here, why don't you come and share the business with me. I've no children to take over from me. My next of kin is a distant relative."

With her dark hair hanging loose over her bare shoulders, Sue looked sideways at him in a speculative way. "You've given me an idea,

Claud," she said slowly. "I'll sleep on it. That might solve a few of my problems."

"Good night, Sue." Claud bent down and kissed her. "I'm not such a bad old sort, you know, once you get to know me."

13

A Crooked Friend from the Past

AFTER two idyllic weeks, the holiday came to an end. Tears had filled Sue's eyes as she said goodbye to old Claud at the station. Confident that they would meet again soon, Claud had been more cheerful. "Think about my suggestion, Sue," he had said. "I'm sure you'd be happy here, and it might be a good proposition for you. The life you lead now will beat you in the end."

"Well, Gladys," said Sue as they sat in the train, "it's back to the old grindstone."

Gladys sniffed. "Never felt warm the whole time I was there," she grumbled.

Sue grinned. "You're getting old, Gladys," she said. "Can't take the fresh air no more."

"Aren't we all?" replied Gladys disagreeably. "Hasn't done your looks any good, all that sunbaving. Yer got bags under yer eyes now."

"I guess I'll just have to get a facial," returned Sue, good-naturedly patting her face. "I certainly don't want to go home, I loved it and felt so free."

"Free's the right word and all," sneered Gladys. "I didn't see no men there who wanted to part wiv an 'undred quid. They would all want it free."

"Oh, you're a depressing old bugger," snapped Sue. After that exchange, she fell silent and sat looking out of the window. As usual, her thoughts went back to Billy. He had had practically no freedom; he was just locked up in a cage. She wondered if he had ever seen the seaside. It was very likely that he hadn't, having also been reared in a back street of the East End. He used to tell her about how, in his youth, he and his mates would go scrounging along the Thames shore at low tide finding rings and coins, anything to raise money. Seeing him now in her mind's eye—his rosy cheeks and his strong, fair body—she wondered if they would ever get together again. If she married old Claud and lived respectably, she would write to Billy but then he could never be her lover again. So that was not the way. But the present way was not right, either. He hated prostitutes. "Get them whores out of my house," he used to yell whenever Ida or Fat Florrie came visiting.

She sighed deeply. She really was between the devil and the deep blue sea. There was no end to her problem. Still, she decided that it was better not to think about it. She would not cross her bridges until the year was out.

Having made this decision, she returned to Soho, she plastered on her make-up and lounged on the pink divan draped in her lovely negligee awaiting her customers. And life went on as usual.

Back in the flat, Gladys was in her element. She always kept the place perfectly clean, cooked appetizing dishes for Sue, and opened the door each evening to the eager clients. In her hard manner, Sue coped with it as always, but now she pushed all thoughts of Billy from her mind and refused to recall the smell of the salt sea or the warmth of that cosy hotel on the Devon cliffs. Business always livened up in the winter because many more conferences were held in the big hotels and more businessmen were in town. The money rolled in for Sue from her work, and then, in the New Year, she received her first dividend from the Maritime Holdings. It was a very substantial sum.

The night life of the swinging city continued. The vice, the violence and the criminal activity increased. More and more foreign immigrants poured into London, and groups of teenagers on hard drugs sat around the statue of Eros in Piccadilly. The pushers and the pedlars invaded the coffee bars and loud reggae music blasted out into the streets so loudly that it could be heard over the noise of the traffic.

'It's becoming such a bloody noisy town," commented Sue one night.

"Better than being bored out of yer mind at some old seaside," retorted Gladys.

Deep in her heart Sue longed for the peace and

beauty that she had had for those two weeks in Devon but stoically she plodded on. She was taken out most nights by her clients to posh restaurants or business parties. And deep in her heart she hated the muscular young men who used her body night after night. Slowly she began to allow herself to think again of the future and she would jubilantly turn over the idea that as soon as spring came she was going to escape from this sordid life.

Coming home early one morning with one of her clients, a big blond West German called Jurgen, she saw a shadowy shape in the porch. She hesitated. There were so many dangers at night now in Soho—muggers and pickpockets who waited for the prostitutes and their escorts going in late at night. The German's hold tightened on her arm as a gruff voice said, "Is that you, Sue? It's Freddie, that old gel won't let me in."

Now she could just see his features. The shadowy figure was Freddie the Sly, the wide boy from the past. Another lad from the slums, he had been one of Sam's Boys and a companion of Billy's. Immediately she thought he might have news of Billy.

She released her arm from the young German's grip. "Just a moment," she said, "it's a friend. I must speak to him. You go inside. Gladys will open the door for you."

With some reluctance, the client did as he was

told and Sue took Freddie to one side. "Hullo, Freddie. This is a surprise."

"I can see that you're busy," sneered Freddie.

"Oh, just an acquaintance," lied Sue. "He won't be staying." She took in Freddie's seedy appearance. He was just out of nick, by the look of him, she thought. Slipping him a fiver, she said, "Go down the road to the all-night café and get a meal. I'll see you back here in about an hour."

Freddie grabbed the note and slid off. He did not return for two hours by which time he was a little drunk and somewhat belligerent. By this time, Sue had managed to get rid of the young German and now sat on the settee freshly bathed and dressed in her very best dressing-gown as she waited anxiously for news of Billy.

Freddie was not particularly helpful. He told her that he had seen Billy when he was on remand up north. It was only for one night, though, and they did not get much chance to communicate. But Freddie told her, Billy had looked well and was about to go to the open prison to finish his sentence. Freddie looked nosily around the room. "This is old Elsie's flat, ain't it, Sue?" he said. "How do you manage to keep it? Must be doing well."

Sue's heart missed a beat. Freddie did not know that she had turned professional. Could she trust him?

Gladys stood in the corner with a very sour

look on her face as she stared aggressively at Freddie. She was tense and ready to turn him out forcibly, if Sue required.

"I'm only out on bail," Freddie informed her. "I'm going down on a long stretch this time. I got mixed up in the hijack of a lorry full of gin."

Sue gave him a sympathetic grin but her mind was working hard to think of a way to fool Freddie. She could not trust him, she decided. He must not find out the truth. "I work in a hotel," she finally said. "Not much else doing around here. Wing Wong's Club is closed."

"So you're not on the game, then?" Freddie seemed a little surprised.

Sue looked shocked. "Me? On the game? Of course not, for Christ's sake. Billy would jump the wall and slit my throat if I was."

Freddie nodded knowingly. "Oh, so you're still a goner for him. Then what's with the German guy?" he asked slyly.

"Just a fellow escorting me home from work," Sue replied blithely. "Going to have a drink, that's all."

Freddie shrugged. "Well, I should have thought you would do all right here, Sue. It's a nice little flat, this. I remember poor old Elsie —what a junkie! You never heard from her, I suppose."

"No, Freddie," said Sue. "I keep the flat on because it's handy but I'm perfectly straight, I can assure you."

174

"It's your business, Sue," said Freddie. "Can I kip down here till tomorrow?"

"If you want to," relieved that he had stopped asking questions. "Get him a blanket, Gladys. I'd better get some kip myself. It'll soon be daylight."

Muttering loudly under her breath, Gladys threw a blanket at Freddie.

"Who's the dragon, Sue?" Freddie asked as he made up a bed for himself on the sofa.

"That's Gladys, my maid and she's okay, Freddie, as long as you don't upset her."

Soon they had all settled down for the night— Sue in her bedroom, Gladys in hers, and Freddie on the sofa. Sue was very tired and she slept heavily, waking up very briefly only once when she thought she heard a movement in her room. But then she sleepily dismissed it and dozed off again.

She was awakened at daylight by a series of loud thumps and Gladys' voice calling her. Staggering out of bed, she opened the door to the sitting room and groaned. There was no sign of Freddie, and the room was in a total upheaval. Drawers were open, the carpet was ripped up and cupboards had had all their contents spilled out onto the floor.

"Oh, dear!" cried Sue. "The slimy bastard!"

Gladys had been locked in her room and was hammering loudly on the door. When Sue unlocked the door, it was as if she were releasing a wild animal. Gladys charged out and ran back and forth across the room, picking up an article here and there. "I knew it!" she exclaimed. "Should never have let him in, Sue. He had the look of a crook written all over him."

But Sue had gone very quiet. Stepping quickly back into her bedroom, she looked into the wardrobe and there, staring at her, was the precious cashbox lying upside down and empty. "Oh no! he's pinched everything!" she cried. "All my letters! And Billy's ring—whatever am I going to do?"

"Inform the police," said Gladys. "Put 'im where 'e belongs."

"No," said Sue, "he can have the money and I'll try and get my letters back. But, oh, I feel so lost without my Billy's little ring. It was the first one he ever gave me."

"All that damned 'ard work for nuffing," complained Gladys.

Sue threw the blanket which had covered Freddie onto the floor and lay languidly on the sofa. "Right," she said. "My mind is made up. I'm quitting in the spring. I've really had enough. Put the kettle on, Gladys."

The next day, Sue visited all the shady bars and low-class cafés in the area looking for Freddie, but did not find him. Later that night she got news that Freddie had been put away for five years. A young newspaper reporter told her. He had been at court that morning.

"Well, that's that, then," said Sue. "He might have torn up the letters. I'll probably never get them now so it's no use worrying."

But she could not help worrying a little. Some of those letters were pretty sharp and were from old customers who had put pen to paper. Some were not very nice and some just thanked her for her services . . .

Her determination to start a new life remained with her. "I'm bloody well going to kick this game," she said. "I'll give it up. I want to be clean and free." Each day the desire became stronger. Increasingly she longed to escape, to get away from this stinking web of vice. She loathed the crime and the evil that clung tenaciously on to her way of life like a big maggot eating into a fresh cabbage. It all revolted her and she thought it strange that she had not thought of it like this before. It was the big fleas living off little fleas. Her attitude to her life had been changed by that holiday by the sea. Soho had not been so bad a few years ago—of course, the ponces had beaten up their girls if the girls did not hand over the money, but that was an accepted thing. Nowadays they stripped the girls naked, man-handled them and then dumped them onto a rubbish tip. Sue often read the *News of the World* on Sunday mornings and reading about all the vice sickened her. Afterwards she would lie on her divan resting and dreaming of the blue skies and stretches of golden sands. How she had loved those rocky coves where the huge waves dashed themselves against the rocks, and where the high winds seemed cool! The whole shore had had a peaceful air. She often thought about those large herring gulls screeching overhead and fighting persistently with each other on the beach for scraps. The big ones were so beautiful—smooth and white with grey wings, but the smaller ones had been grey and very ugly.

"They are the squeakers," Claud had informed her. "They remain that dirty grey colour until they're adult, just like young swans."

Sue had been amazed by all the new wonders that Claud had shown to her during those two weeks. Now she lay thinking about them in her little flat in the centre of London amid the roar of the traffic which sounded loud through the window. Although it was still just a dream, she knew that she had to go back to East Bay. She was not ready yet, since Sly Freddie had stolen all her spare cash. She had to save up a fair bit again. It was just as well she had put that five hundred pounds away, she told herself, otherwise he would have had the lot. It was the loss of the letters that bothered her most now, but she hoped that Freddie's conscience might prick him after he had read the letters. He might, she hoped, send them back to her. So, forcing herself to be optimistic, she concentrated on her work, satisfying the desires of an endless procession of stupid, drunken men as well as her regular clients. She had to take on the extra work to earn back what she had lost.

Finally, in February, she put an advertisement in the paper: "Flat fully furnished for sale."

Gladys was horrified. "Oh, Sue! You can't do that. Don't burn your boats yet, it would be a disaster."

"Shut your face," snarled Sue. "I don't need the furniture so I might as well have the money for it."

"But, Sue," wailed Gladys, "you'll never be able to find another flat in London."

"I don't want one in London. I'm not coming back," Sue announced firmly.

"But what about your business?" cried Gladys. "You can't afford to lose those regular clients."

Sue grasped Gladys firmly by the back of the neck and shook her till that frizzy head with its golden earloops rattled. "Get it into your thick head," she yelled, "that once and for all times, I'm quitting this lousy game while I'm still in good health. I don't want to end up like those whining, grizzling whores scrounging drinks at The Duke."

Gladys' slant eyes looked for a moment as if they might produce tears but they remained dry. She just sat on the sofa looking crestfallen and very sorry for herself.

"Don't just sit there," raved Sue. "Get up and start packing!"

Gladys got up and did as she was bid. Instant

obedience had been instilled in her by the convent.

"Don't know why you're complaining," continued Sue. "You're retiring to a nice rest home by the sea."

Sue had a whale of a time, smashing up the rest of Elsie's knick-knacks, tearing up old negligées and fancy underwear, and stuffing shoes and dresses into a plastic bag. "I'm not taking any of this rubbish," she declared. "You can phone Oxfam and tell them to come and collect it."

Gladys did not answer but watched with mournful eyes as the sequinned dresses, low-necked blouses and many other lovely things disappeared into the bag.

"I'll buy some sober kind of dresses," declared Sue, "and have a new start. We'll both have a new start."

14

East Bay

THE journey down to Devon that spring was an exciting one for Sue. She had accomplished her task and saved a lot of cash and, at last, left Soho behind for good. She had no regrets at all and was determined to begin a new kind of life.

As Sue expected, Gladys was very depressed, but Sue had been firm with her. "If you really don't want to come to Devon with me," she told her, "I suppose you can go back to the bloody convent."

"No, Sue," Gladys had pleaded sadly. "Never that. I'd sooner stay here and get a job somewhere else."

"You want to desert me after all this time?" Sue had stared at Gladys in astonishment.

At this accusation, the wizened little face had crumpled up in grief. "Not unless you don't want me," Gladys had wailed.

Immediately, Sue had repented. "Don't be silly," she said, cuddling Gladys tightly. "Of course I want you. Why, we'll have the time of our lives down there at the seaside—you should think yourself lucky." Gladys had then smiled and cheered up slightly.

Now as they sat in the train, Gladys said quietly, "No one ever wanted me but you, Sue. My parents gave me to that rotten convent when I was born. I was too ugly and unsightly, they thought, to be owned by them."

"Didn't you even know who they were?" asked Sue gently.

"I did hear that they had plenty of money and gave to the Church. That's why the convent took me. Once I heard Sister Winifred remark, 'Conceived in drink, God save us', and I think she meant me."

"Oh, don't think back, Gladys. Let's look forward now," said Sue. She smiled. "I must say, you look very smart today. That beige suit is nice —much better than that drab old brown."

Gladys' mouth twisted into a little smile and her tiny rough hands reached up to adjust the new straw hat that matched the suit. "Do I, Sue?" she said anxiously.

Claud was at the station to meet them. Sitting in his little pony cart, he did not look well. His old face seemed more lined and was pallid and drawn.

"Had a bad dose of flu in the winter," he explained. "Haven't quite got over it yet." He gave Sue a hug. "It's great to see you, love. There'll be plenty for you to do down here when the season starts. Why, hullo little donkey . . ."

He gave Gladys a friendly pat. "Going to put you out to grass—how's that?"

Gladys was not at all amused, and she pulled away from him with an angry scowl on her face.

As the pony cart rattled along the cliff road, Sue thought that East Bay looked magnificent on this fine spring day. There again was the lovely view across the bay, and the long line of cliffs stretching round the cove glowed white and green in the brilliant sunshine. The air was so fresh and clean and smelled of the sea. There was not a soul down there on the little patch of sand, for it was still too early for the holiday-makers. But her old friends, the herring gulls, gracefully circled the bay, their cries echoing over the land. "It's all so clean and bright," Sue said. "It's as if everything has just been newly washed—even the houses look scrubbed."

"I expect the winter gales have cleaned them up a bit," remarked Claud. "It's been a long, cold winter. We had some very heavy storms in December—we lost a couple of fishing boats, with all the crew aboard."

But Sue was not listening as they drove up the steep slope to the hotel for her heart was pounding with excitement as she saw the huge waves crashing against the rocky shore. This was to be her home now, she thought. And it felt like home, as no other place ever had before. That made her very happy.

It did not take long for them to settle in. And

even Gladys was content once she realized how much she was needed to keep the huge, rather neglected hotel in order. She became her old self once more, and even acknowledged Claud's jovial banter with a sly grin. Her convent training made her such an asset to the hotel. The old brass coal-scuttles and wall-plates were all grimy and black from neglect. Claud was not fit enough to do them and the domestics who came in every day were not reliable enough to see that the brasswork was done. But Gladys burnished and polished them all until everything was bright and shiny. And she kept it up, vigorously polishing everything each morning until it all shone brilliantly. Gladys would stand back and smile proudly at the sight.

"My word," Claud would declare to Sue, "what a worker that little one is. Those horse brasses around the fireplace haven't looked like that since my wife died. Now she was a stickler for cleanliness."

"Gladys will be all right as long as she's needed," Sue told him. "She's hard as nails and will work like the donkey you're always calling her."

Sue learned to serve drinks in the bar and had a way with all the customers, whether they were in the public bar or the hotel. She also loved to pick flowers from the garden and arrange them in vases. Since it was spring, the hotel was scented throughout by pink and mauve hyacinths, and large clumps of yellow daffodils brightened up the gloomy hallways.

Claud was very pleased. "They've done wonders," he would inform his customers. "Can't think how I managed without them."

During the day, in a smart tailored dress, Sue would look after the reception desk and see that the guests were booked in and out. Tall, elegant and bursting with energy, Sue was everything that Claud needed to keep his business and his home going. "Made no mistake there, old son," he would tell himself repeatedly.

What Sue enjoyed most was the early morning, when she went down to the small harbour to watch the fishing boats come in. On the quayside she would wander between the huge baskets full of shining mackerel which could be bought for a few shillings, or freshly caught crabs and lobsters struggling to climb out. It all fascinated Sue, and in her chatty manner she got to know the various boats and the fishermen, who greatly appreciated her smart slacks and tight jersey. She liked them all; they were her own kind of men—solid, earthy types she was always at ease with. She could sit on the harbour wall laughing and talking with them for hours.

When summer finally arrived, Sue would spend her leisure hours lying on the beach clad in a brief swimming suit and wishing she could swim. Sue had never learned to swim, for there had not been the time or the opportunity in her cramped youth.

185

Now she would look on enviously as the holiday-makers romped confidently in the waves. She would often imagine herself and Billy floating out there on a calm sea. She knew that Billy could swim, for he had learned the hard way by playing on the muddy banks of the Thames and falling in.

She smiled to herself now as she thought about him. How he would love it down here! Billy would be just finishing his sentence, now, she thought, in that open prison. She still remembered his prison number—it was stamped on her heart. Suddenly she leaped to her feet, scattering sand everywhere. She knew what she had to do . . . She would go home and write to Billy. She would write him the first letter in years to find out if he still loved her. She now had a respectable address for his letters to come to, so it could not do any harm.

The hotel bar in mid-season was busy, so it was long after midnight before Sue finally sat down in her room to compose a love letter to her man on Claud's headed notepaper. East Bay Hotel, Devon: it looked nice and sounded very respectable, she thought with pleasure.

Dear Billy,
After all this time I felt I must write to you. I expect you will be going home soon. I am working down in Devon in an hotel. It is very nice here. Do hope you have not forgotten me.

I have never forgotten you and my love for you is as strong as ever. So if you will drop me a line perhaps we can keep in touch once you are out.

Love Susan.

Sue read the letter through and sighed. It was not much of a love letter but then she had always found it difficult to put words on paper. But at least her handwriting was strong and clear.

On her way to the beach the next morning, she posted the letter and stood by the letter box with fingers crossed. "Oh, please, Billy, please still love me," she whispered.

Billy's reply came two weeks later. Claud picked up the mail and gazed curiously at this particular letter addressed to Sue. The blue envelope was marked "OHMS, Strangeways Prison".

"Is this yours, Sue?" he asked.

Sue quickly snatched the letter from him. "It's from my brother," she explained. "I wrote to him. He's in trouble but we correspond." With that, she dashed off to her room to read it.

Billy's handwriting had improved quite a lot since the last letters he had written. A feeling of happiness washed over her as she read his words.

Dear Sue,
So pleased to hear from you, Sue. Also so glad that you have left London and are now

working. I often used to worry over you but now you have given me hope that we can begin again, my love. I lost my old Mum since I was inside so I have only you to care for now. I've still got three months to do but it will soon pass. In the meantime, keep writing. You don't know how good it made me feel. All my love,

Billy.

Sue wept and kissed the letter. After that she kept it in her pocket and every free moment she would take it out and read it over and over again.

Gladys did not think much of this. "Don't tell me you're still mooning over that bloke who got put away?" she sniffed.

"Mind your own bloody business!" snapped Sue. "And keep your mouth shut."

"Who cares? It's your pigeon," retorted Gladys, going off in a huff.

Throughout that beautiful and bright summer, Sue got a letter every month from Billy. She in turn wrote to him every week without fail to tell him of her plans to get him to come down to Devon. She had saved quite a bit of money, she told him, and would get a little beach cottage for them to live in. Inwardly, she was concerned about Claud and what his reaction would be to this plan of hers. Claud always gave her Billy's letters with a sort of questioning look on his kind face. But Sue adamantly refused to discuss anything with him which concerned her plans.

As autumn approached, the early morning mists lay over the sea and a sharp breeze blew in from the east. The hotel began to empty as the holiday-makers went home. There was much less to do in the hotel now and Sue would often sit with the others in the dining-room around a log fire. Claud and Sue would chat while Gladys sat crocheting, a hobby she had recently taken up. She had become very good at it and had started to make things, like lace doilies and pretty tablecloths. Once she even gave Sue a present of a pretty open lace-work jumper she had made. Gladys had settled down at the hotel and become as contented as a sleek old cat.

"Would you like to go up to London with me for a week, Sue?" Claud asked one evening. "Do a bit of shopping and visit old places. The hotel's done very well this year, thanks to you, and I'd like to repay you, Sue."

Sue hesitated and then said, "No, you go, Claud. I'll look after things here."

She knew that Claud was disappointed that she had turned down his offer, but Billy would be arriving any day and she was determined not to miss him.

So Claud went off to London on his own one misty November day. "I'll see about our investments while I am in town," he told Sue. "We should get an extra dividend this year."

As soon as he had gone, Sue called Gladys. "Come on," she said, "help me get the best suite ready. We're going to have a very important visitor."

"I ain't never 'eard of no important visitor," complained Gladys. "I thought the 'otel part was shut for the winter."

"Well, it's not," Sue informed her. "I've got a very special guest coming."

Gladys' eyes gleamed. "A man, Sue?"

"Oh yes!" replied Sue with a coy smile. "A real male, a he-man, my lover, Billy."

Gladys gasped. "Oh, no, Sue, you can't do that to Claud!" she cried. Now that she had got to know Claud better, she was steadfastly loyal to him.

"Who says I can't?" Sue challenged her. And the determination in her eyes made Gladys retreat. She knew her wilful mistress very well, and there was no point in trying to change her mind.

When Sue went to meet Billy at the station, she wore her fur coat and a little beret. He had a week's parole to adjust himself to life outside the prison walls before his official release. At first she did not recognize him as he stood there on the station platform. He wore a cheap, ill-fitting suit and had lost a lot of weight. His hair line had receded and his high polished forehead made him look much older. But Billy knew her instantly and swept her into his arms. Regardless of who saw them, they stood locked together on the little station in a close embrace for several minutes.

Then, hand in hand, they walked up the High Street with smiles on their faces. "Quaint little spot," said Billy. "How did you find it, Sue?"

"The job was advertised in the paper," lied Sue. "The boss has gone off on a holiday and left me in charge. I'm going to smuggle you in there. Is that all right with you, Billy?" She stared lovingly at him.

"I have to be very careful, Sue. I'm only out on parole and I can't afford to get into any trouble."

"There won't be any trouble, darling," she assured him. "It's all laid on. Just trust me. The only thing is that I've told the two servants that you're my brother. There are no other guests. The hotel is closed for the winter and only the bars are open."

Sue called a taxi and soon they were at the hotel where Billy was booked in as an unofficial guest, and Sue's brother. The cook and the lounge barman, the only staff retained for the winter, accepted this as the sort of thing that happened when the boss was away.

Billy stared around the huge bedroom and at the bathroom next door. "Blimey, Sue," he exclaimed. "What's this? The honeymoon suite?"

"Yes, darling," said Sue, already removing her dress.

It was early afternoon when they went to bed and made passionate love. Billy was a little shy at first but Sue, experienced in these matters, soon made him lose his fears. She had never been so happy. This was her man, her true mate. Not since she was a teenager and had fancied Dodgy Roger had she been so eager for love. They made love over and over again, and did not emerge from the guest room until the next morning.

15

Poor Old Claud

IT was a sad moment for Sue when the week was up and Billy had to return to the nick. Their brief honeymoon had been a great success. Billy had lost his prison pallor and had even put on a couple of pounds in weight. But best of all, they had taken the opportunity to get to know each other again and neither had been disappointed. Sue loved Billy's rough, possessive ways which made her no longer feel like an aggressive woman with a chip on her shoulder. She felt that she had put her past life well behind her and was most decidedly a reformed character; indeed, it showed in the subdued way she dressed and the nice upright way she walked.

"Sue, my love," said Billy, as they lay in bed together on that last day, "you've certainly grown into a very nice, mature woman. I'd be proud to have you as my wife, if you still want me . . ."

"Oh, Billy!" cried Sue ecstatically, flinging her arms about his neck. "I love you so much, I can't bear the thought of you leaving me."

"I'll be back, darling," replied Billy. "But remember that I haven't got a job, and I've never held on to a regular job. I've always been a tearaway, you know that."

"That doesn't matter," she cried, holding on to him fiercely. "Billy, darling, if you desert me I don't know what I will do now that I've had you back with me for a short while. But we'll get by, I've got some money saved. I'll quit the hotel and find us a little cottage, or something. There are a lot of things we can do together."

"Well, I ain't no bleeding gigolo," announced Billy, "so don't count on it, Sue. It's fine down here for a holiday but whether I'd get a living is another matter."

"But you could get a boat and go fishing—a lot of the men do that down here."

"There's no money in fishing, Sue," said Billy, shaking his head. "I like it here, the sea fascinates me, but we've got to eat."

Sue hugged him tight. "I've told you that there's no need to worry. I've got money saved up for us."

"We could get spliced when I come out and then go back to London," he told her. "Me brother-in-law is in the transport business and might give me a job."

"Oh, Billy, Billy, darling," she cried. "Please be quiet. Don't spoil our last day together."

He kissed her hard on the lips. "Don't worry, I won't," he said with a smile. "And I promise you that I'll go straight once I'm out. I've had enough of the bloody nick."

194

"Good, good, darling," Sue cried, covering his face with kisses. "Now, love me so I will have so much to remember . . ."

Sue's eyes were still red with crying when Claud returned from his London trip. For Billy had gone back to his cage and would not be out again for several months. Claud looked at her strangely when he first arrived home, but it did not take long for him to find out at least some of what had been going on in his absence. The cook was the first to let on. "We had a guest in the best suite all the week," she informed him.

"A honeymoon couple?" Claud enquired.

"Well, it could be," the cook said with a shrug. "It was supposed to be Sue's brother but she spent most of her time with him up there."

Claud looked annoyed but was reluctant to jump to conclusions. "Ah well," he said, "Sue was in charge and it was up to her what she did."

That evening it was a very subdued Sue who served behind the bar. It was Saturday and, as usual, the locals came in force to the public bar.

The women all huddled together on a long seat swallowing their stout, and whispering and gossiping while the men played darts and shove ha'penny or simply lounged against the bar. It was a nice homely scene and usually Sue felt very much at home there; she liked the locals and they in turn were fond of her. But tonight she was feeling a little shifty about her behaviour the week before. She had come down to the bar on Saturday evening with Billy and, unfortunately, they had had a few drinks too many. Without thinking, Sue had lolled all over him, fussing and petting him, and practically raping him with her dark, passionate eyes. The locals had been shocked at this display.

"Ah, ee's no brother," Dora had said in her Bristol accent.

"Oi ain't never bin *that* fond o' me brother," said her daughter Bess, who was sitting beside her.

Regardless of the locals' sharp scrutiny, Sue had continued to love and fondle her man.

"Blimey," remarked Bess, "she's even turning me on." Bess' husband, who was playing darts across the room, was a Cockney and known to everyone as Titch.

The gossip zipped around the bar like a forest fire, and there was a series of nudges and winks as Sue kissed her man and fondled his knees. Billy had begun to look very embarrassed as his penis stiffened and showed through his tight jeans.

Then the men passed coarse remarks among themselves and laughed loudly.

"Who is he?" demanded Dora. "I've never seen him afore."

"He's a Londoner," said Titch. "Spoke to him down on the quay. A nice chap."

"Never seen Sue act like that before," announced Bess looking very concerned. "I thought she was old Claud's woman. He's certainly very fond of her."

"The cat's away and the mice will play," said Dora's friend Marie. "He's nice," she added. "I could fancy him myself."

"Tut, tut!" declared Dora. "What a disgraceful thing for an old woman like you to say."

"Oh, who cares?" replied Marie. "My old man can't supply me any more, and there's no harm in wishing."

And so the conversation in the bar continued until Wendy, the part-time barmaid, rang the bell for time. "Come on," she called. "Let's get home, it's past time."

The locals began to leave, but Sue and her man had already disappeared—back to bed. Then, as always, Jim the butcher came to the bar. This was his Saturday routine: always at eleven o'clock he would come in for a drink and also catch the last few customers going home who might have forgotten their Sunday joint. After he had had a drink, Jim would supply anyone from his mobile van. Tonight he had to needs listen to all the goings-on in the bar with Sue and her so-called brother.

"What? We having incest now?" he joked. "That makes a bloody change down here. It would cause a bit of excitement in the local paper, that would."

"He's not 'er brother," decided Dora.

"No," agreed Bess, "I think they know each other, if you know what I mean." She was always very precise, was young Bess.

"Ah well, Jim," said Titch, "got a nice bit o' steak, have you? I better get going—all that sex talk has turned me on."

"All as I hope," said Dora's husband, Alfred, who was a very quiet man, "is that old Claud don't get a wheeze of it. It'll upset him a lot, it will."

But old Claud had quickly got the wheeze of it when he got back from London. In fact, he was fed up to the teeth by the number of people who wished to talk to him of Sue's misdemeanours. He only had to walk the dog down to the village post office to be stopped several times by people who "thought he ought to know . . ." He returned to the hotel feeling despondent. His shoulders were slightly bowed and he felt he had little to say to Sue.

So now Saturday night had come round again and Sue had to face the consequences of last week's behaviour. "I wonder what the gossips will have to say tonight," she muttered somewhat anxiously to Gladys, who was drying glasses.

"Well, you were a bit naughty, Sue. The cook heard all sorts of things about your goings-on with that Billy."

"Oh, sod them!" declared Sue. "If old Claud asks me, I'll just tell him the truth."

"Just as well," said Gladys. "Then perhaps we can go home."

"Go home?" yelled Sue. "You are home!"

"Back home to Soho, I meant—that's home to me."

"Oh, Gladys," sighed Sue, "will you never change your ways?"

When Claud came in with the dog, he slowly put his stick into the umbrella stand and wearily wiped his feet on the mat.

From her position in the bar, Sue watched him. He looked pale and his features were drawn and tired-looking.

"Feeling tired?" she asked brightly. "I expect you've walked too far."

"Not far enough, Sue," replied Claud. "Can't get away from the buggers all keen to tell me about your goings-on."

Sue blushed but she decided to take the bull by the horns. "Well, that's how it is, Claud. Do you want me to tell you the truth?"

Claud nodded. "I'd be much obliged if you would, Sue."

Sue took a deep breath. "Okay, then," she began, "the man they are all talking about is Billy Rafferty. He's just out on parole after seven years inside."

Claud nodded as if he was not surprised. "But surely you could have gone to stay in town with him," he said. "Why poop on your own door-step?"

Claud's attitude suddenly made Sue become extremely angry. Why should she make excuses? After all, she was still a free agent. "If you mean shit why don't you say shit?" she snapped irritably.

Claud drew back and looked offended. He was, in all circumstances, always a gentleman. "The folks down here have learned to respect you, Sue. It'd be a pity to spoil it for yourself."

Sue tossed back her hair. "Oh, they can go to Hell," she declared, "because I don't care any more. When Billy comes out in a few months' time, we're going to be married."

Claud paled a little. "Well, that's your prerogative, Sue, but I had hoped that you'd settled down. If you marry an ex-convict now, you'll be back on the game in no time."

Two scarlet patches appeared on her cheeks as one of her terrible rages overwhelmed her. "Is that what you think?" she screamed. "Well, my Billy hates whores. He was my man before I went on the game. I said I'd keep straight and I am going to."

"All right, all right," said Claud, trying to calm her. "That's all up to you, but give me time to replace you. You've been a great asset to me here and I'll miss you. You know I'm not as fit as I was." As he spoke, his old hand trembled and he grabbed the back of the chair to steady himself.

Instantly Sue was at his side. She put her arms about his neck. "Oh, I'm so sorry," she said. "Sit down now, and don't let me upset you, please, Claud."

"It's all right, pet." Claud patted her shoulder; his voice was choked. "I suppose I've got fond of you but it's possible I expected too much of you." He sat down in the chair as Sue went to the sideboard and poured him a glass of brandy. She gave him the drink and sat down beside him.

"Let me explain, darling," she said. "I'll never stop being grateful to you for what you've done for Gladys and me, but I love this man, you have to understand that. He fathered my second child and because he was sent to prison I had it aborted. Please understand, Claud, I have this dream of living a clean and full life once more. Am I a fool for wanting that? You tell me."

Claud shook his head and patted her hand. "No, Sue, you're probably right, and I'm just an old fool, so let's not cross our bridges till we come to them, shall we?"

She kissed him on the brow. "Now you sit there. I'll go and open the bar. I'm quite ready for those gossiping old women, so don't you worry."

After a few weekends the whispering and the chuckling in the public bar had died away and Sue was once more a well-loved figure there, part of the community again, rather than apart from it. Life settled down once more and Sue was quite content. Poor Claud's health, however, deteriorated over that winter, and he began to rely on Sue more than ever.

Meanwhile, Sue wrote regularly to Billy outlining her plans for their future, and she visited a local house agent to investigate the possibility of renting or buying a small cottage.

In January, there were some terrible gales. The sea roared angrily and ceaselessly up over the front and the lifeboat had to be called out several times. On these occasions, distress rockets whizzed up into the night sky, and the villagers huddled together on the cliffs in little groups to watch the rescue. This was an element of the coast that Sue had never known before—the wild wind and dangerous deserted shore made her shiver with fear at times. In this appalling weather, the little fishing boats were lying at anchor in the bay while their owners spent their days in the public bar. That nice world Sue had known had temporarily come to a halt. But despite the stormy scenes, she still had her inner peace and every day she marked off the calendar another day towards Billy's release.

Poor old Claud's health was getting worse. He coughed repeatedly all through the night and often spent the day in bed. One very cold night, he crept into Sue's room and asked pathetically, "Can I get in bed with you, Sue? It's just to keep me warm. I feel so cold I can't get to sleep."

Sue sighed and moved over to make room for his bony old body next to hers. The smell of the embrocation which he used to rub on his chest was disgusting, but big-hearted Sue cuddled the old man up to her warm smooth body and Claud, sighing like a contented child, finally went to sleep.

After that, Claud often came to be warmed by Sue's voluptuous body. But one night, after Claud had gone to sleep in her arms, Sue woke up, to find her arm trapped uncomfortably under Claud's head. She pushed him over in order to try to dislodge it, and switched on the bedside light with her free arm. "Gosh, Claud," she said, "you are heavy. Move over, love."

Awkwardly, she managed to sit up. Claud had still not moved. His mouth was wide open but no sound came from it and he had a strange pallor on his face. Sue gave him another push but his head was very heavy and did not budge. Suddenly, in panic, she wrenched her arm away. Now his old head lolled to one side and Sue knew immediately that he was dead. Her screams made Gladys dash in wearing her nightgown. Her head was a mass of curlers. Gladys took one look at Claud and then rushed to Sue. "Don't look, love," she said. "He's snuffed it."

Sue howled with horror and then passed out.

Claud's death badly affected Sue. She had always dealt with the living before and had an inner horror of illness or death. She recalled how shocked she had been to see her father return from prison as a bent-up cripple, and now poor Claud was gone. It was with great sadness that she remembered his sky-blue eyes which always had such a lovely humorous twinkle . . . But now he was no more. She shuddered every time she thought of his cold stiff body lying in her arms all night. The memory made her want to vomit.

An inquest was held and the nosey crowd from the village attended. The verdict was simple: death from natural causes. And Sue discovered that Claud was a good few years older than he had ever admitted to being.

In the village churchyard they laid him to rest beside his wife, who had been a local woman. The mourners included many friends and neighbours. Sue served them all drinks and sandwiches in the hotel bar. Only one close relative turned up—he was a nephew on Claud's wife's side. He was a big fat fellow who stayed to enjoy the free drinks. In fact, he had started to drink as soon as he arrived.

Later that afternoon, the will was read in the sitting-room. In a solemn voice the lawyer read Claud's will. ". . . I bequeath the hotel and all money in my bank to Susan as long as she will continue to run the hotel in the same way as my wife, Nadia, had always done." There followed a few bequests of his guns and his collection of coins to old friends. The big fat nephew was left a mere five hundred pounds, which probably only covered the expenses he must have incurred attending the funeral. All other monies owed to his estate were to be forgotten. At the end of the reading, the nephew got up and marched out of the room. "I'll contest it," he muttered. "Who is she anyway? Just a mistress."

Sue was astonished by the contents of the will. She really had not expected anything. Dumb, she sat trying to comprehend this generous and wonderful gift. Finally, she turned to the lawyer and said, "If that is what old Claud wanted of me—to take care of the business—then that's what I'll do." Inwardly she could not believe her luck. This was a nice little hotel and it had dropped right into her lap. What more could she and Billy want? The fact that the villagers were a little suspicious of Claud's sudden death did not bother Sue. In that respect her conscience was completely clear.

The gossips started on the following Saturday night. "Ah, he took to the bottle those last few weeks," cried Dora in a loud voice.

"Had a bit of a shock," agreed Albert. "That were what triggered him off."

But Sue just cast cold glances in their direction and, knowing that it would upset them, had them all out of the bar dead on time.

"Gladys," said Sue, "in a couple of weeks, when all this is settled, you and I will have a very comfortable home here for the rest of our lives."

Little Gladys' face wrinkled suddenly with grief. "Poor old Claud," she said. "He wasn't so bad, was he? God rest his soul." Then she made the sign of the cross.

Sue stared at her in amazement. "Why, you

don't still keep up that old hocus-pocus they taught us in the convent, do you, Gladys?"

"Oh, yes I do," replied Gladys defiantly. "And it would do you good to say a little prayer now. He has taken good care of you."

Sue looked slightly alarmed and gazed towards the bed where Claud had died. "You know, I think I'll move out of this room to that nice big double down the corridor. Come on, let's get cracking, we'll move everything tonight."

Gladys stared at her and mumbled, "Don't know why you should be frightened of that poor old man. He was very fond of you."

Sue stalked angrily past her. "I am not afraid, but illness and death give me the creeps."

As always, Sue got her way and moved her bedroom. Then she began to prepare it for Billy's return. She bought colourful new curtains and covers, installed hi-fi equipment and a bookcase full of paperback books. Her Billy was not going to be deprived of anything any more, not like he had these last years spent in prison.

16

The Boss

THE first thing Sue had to do when she took over the hotel was talk to the staff. She was determined to show them her authority and gain their confidence. There was Frannie, the big, moonfaced cook; Tommy the tall, thin old gardener; small, robust Mary who combined the duties of chambermaid and below-stairs helper and was a sort of tweeny, and finally, the tall bright barmaid. They all lived outside the hotel and off-season, they worked a rota system between them. Most of them lived in the village and had held down these jobs for years. They were all good and Sue did not wish to lose any of them.

They were all assembled in the large kitchen downstairs, and they looked rather anxious. "There's tea and cakes there," indicated Sue. She smiled at them. "No need to look so scared," she reassured them, "I'm not going to sack anyone. But I do want to know if I have your cooperation to help run this place. I'm a relative newcomer to the hotel business and you all know more about it than I. So I'd like to establish a good working relationship between us all. I shall be getting married soon so you'll have a new boss. Meanwhile, I'd like to think that we can all work together in harmony. I know you all tittle-tattled to poor old Claud about me but I hold no grudges. I'd like you to state now if you wish to stay and work with me because I'll have no whining or complaining behind my back. If you do stay, I hope you'll always come to me with your complaints and I will always do my best to put them right. But I would like loyalty and trust from you."

Gladys looked amazed, for this was a long speech for Sue whose normal conversation was fairly limited. Yet here she was making a speech in a clear and precise voice, looking them all straight in the eye.

When Sue had finished, the staff started to fidget. Then Wendy, the barmaid, said, "I'd love to stay with you, Sue, but I'd already told Claud that I'm booked to go and work in Switzerland for the summer. I thought I'd get out of this dead-end place. Might find a rich husband out there . . ." She grinned at Sue.

Sue nodded. "That's it, Wendy, see the world while you're young. And thanks for being straight with me. Is there anyone else quitting?" she asked, looking at the others.

"Oh no, Sue," they all protested in unison. "We're quite happy at our work."

"Good," said Sue, most satisfied with the outcome of this meeting. "Get stuck into the cakes, now. We all know where we stand, don't we?"

But there was no reply, only the nodding of heads as they stuffed the cakes into their mouths.

From then on, life in the hotel went more or less smoothly. The season began again and the holiday-makers arrived as the front brightened up with vendors' kiosks, Punch and Judy stands and cockle stalls. Sue liked to stroll down to the harbour every morning to buy fresh fish and chat with the seamen and she loved to see all the colourful signs of the new season. She longed to share these sights with Billy when he finally returned to her.

The week before Wendy left, Sue advertised for a new young barmaid. She wanted a girl who would live in so that she could train her the way she wanted her to work. There were plenty of applicants and Sue spent many hours interviewing, but so far she had not seen anyone who was quite suitable for the position.

One day, a young couple arrived on a motor cycle. They parked outside the hotel and the young man took off his crash helmet and sat on the grass while he waited for his girlfriend. The girl came in while Sue was getting the morning bar ready. The sun was behind her and Sue was struck by her fair beauty as a shaft of sunlight shone on her silvery gold hair. As she approached Sue could see how neat she was—tall and slim and dressed in a tight-fitting summer dress.

"Ah coom aboot the joab." The girl spoke slowly and politely.

"Come in, love. Sit down. I'll be with you in a minute," said Sue. Grabbing her book and pencil, she sat down to interview this young girl who was from the big town of Bristol, quite a way from East Bay. She spoke slowly and so quietly it had a fascinating lilt; she seemed somehow to swallow her words.

"Bristol's a long way," commented Sue.

"Ah noa," replied the girl, "me boyfriend broaght me on his boike. But a'd loike to live in, ef et's possible."

"Well, that's what I am looking for," said Sue. "Are you experienced in hotel work?"

The girl shook her golden head. "Noa I worked in the bacon factree. Am saving ooop to get married and me young man goes to sea. A'd like to work away from home so ah can save more money. Ah doan't like the factree an ah ain't niver bin away from Bristol afore."

Sue looked her over. She was pretty dim but nice and clean with a clear white skin, and her shoulder-length silvery golden hair was very attractive. "I'll take you on a month's trial. Is that all right?" asked Sue.

"Ah yeh! that'll be fine," replied the girl, giving her a sweet smile.

"By the way, what's your name?" Sue asked. She had been so taken with this nice girl that she had forgotten to find out her name.

"It's Mandy," she said with her slow drawl.

"How about your young man, Mandy? Will he mind you only getting one day off a week and not much time off at weekends, especially at the height of the season?"

"Ah knows," smiled Mandy. "Andy says it will be good for us to be apart for a while afore ee haas me." Sue wanted to laugh at her words. Mandy was nearly eighteen, and Sue thought about herself at eighteen: a lot of men had had her by then. She had learned quite a lot. Mandy seemed so sweet, naïve and innocent, it hardly seemed possible that she was that age.

Naïve or not, Mandy seemed to adapt very well to life at the hotel and everyone liked her. She was open and friendly, and if she got a tip from a customer she would put it in a little box towards her wedding dress.

Sue quickly became so fond of Mandy that Gladys became jealous. Every time she got near Mandy, she would give her a vicious jab in the back with her elbow. But mild Mandy would only open her wide blue eyes and say, "What be the matter, leetle Gladees? Oim big enough to see, eren't I?" She certainly never lost her temper.

On her day off, Mandy's boyfriend would arrive from Bristol on his motorbike and they would spend the day on the cliffs together.

"You can bring your young man in here," Sue said to her one day, "and spend a little time in your room if you want to, I won't mind."

211

"Oh, he wouldn't do that," asserted Mandy.

"How long have you been courting?" asked Sue.

"We bin engaged six months," Mandy replied proudly.

Sue stared hard at her in disbelief. "You mean to say you never got to know each other yet, not once?"

Mandy blushed and hung her fair hair. "Ah noa," she murmured. "Andy wants me to be very pure when he haas me. So we are going to wait till we marry."

"Oh, crikey!" exclaimed Sue. "What sort of a nut is that boyfriend of yours, Mandy?"

"Ee be very nice," said Mandy stiffly. "Oi loves eem."

"All right, darling, forget what I said." Sue suddenly felt ashamed, and stopped herself from making any more comments. She liked Mandy and did not want to hurt her.

Although the atmosphere in the hotel was generally pleasant, it was inevitable that the gossip would start up again at some point. "Where's this fella she was going to marry then," remarked Dora. "And is it the same one she cut all those capers with last year?"

"I think so," replied Bess. "I believe he works abroad in Saudi Arabia, or some such place like that."

"Never! Not on your Nelly," piped up Marie.

"Why, he was as white as an 'addack. Ain't seen a lot of the sun for years."

"What are you getting at, Marie?" demanded Dora who liked to be top dog.

"I'm not saying," Marie replied haughtily. "It's not going to be me that said anything."

Bess leaned over and whispered in her Mum's ear. "I know what she's getting at—he's been in prison."

"Well, if that's the case, I'm sorry for the poor devil," said Albert, who heard his daughter's whisper. "And I for one will make him welcome."

Dora sniffed. "It depends what he's done," she muttered.

"Now, if I was you I'd mind me own business," said Marie. "You know what Sue's like in a temper . . ."

So they all agreed and waited anxiously for the arrival of Billy Rafferty.

Sue kept very busy and was extremely happy. She seemed to blossom like an over-blown rose, her eyes shone and her cheeks were pink. Bursting with energy, she worked from early morning to late at night to keep the hotel in order and running smoothly.

Soon the season was over. A cool wind blew across the pier and the boys who fished from it put on their big woolly jerseys. The hotel emptied, and Sue was glad to have a few weeks' respite before Billy came to claim her for his bride. They had already decided to make it a secret wedding. They planned to go into the small, nearby town of Bideford to get a special licence, stay overnight in a small guest-house, and return to East Bay the following day as legal man and wife.

"I think it's a good idea, don't you, Gladys?" asked Sue. Gladys was the only one she told of her plan.

"I think it's a very silly idea," grumbled Gladys. "One man isn't going to be enough for you, Sue, and he's the kind that'll murder you if he ever does find you with another man."

"Gladys!" yelled Sue. "Don't you ever let me hear you saying things like that again! As far as we are concerned, the past is well gone."

"Please yourself," snorted Gladys.

It was a misty September morning when Sue crept out of the hotel by a side door and got into a waiting taxi. She looked extremely smart in her tan suit and pink accessories, and her heart was thumping with joy as she sat in the back of the taxi as it ferried her to the main station to meet her Billy.

The train was late but contentedly she waited on the platform until it arrived at last. Eagerly, she jumped up and, as Billy finally appeared, his tall figure stepping off the train, she flung herself at him.

Billy looked very smart in a light-grey, tailored

suit and his hair was neat and short. In his right hand he carried a small suitcase.

"Oh, Billy, you look fine!" cried Sue as she held on to him.

"You like the whistle and flute?" he asked, turning around to show off his suit. "My sister got all the family to chip in and they bought it for me. She's a champ."

Sue immediately felt a pang of disappointment and jealousy. He had gone back to the East End to see his family before he came to her on their wedding day. How could he?

"I didn't tell them I was getting spliced," continued Billy. "Still, I'll take you up to see them one day," he promised.

Sue ignored what he had just told her. "We've got to be at the registry office at three o'clock," she said. "We'd better get some lunch."

"As soon as that?" Billy exclaimed a little nervously.

"Yes," said Sue with a laugh. "You're not getting away from me so easily this time."

Billy bent down and kissed her lips. "I'm quite sure that I'll never want to," he said.

Sue's happiness knew no bounds. The wedding was a short ceremony and two witnesses were provided by the registrar. Afterwards, as the newly-wed couple, they walked to the small guest-house without uttering a word. Their happiness and contentment was too great. At last Sue had captured her Billy and now wore a beautiful gold wedding ring like any other self-respecting woman.

Billy clutched her hand tight as they walked up the red-carpeted stairs of the guest-house. "Want a drink Sue?" he asked.

She shook her head. Little tremors of passion ran through her body and all she could think about were Billy's strong arms encircling her.

"I'd carry you over the threshold but I might rupture myself," jested Billy, and Sue began to giggle.

Once inside their room they closed the door on the world outside and made love tenderly and closely for hours. Sue had never been so happy in her life. At last her life was complete.

Of course news of the secret wedding had leaked to the East Bay Hotel so when Sue and Billy returned the following evening, a special dinner had been laid on for them in the dining-room. Cook had baked a cake with silver trimmings and "Congratulations to Billy and Sue" written on it with pink icing. Sue ordered champagne to be brought out from Claud's secret hoard down in the cellar and the toasts were made with real bubbly. The staff then presented the newly-weds with a silver tray, and there was more drinking while the cake was eaten. It was a jolly party and a good time was had by all.

With their arms linked, Sue and Billy watched everyone finally depart on unsteady legs. "It seems impossible that I can be so happy," Sue murmured. "I'm afraid to think about it."

Always spontaneous in his affections Billy kissed her gently. "You've earned it, Sue. They all seem to like you down here, and this is a swell placc."

As they finally settled down for the night, a few doors away, Gladys sat hunched up on her bed with her mouth in a tight grim line. She was feeling very unhappy and sadly neglected, having lost her Sue who had been everything to her in her uneventful life.

The next morning Billy got up very early and put on some old jeans and a warm woolly.

"Oh Bill," moaned Sue looking at the clock "it's only five o'clock."

"Sorry, Sue," he explained, "but I'm used to rising early and I must get out for a bit of exercise. I'm going to take a trot down to the harbour and watch the fishing boats come in."

"Good," said Sue from the depths of the blankets, "you'll like that, Billy, I always do."

Later that morning, after Billy had returned looking very refreshed and sounding very interested in the boats, he helped Sue with her chores and then they discussed the future.

"I see no reason why we can't be happy here, Billy," said Sue. "We can work together and improve this place—make it a bit more modern."

"All I am hoping, Sue, is that I don't let you down. I'm a pretty restless guy, as you know, and I've been cooped up a long time. I might find it hard to stay put."

"No, you won't," insisted Sue. "We can work hard in the summer and go abroad in the winter. That's what most of the hotel keepers do in these parts."

"Yes, but that takes a lot of lolly," replied Billy.

"That's not a problem, Billy," Sue continued. "Claud left me this hotel, lock, stock and barrel. And I've certain little investments of my own if we can't make it pay."

Billy looked worried. "Why did that old boy leave all this to you, Sue? What was there between you?"

Sue looked annoyed. "Oh, there you go, Billy, starting to get jealous. I worked for him, that's all, and he needed me. We were just very good friends."

Billy poured himself a pint of beer and sat down to drink it. "Well, it's good to be able to get a pint like that. Where I've been that was only a dream."

Sue sat in his lap and kissed him. "I know, darling, and I'm going to make it up to you," she said gently.

"Oh, well," said Billy philosophically, "perhaps I'll enjoy being a kept man."

Sue laughed. "Oh, no, you won't. You'll work the same as I do. Come on, now, it's time to open up."

So Billy became mine host at the hotel and made a very pleasant landlord, mixing well with both the lounge and public bars. He played cards with the older guests and learned to play golf and go fishing with the younger ones. And he never stood any nonsense in the bars. One gesture of Billy's big fist and all argument ceased. He also became very popular down at the quayside with the fishermen. The shimmering sea seemed to fascinate him, he would often go out in all weathers with his new friends and come back full of beans and with a great yearning to own his own boat.

"We'll see how we've done at the end of the season and then I'll buy you one," Sue promised.

After his time at the hotel, Billy was now looking very healthy and sun-tanned. He always wore a skipper's cap jauntily on the back of his head and talked of fishing and boats with the rest of the skippers down on the quay. Watching him, Sue would think that there was little trace of the old Cockney tearaway left in him, and this made her exceedingly happy.

But still Gladys was full of gloom and had little to say to Billy, who ignored her anyway, and certainly never allowed her into the bedroom while he was there. So poor Gladys was left to her own devices quite a lot, which she resented.

One day she and Sue were sitting out on the balcony overlooking the sea. "Oh, Gladys," sighed Sue. "Who would think we could be so happy and comfortable?" She was dressed in a cool summer dress and stretched out her legs in a leisurely manner, as she used to do on Elsie's pink divan.

Gladys was busy with her crochet hook, her hunched figure bent over her work. "I shouldn't court the bleeding devil if I was you," she snapped.

"Oh, you're getting to be a miserable old bugger," said Sue, getting up and stalking inside.

Gladys looked up to watch her disappear and a wry grin appeared on her wrinkled face.

17

The Return of Freddie

THE atmosphere in the lounge bar on Saturday night was warm, comfortable and congenial. Dressed in their light summer clothes, the relaxed customers drank, chatted and laughed gaily. The bar was looking very attractive with large tanks of exotic tropical fish swimming peacefully amid the coloured lights, graceful plants climbing up the walls and tubs of bright flowers in every corner. The large window offered a wonderful view across the bay. It was still not completely dark outside so it was still possible to see the shadowy line of the cliffs above the bright lights of the funfair which was in full swing down on the front. The gay music from the carousels drifted across the village.

Tall, slim and exceedingly graceful, Sue served behind the bar. With an enigmatic *Mona Lisa* smile on her face, she kept a weather eye on Billy who was chatting to the fishermen in the next bar. Just looking at him now made her heart swell with pride. Billy was wearing his white yachting cap at a jaunty angle on his head, and his blue eyes were shining with excitement and the effects of the booze. His broad, strong shoulders bulged out of his white roll-necked sweater, and, watching the muscles flex in his arms, she thought that he was such a fine specimen of a man.

Sue served those thirsty Saturday night revellers with great skill, and she was assisted by Mandy, the young girl from Bristol. Fair as a lily, even when she was harassed with the rush of customers, Mandy looked fresh, sweet and still very young. The days in the sun had given her skin a mass of golden freckles and tonight she wore a pretty, low-cut pink dress. Looking round the bar, Sue reflected on how lucky she had been since old Claud had died. She had both a very prosperous business and Billy who, much to her relief, had settled down to a life of leisure by the sea. She had no regrets whatever. And if Billy got restless in the winter they could, she was quite sure, take a nice long holiday in the Bahamas or Spain, where it was pleasant and warm. How happy she felt, so warm and mellow—life could not be better, she thought.

It was then she noticed that Billy had moved into the centre of the bar and was heartily slapping a newcomer on the back. This person was short and thin with a shock of lank sandy hair; his face was pallid and he had a long pointed chin and deep-set eyes. It was none other than Freddie the Sly, who met Sue's startled gaze with a sneering smile. Sue only just stopped herself crying out aloud and she nearly dropped a glass as she heard Billy giving his old friend an over-whelming welcome.

"Well, I'll be blowed!" exclaimed Billy, "if it ain't me old mate, Freddie. What are you doing down here, old son?"

Sue felt quite faint as she watched Billy get Freddie a bar stool to sit on and order him a pint. Billy then stood beside Freddie, waving and gesticulating in a very excited manner, and talking about old times and new. Her head was swimming as she tried to go about her chores, and the voices in the bar around her grew louder, adding to her confusion. Freddie the Sly spelt trouble, she knew that. What did he want? He was just out of the nick, by the look of him. And however did he find her?

After time was called, a well-boozed Billy brought Freddie over to meet her. "Remember Freddie?" he asked. "He was one of old Sam's Boys," he told her.

Sue stared at Freddie with burning hostility in her eyes, but she murmured coolly, "How are you, Freddie?"

"Walked in out of the blue," said Billy, looking very pleased with himself.

Freddie seemed a little sheepish. "Got a nice place here, Sue," he muttered. "Was on me way home. Just off the island, you know, so I thought I'd have a little holiday. Was astounded when I walked in, seeing Billy all poshed up like that, and he tells me he's the landlord."

Sue's gaze did not flinch. "Amazing," she murmured, her voice loaded with sarcasm.

"Nice to meet up with old pals," continued Freddie, with a semi-concealed sneer on his lips.

Sue just stared back at him wide-eyed with fear. Freddie was not going to go away easily, she told herself, not without a rip-off of some kind. She knew him well enough to be quite sure of that.

"Hand us a bottle of Scotch, Sue," Billy called to her. "We'll go into the dining-room and talk over old times."

With fear and hatred in her eyes, Sue watched them go. Asking Mandy to clear up for her, she ran upstairs to find Gladys who was in her room, watching a horror film on her portable television.

"Oh, Gladys!" Sue cried breathlessly. "That evil Freddie has just walked into the bar."

At first Gladys turned her wizened face towards Sue impassively, but then noticing how distressed her friend was, she turned off the television set and looked concerned. She was needed once more.

"Oh, dear, what am I going to do?" wailed Sue.

"Billy seen him yet?" asked Gladys.

"He's with him now. They are both getting drunk in the dining-room."

"Well, Sue," said Gladys, "looks like you are going to have to face the music. But don't worry,

I'll stick by you." Her funny looking face wrinkled in a smile.

Sue sat down and chewed her nails in agitation. She had completely lost her cool. "I don't trust that little swine," she muttered. "Supposing he's still got those letters?"

"Well, if he has he'll want a price for them," said Gladys shrewdly. "But he won't show his hand yet. Now, don't lose your head, Sue, he might even push off if we butter him up a bit."

"Let's hope so, but he's such a vindictive little swine," replied Sue, in a hard voice, but then, as she thought about the threat he represented, she wailed. "Oh Gladys, after all we've been through, some dirty little crook is going to spoil the happiness we've found here. It makes me so furious!"

"Go to bed, love," said Gladys turning on the television once more. "Nothing will be gained by worrying."

In bed, Sue pulled the sheets up over her head and tried to shut out the drunken sounds coming from the dining-room as Billy and Freddie sang bawdy street songs. She clutched her hands nervously. She had to get rid of Freddie at all costs, she told herself. She had to. Inside she felt desolate and empty. At one point she even toyed with the idea of murdering him. She just wished she could do something to get him away from there. For she was quite convinced that he would bring her nothing but trouble.

In the middle of the night, Billy crawled into bed fully dressed and very drunk. Lying on his back he fell asleep immediately and snored loudly. Sue crept out of the room to rout out Freddie, but he was lying on the dining-room floor absolutely out. Although Sue gave him a sharp kick in the ribs with her pointed slipper, he did not stir. How easy it would be to hit him on the head with something hard and get rid of him, she thought angrily. But she instantly checked herself. How could she seriously think such murderous thoughts? That was not any solution at all . . .

She went into the kitchen and made herself a cup of coffee, and then returned to bed. Perhaps she could face it better in the morning.

The next morning, she woke up to the sound of Billy singing in the shower next door. Her head felt like a pumpkin and she felt terrible. Yet morning was here, and she knew that she had better face the music.

Billy blustered in, rubbing himself briskly with a towel. "Going out in the boat, Sue," he yelled. "I've put Freddie in one of the rooms. Poor old sod ain't fit for nothing this morning."

Pretending to be asleep, Sue did not stir. Thank God, she thought, as Billy left, now she had the chance to tackle Freddie and find out just what he was up to.

At eight o'clock, she took a tray of tea up to

Freddie. She locked the door before she roused him.

"Christ!" said Freddie, sitting up in bed. His long lank hair hung down over his eyes. "Phew!" he groaned, "what a bloody hangover!"

She poured him a cup of tea and sat on the end of the bed. Her teeth showed in a fixed smile.

Freddie drank his tea and as soon as he finished she snatched the cup back. "Now Freddie," she hissed, "tell me what you're doing here."

"Me? Nuffink. Why, I only came here by accident. Got the shock of me life when I saw old Billy all ponced up in his yachting cap."

Sue stared at him with narrowed eyes. "Don't give me that," she snarled. "How did you find us?"

"I swear I never knew where you were, Sue. I've been on the island a year. I just wanted a break from the smoke, that's all."

Sue sighed. How she wanted to believe him! She got to her feet and looked down at him threateningly. "Well, then, you can come up with me bleeding letters," she declared reverting to her Cockney dialect.

"I ain't got 'em, Sue," whined Freddie. "Sorry I pinched yer money but I got on the booze and some tricky bastard dipped me wallet."

"I'd like to believe you, Freddie," said Sue, "but I don't. So get your arse out of here before Billy gets back."

"Oh don't be like that, Sue, I can keep me

mouth shut. I know what Billy's like, slice yer head off if he knew about your Soho capers." He let out a little snigger.

Sue instantly lost her temper and struck out at him with her fist. But Freddie dodged out of the way and in seconds he was pointing a flick knife at her. "Cool it, Sue," his thin mean voice said. "I'm still very handy with the old flicker here."

"You bastard!" yelled Sue backing away. "Get out of my hotel! I'll not let you mess up my life with Billy."

Freddie grinned slyly. "I don't want to, Sue, honestly I don't," he whined.

As Sue let herself out of Freddie's room, the tears were falling fast.

Gladys was waiting for her outside. "Don't let him upset you, Sue," she comforted her. "Where there's a will there's a way, as we learned in Soho. Come on, love, have a nice cool wash and forget him for a while."

Sue took her advice and went down to help with the breakfasts in the kitchen where she snapped and snarled at everyone.

"She's got out of bed the wrong side, ain't she?" remarked the cook.

There was no way in which Sue could dislodge Freddie from the hotel. He stuck there like glue and stayed close to Billy. Every time he passed Sue in the corridor, he would give her an oily smile.

Gladys pushed her luck with him one day and

stood in front of him. "Why don't you piss off?" she muttered.

But Freddie just smiled, spun her round by the shoulders and gave her a sudden kick in the rump that sent her reeling. After that, she avoided him.

"How long is Freddie staying?" Sue asked Billy.

"He's just done a stretch. I thought you, of all people, would have a bit of understanding."

Sue looked forlorn. "It's not like it used to be with him around all the time." She put her arms around his neck. "We don't seem as close to each other as we were."

"The bleeding honeymoon can't go on forever, Sue," he said impatiently and pulled away from her.

A hard lump came to her throat and seemed to go on down to her heart. Boiling rage and hatred churned inside her for Freddie whom she knew was her enemy.

18

Mandy's Dilemma

NOW that Billy and Sue were at loggerheads over Freddie the Sly, Gladys had come into her own again. Freddie also seemed to wallow in the fact that he had come between them and still did not show the slightest inclination to leave East Bay Hotel. He swaggered around in Billy's wake with a sneering smile on his face.

This situation made Sue sad, very depressed and extremely bad tempered. And she vented her feelings on the staff in a relentlessly vicious manner, day and night.

Even her favourite, sweet Mandy, commented, "Eeh, what's oop wi't'missus? 'Er be loike a bear wi' a sore head."

"It's that slimy git Freddie," the cook informed her.

"Why! eeh be a very nice boy," Mandy said with her blue eyes wide open. For Freddie was exceedingly charming to Mandy and she, in turn, chatted to Freddie about her boyfriend, Andy, and her forthcoming wedding at the end of September. With a twisted smile, Freddie would listen affably to her and Mandy would give an extra flick of the wrist whenever she poured him his drinks.

When Freddie was not lounging at the bar talking to Mandy, he was out in the boat with Billy. A cold atmosphere had built up between Sue and her Billy. He now kept as far away from her as possible, and there was a sulky expression on his face when they met at meals or in their room.

"I don't think that I can stand much more," Sue confided to Gladys. "I feel as if I am living on the edge of a volcano. Something's going to blow any minute."

"We'll both attack Freddie and beat him up," suggested Gladys. "Then he'll go."

Sue sighed and shook her head. "No, Gladys, that's not the answer. Freddie's very vicious with that flick knife. I know, because I've seen him in action. But we're not going to let the grass grow under our feet, I can assure you. The next time he goes out with Billy, we'll search his room systematically. If he's still got those letters we had better find them."

So the next day, once Freddie had gone out in the boat with Billy, Sue and Gladys searched every nook and cranny of his room. They looked everywhere—all the pockets of his clothes, all the articles packed in the battered old suitcase he had brought with him, under the bed, inside the wardrobe—but they found nothing of interest. Defeated, they sat on Freddie's bed wondering what to do next. Suddenly they heard footsteps echoing along the corridor and before they could move, Mandy walked in. In her hand she was carrying a glossy magazine. "What be you doing in Freddie's room?" she asked innocently.

"Cleaning it up," complained Gladys. "It's a bleeding pigsty."

"Look!" cried Mandy holding out the magazine. "Isn't that lovely, that long wedding dress? It's just what I want. 'Mandy', oi said to meself, 'that's the dress for you', and now I've got enough money in me box to buy it. Wait a minute, I'll show you." She dashed off and returned moments later holding the cash box that she saved all her tips in.

Sue and Gladys exchanged glances of amusement.

"Nearly twenty pounds oi got in there," said Mandy, proudly. "It's enough to buy that dress —isn't that exciting?"

"That's nice, dear," said Sue kindly. "Now you go and put your little box in a safe place."

With the box clutched under her arm and still admiring the dress in the magazine, Mandy went off down to the kitchen to talk to the cook about it.

When she had gone Sue and Gladys still sat gloomily on the bed, returned to their problem.

"The fact is," said Sue, "we could knock him off but sure as eggs is eggs we'd get caught and end up behind closed doors again. It's just not worth the risk."

And Gladys regretfully agreed.

Meanwhile, Freddie was out in the bay with Billy in his boat. The sun was shining, the sky was blue and in the hold there were several crates of beer. Billy pointed to the shoals of mackerel dashing past the boat, darting here and there like slivers of silver. "There'll be a porpoise chasing them," said Billy, "driving them inland. Watch for him. You see, I've learnt a few good tricks from the local fishermen," he added proudly as he threw out his nets with great skill.

The two men laughed and chatted about the old days. "The fellas would larf their 'eads orf if they saw us now," commented Freddie.

"Oh well, it's certainly a great life," said Billy. "I'd never turn back."

"Did you know that Sue resents me, Billy?" asked Freddie, cautiously sounding out Billy.

"She's a little jealous, I suppose," replied Billy. "Not to worry, old son. I'm still the guv'nor."

"Yes," sneered Freddie. "You've both come a long way since she was a kid skivvying for the old prostitutes in Soho."

Billy shot Freddie an angry look. "We never look back," he said sharply. "Sue and I live for each day." He pointed to the silver glint of the mackerel shoal to the right. "Come on, lad!" yelled Billy. "Get your finger out! Here they come!"

At mid-afternoon Billy slopped into the hotel kitchen and began hauling off dripping oilskins and heavy rubber boots. He was jubilant. "Fifty mackerel in one haul," he boasted.

Sue cast him a side-long look and then went forward to pull off his boots as she used to when they were more friendly. She knelt down and looked up at him whereupon Billy bent forward and kissed her full on the lips. "Oh, Sue, don't let's quarrel," he pleaded.

With a wonderful sense of relief, Sue put her arms around his neck and immediately they were clenched in a passionate embrace.

"Help me out of me gear," Billy whispered, "and let's go to bed."

Sue gasped, pretending to be shocked. "In the afternoon, Billy?" she asked.

"Who cares?" said Billy, his big rough hands fondling her breasts.

And so they disappeared into their bedroom where they spent the rest of that hot afternoon making love to each other, oblivious to everything except themselves.

"Seen the missus?" everyone asked, but no one needed to answer.

Like an old watchdog, Gladys prowled up and down the corridor outside the bedroom while Sue slept a deep sleep of exhaustion and did not emerge till the morning. As she patrolled, Gladys passed Mandy and Freddie chatting to each other, but she did not hear the conversation between them.

"Andy be away in the deep sea," Mandy was telling Freddie. "And when he come back in three weeks' time, then oi will go home to be wed."

"Good for you," remarked Freddie, looking very interested.

"Oi be going to buy this nice wedding dress," she waved her magazine at him. "Look at that!"

But Freddie's mean, narrow eyes missed the page and focused on her neck and soft bosoms. Reaching out with his finger, he touched the tight pink jumper stretched over them. "Got a nice lot of tit in there," he said cockily.

"What a naughty boy you are, Freddie," replied Mandy, drawing away and blushing.

But Freddie just sniggered and ignored her. "What about a date, then, Mandy?"

"I told you," replied Mandy, "I've got a boyfriend." She walked away hurriedly, her bottom waggling in her tight skirt.

"Okay," Freddie called after her, "so yer said."

The next morning, after he had dressed, Billy kissed Sue again with great passion. "You were right, Sue," he said. "At the end of the season we should close up this part of the hotel and go off to Spain for a holiday. That's when I'll give Freddie the elbow."

Sue was overjoyed. "Do you really mean it, Billy?" she asked.

Billy nodded. "But for the time being, leave Freddie alone. He's useful and gives me a hand with the nets when I'm out in the boat."

It was a very radiant Sue that agreed.

That evening, Sue sailed into the lounge and took over the bar looking more like her old self than she had for days. She wore a nice tailored black dress and some pretty jewellery to liven it up.

She noticed that Mandy seemed a bit overexcited, and kept doing everything wrong.

"What's wrong with you, Mandy?" asked Sue sharply, after she had smashed a second glass.

"Oi doan't feel well," cried Mandy, with tears welling up in her blue eyes.

"All right, take an early night," said Sue kindly, "you're getting too worked up about this wedding."

As Mandy gratefully went off duty, she passed Freddie playing darts in the public bar. He looked furtively at her as she hurried past. Noticing this, Sue reminded herself to keep an eye on them, since she knew how easily Freddie could corrupt innocent little Mandy, who was obviously missing her boyfriend.

Early the next morning, everyone was woken up by such a to-do. A distraught Mandy was running about the place weeping madly. Someone had rifled her money box and taken the nineteen pound notes but left behind the coins.

"That slimy bastard, Freddie, is at it again," declared Sue to Gladys.

Mandy was almost hysterical. "Now oi can't buy me nice wedding dress," she wailed, wringing her hands in distress.

"Now, pull yourself together, Mandy," begged Sue. "I'll replace the money so you can still buy the dress. I've always warned you to lock your bedroom door. I'll give the money to you on Friday when you get your month's pay. Then on Saturday you can go into town and take out a Post Office Savings book. You can let the money stay there until you go home at the end of the month."

"Thank you, Sue," said Mandy, wiping her eyes.

"Now, go and get dressed and start work. And forget about it," Sue told her kindly. When the girl had gone, she sighed to herself. "I for one shall be very pleased when Mandy is finally wed," she murmured to herself.

"He's after her," Gladys announced later.

"Who's after who?" asked Sue.

"That Freddie, dirty little sod," declared Gladys. "I saw him talking to her in the passage upstairs, yesterday evening."

Sue looked alarmed. "Surely Mandy wouldn't be so foolish," she said.

"She's hot," cackled Gladys, "only waiting to be laid."

"Now don't be so coarse," said Sue. "I certainly shall be relieved when she finally goes at the end of the month."

On Saturday morning Mandy caught the bus into town. She was looking very pretty, with her hair freshly curled and wearing a plain white summer dress and carrying a big white handbag. In the bag she had all the money that Sue had so kindly given her.

When she arrived in town and had been to the post office, to her astonishment, she met Freddie. It was such a coincidence, she told herself, but she wasn't displeased to see him.

"Wot abaht a cuppa?" asked Freddie, piloting her into a posh teashop. She was happy to be with Freddie and enjoyed sitting at the table and pouring tea from a silver-plated teapot. "Oi must remember the time the bus goes," she said. "Oi promised Sue I'd be back by one o'clock."

"Well, that's it," grinned Freddie, pointing out of the window. "It's going up the road."

"Oh dear," cried Mandy in dismay, "I've missed it."

"Not to worry," Freddie reassured her, "there'll be another along in two hours. How about a trip to the funfair in the meantime? Would yer like a ride on the bumper cars, eh, Mandy?"

His suggestion sounded very exciting, particularly since she had to hang around for a couple of hours. "If you like, Freddie," she replied sweetly.

"Right, then," said Freddie, swaggering to the cash desk to pay the bill with one of the many pound notes he had stuffed into his pockets.

They walked along side by side down the streets. Mandy was shyly silent but Freddie walked with his hands in his pockets, whistling a tune. At the funfair they had a ride on the bumper cars. Freddie behaved very badly, bashing violently into the other cars, and yelling and swearing at their drivers.

"Oh, dear," cried Mandy. "I feel sick, Freddie, let's get off, please."

"Nice bit of fresh air will do you good," said Freddie leering at her. "Come on, then, let's go up the cliffs."

He pulled her up the steep path and they sat right on the edge of the cliff in the long grass. Quite unexpectedly, Freddie grabbed hold of her knee.

Mandy pushed him away. "Now, Freddie," she said mildly, "doan't ee be so rude."

But Freddie ignored her. "Come on," he urged. "Give us a kiss." With that, he pushed her back down into the long grass.

But Mandy was big and strong and she fought like a tigress to get free.

Seeing that she was going to be so much

trouble, Freddie jumped up at last. "Mingy cow," he sneered.

Mandy got to her feet and, from her greater height, looked down at Freddie with an air of superiority. "You know I have a boyfriend," she said, "so you behave yourself. I'm going to wait for the bus at the bus station, now."

"Please yerself," shrugged Freddie. "I'm going to get meself a bloody drink. Thought you'd be a bit sporty," he taunted her. "Don't see why you're hanging on to it." With that, he swaggered off.

Mandy carefully climbed down the steep slope and sat in the bus station to wait for her bus. At last it came but it was just pulling out of the bus depot, when Freddie, looking a little worse for drink, shuffled out of the pub opposite and jumped aboard. He plonked himself behind Mandy, giving her an occasional poke in the ribs and offering her a cigarette.

"No, thank you, I don't smoke, Freddie," she said in response.

"Why can't yer be a bit bleeding sociable?" demanded Freddie aggressively.

Mandy blushed and decided not to speak to him any more. But when they got off the bus at the end of the road that led up to East Bay Hotel, Freddie ambled along beside her. Mandy did not protest because she had always been a little afraid of the lonely winding cliff road, as though somebody might jump out at her from behind a bush. So she did not complain when Freddie shuffled along beside her, particularly since he seemed to be in a better frame of mind.

"This bloke of yours, what's he do for a living?" Freddie asked quite sociably.

"He be a sailor," replied Mandy proudly.

"'Ow long since yer seen 'im?" continued Freddie.

"Well, tiz now three weeks," said Mandy innocently, "an' in another two weeks I go home and we be wed."

"Well, you must be getting bleeding hungry," returned Freddie with a change of tone.

"Oi don't know what you be getting at, Freddie," Mandy replied mildly.

"Git orf it," Freddie said, "mean ter say that yer don't fancy a bit of the uvver?"

As she realized what he meant, Mandy stopped and stared at Freddie looking very shocked. But with a quick shove of his shoulder Freddie sent her spinning towards a dark spot where the cliff dipped into a deep cavern.

"Stop it, Freddie!" Mandy screamed out with fear, but his fist landed her a blow to the chin. Her handbag flew out of her hands and she fell on her knees.

He was on her in a flash and had her spread-eagled on the ground. His knees held her legs apart as he tore at her dress. Mandy bit and scratched and fought, but when she tried to scream again he shoved his hand over her mouth.

"Shut up, you silly bitch!" he hissed. "Because I am going to fuck you whether you like it or not."

So Freddie stole Mandy's virginity in a very brutal manner, that precious thing she had hung onto with such tenacity for the sailor boy she loved.

When Freddie finally released her, Mandy got up and ran blindly up the cliff path towards the comforting sight of the lights of East Bay Hotel. She did not even notice that she had lost one shoe and her big white handbag, which Freddie immediately rifled—taking her purse and the Post Office Savings book—before throwing it in the sea. Freddie then ambled quickly back down the road to lie low until things had blown over.

When Mandy burst into the hotel kitchen, Sue was refilling an ice bucket for the counter. "Oh, Christ!" cried Sue when she saw the state of Mandy, she rushed forwards to the young girl. Mandy's dress was torn to ribbons and there was blood running down her face. "Whatever's happened to you? Oh Mandy, Mandy." Sue held her tight.

"That Freddie, he done it to me," sobbed Mandy.

"Gladys, come down here!" yelled Sue. Whereupon Gladys left her television and came to the aid of the distressed little Mandy.

They took the girl upstairs and bathed her gently. They gave her a hot toddy and then put her to bed. Throughout this time, Sue was white-lipped with rage. "The bastard," she muttered, "the slimy git, he's done it this time. Stay with her, Gladys, and lock the door. I've got to go back to the bar."

White-faced with rage, she stalked into the bar.

"What's up, Sue?" asked Billy.

"Where's that bloody mate of yours?" she hissed.

"Who? Freddie? He's gone to town. Why, what's the matter? What's he done?"

"Never mind," replied Sue, her face set hard with hate.

"I'll go and get ready now, Sue," Billy said. He always went out with the local fishermen on Saturday nights but Sue hardly heard him, her rage was so great.

When the bar finally closed and Mandy lay in bed sleeping, Sue called to Gladys. "Come out now, Gladys. Lock her door and we'll wait for him. He's bound to sneak in the back door. Lock all the other doors and we'll wait for him here."

The two women then waited in the wine cellar next to the pantry until at last they heard a well-boozed Freddie come whistling up the garden path to the back door. He breezed into the lavatory. While he was busy in there, Sue took off her high stiletto shoe and, as Freddie came out, she made a mad dash at him waving the shoe and crying out, "You bastard! You slimy bastard!" She struck him on the head and about the face with the sharp heel of the shoe.

Freddie was taken completely by surprise and instinctively backed away, but from behind him another sturdy figure jumped on his back and pulled him down on the concrete floor where his head struck the floor with a decided thump. Gladys then grabbed his long hair and proceeded to bang his head on the floor while Sue hammered at him with her shoe, and kicked and jumped on him like a maniac.

Freddie's eyes rolled in terror and he gave a loud gasp as he passed out.

"Oh, Gladys," cried Sue, suddenly backing away. "I think we've killed him."

"No such luck," said Gladys giving him an extra kick in the ribs. "Let's drag him along and aim him out of the back door," she suggested.

So they dragged him down the passage and pushed him out of the back door down a steep flight of steps so that he lay on the path in an unconscious heap.

"Now, lock the doors, Gladys. Billy won't be home till the morning. Then get Freddie's belongings and throw them out on top of him in case he gets any ideas about coming back in. I'm going to have a stiff drink."

Gladys took the old suitcase and all Freddie's clothes and threw them out onto the grass.

Sitting in the bar Sue sipped a big brandy. "Well, I feel much better," she said with satisfaction, "we have really done it now, Gladys."

"Good job, too," announced Gladys, looking quite invigorated. "I enjoyed that."

It was a rosy morning over the harbour when Billy came ashore. He spent a while with the other fishermen sorting out the catch and hanging out the nets to dry. In the old boat shed, he joined the locals in a hot cuppa liberally spiked with rum. He always found it strange that he, a London lad, had this affinity with the deep-sea fishermen. He liked nothing more than being out there, battling with those huge Atlantic waves. He had his own little runabout, a motor boat, but that could not compare with those trips out in the trawlers. He never missed the Saturday night trips, if he could help it.

Sue lay in bed restlessly looking out at the grey sky lit with the pink and gold of the dawn, and wondering where Billy was by now. The huge gannets screeched and swirled around the chimney pots as she morbidly imagined Billy coming up the cliff path and seeing Freddie's lifeless body lying there. Or worse, imagining that Freddie had recovered and was now down at the harbour waiting for Billy, to enlighten him of Sue's secret life in Soho. Her body shook with terror and sweat came to her brow, for she was still very afraid of Billy's violent temper. Unable to stand the anxiety any longer, she shot quickly out of bed and ran to the window. From where she stood, she could just see the back steps where Freddie had lain, but there was not a sight or sound of him, and no suitcase or clothes littered the lawn. She drew a deep breath of relief and ran quickly along the corridor to look out of the back window. It was clear. There was no reminder of last night's horror scene.

"Gladys! Gladys!" she called softly, "come out here."

Gladys' squat form arrived, clad in a balloon-like nightie, and a crochet shawl around her shoulders. She scratched her woolly head irritably.

"He's gone!" gasped Sue, pointing towards the steps. "Look for yourself."

"I know," replied Gladys. "I watched him pick up his things and go about half an hour after you was in bed."

"Wonder where he's gone?" pondered Sue.

"He looked very sorry for himself," said Gladys with much satisfaction. "Bunged his clothes back in the case, swearing all the time. I put two fingers up at him, I did," she declared.

"Oh, Gladys, you never!" cried Sue, but she chuckled at the thought.

"Now, if you don't mind, I'd like to catch up on my sleep," said Gladys wandering back to bed.

Sue stood looking out of the window out to sea at the white choppy waves rolling line after line towards the shore. The sea always fascinated her, and Billy, too, since he had come here. He had adapted himself to the life in this little seafaring community so well, it would be a pity if it were all over. She could only hope that it was not. Creeping back into bed, she waited for Billy to return. At last she heard him dump his fishing tackle in the hall and take off his sea boots. Minutes later, he entered the bedroom. "Don't get up yet, Sue," he said. "I'm cold, let's have a cuddle."

She moved over to make room for him, sighing a deep sigh of relief. All was well. Billy was home safe and Freddie had gone away. She put her arms about him. "Oh Billy, Billy, I love you so much," she whispered sleepily.

"Gor blimey!" exclaimed Billy with a laugh, "wait for it, let me get in the bed . . ."

A week passed and there was still no news from Freddie. Billy was very annoyed. "There's a bastard for you," he said. "I've been a good mate to that Freddie and he's pissed off without a word."

Sue made no comment but she knew Freddie. He was an animal, he would stay somewhere and lick his wounds and would eventually come back to his prey.

Mandy, looking very pale and subdued was up and about again.

"Would you like to go home a little early, Mandy?" asked Sue one morning.

Mandy's lip trembled. "Do ee want to get rid of me?" she cried.

Sue shook her head and smiled kindly. "No, no, nothing like that," she said. "I'll pay your wages in advance and that will help with the wedding. You'll need it since you've lost your Post Office Savings book. I'm closing the residential part of the hotel early this year, and Billy and I are going to take a holiday, so you can go home and be nice to Andy and get this wedding over at last."

Mandy's lip continued to tremble and her blue eyes filled with tears. "Oi doan't know, Andy might not marry me now."

But Sue grabbed her by the shoulders and shook her hard. "For God's sake, Mandy, don't be such a little fool! He'll never know if you use your head. All this talk of virginity is an old wives' tale, I can assure you. If you really love each other, it don't matter."

Mandy stared dolefully at Sue. "I believes you, Sue," she said. "So if Andy haas me it won't matter what Freddie did."

"That's the idea." Sue was relieved to find that Mandy had some sense in her. "Now come on, let's get you packed up and on your way and you'll be there when Andy comes home from sea."

Mandy was given a little farewell party and

packed off on a train the next day. Sue watched as the girl waved from the train window, her lovely blonde hair shining in the sun. "Oh, dear Mandy, I hope all goes well with you," she said with a sigh.

19

Peace Before the Storm

EVEN by mid-September it was clear that a very bad winter was on its way. Already there were gale force winds tearing at the rocky coves, howling like banshees and keeping the residents of East Bay awake at night. Massive waves bounded over the sea wall, washing over the empty promenade where all the small kiosks were closed and boarded up, well protected against nature's wild elements. Throughout the little fishing village, anticipation was felt as the residents awaited the long stormy period ahead.

High up on the cliffs, at East Bay Hotel the atmosphere had already become extraordinarily peaceful. Most of the holiday-makers had gone home and now the only guests were a couple of old men taking a late vacation.

Sue herself was kept busy getting the rooms prepared for the winter season during which they would not be in use. She covered the furniture with dust sheets and stripped all the beds; this was how it would all remain until the early spring. She was still determined that she and Billy would take a holiday in Spain during November and get away from the hotel completely. She wanted to take Billy away on a second honeymoon and also to get him away for a while in case Freddie came creeping back into their lives.

"It's strange," Sue remarked to Gladys, "that Freddie just disappeared like that."

"Gone back to his own rotten sty," said Gladys with a vicious tone in her voice.

"I'd feel so much more relieved if I could be sure," replied Sue. "Anyway, I'll be glad to get away at the end of the month, what with the weather and that damned villain on my mind."

"Don't worry, love," Gladys assured her. "I'll be here if he comes back and he'll get another good clobbering."

Sue looked at her little protector with affection. Where in all the wide world would she ever find anyone as loyal and affectionate as sturdy little Gladys?

Billy had quickly forgotten about Freddie disappearing without a word and went back to his seafaring friends. He had recently become very interested in the lads of the lifeboat crew whom he met socially in the bar once a week. Billy had put on quite a lot of weight over the past few months, his face had become red and weatherbeaten, and he had developed a rolling gait. He deliberately seemed to assume the air of an old sea salt and talked of nothing that was not connected with the sea. And now when the lifeboat went out training on Sunday mornings his strong muscular arms willingly pulled at the oars. The lifeboat was housed on the beach not far from the hotel, and when Billy was nominated for the second stand-by crew of the East Bay lifeboat, he was completely over the moon about it all. "Don't be so silly, Sue," he said when she mentioned going to Spain. "How can I go off to Spain? They need more men for the lifeboat in the winter. Why, someone else might volunteer and I'd lose me place on the crew."

Sue was quite upset by this development. "Billy, all this will be here when we get back, and anyway, the weather might improve."

"Do me a favour, Sue," replied Billy, "you go to Spain. Take old Gladys with you. I'd sooner stay here."

"Oh, Billy," Sue wailed again. "I was so looking forward to this holiday for both of us, to get away from this stormy sea and the continuous howling wind. Out in Spain at this time of year the sun will still be shining."

But Billy just kicked off his sea boots and lay back in his chair. "You still don't understand, do you? When I was in London I was a nonentity scrambling for a few quid the best I could. Here I'm accepted without any questions. It means a lot to me, it does."

"Well," snapped Sue, "not only is what you do bloody dangerous but your popularity only boils down to all the free beer you give everyone to drink in the bar."

"You still don't see it, do you?" declared Billy.

"When I'm out in me little boat and the wind is whistling by, I get great excitement. I ride the waves. I'm like a king in a world of me own. I'm not afraid of the sea, and I've never been so happy and so free."

"Now, Billy," replied Sue severely, "this is Sue you're talking to, who knows you and knows that you never saw the sea till you came down here. So don't get carried away."

Billy looked gloomy. "Oh well," he said, "I've found what I was looking for and getting on the lifeboat crew has really pleased me. Do you know that they have saved hundreds of lives in the last few years."

"Yes, and lost a few, no doubt," retorted Sue with irony.

"The lads like and respect me, so I'll not let them down. And that's final, Sue." He suddenly lost his temper and stalked out of the room in his sock-clad feet.

"Oh well," Sue sighed sadly, "I'll have to spend the winter here, then, I suppose."

October slowly advanced into November, dark storm clouds chased over the choppy sea. The air was frosty and the winter sun blood red like a ball of fire.

Sue had dismissed all thoughts of the holiday from her mind, and settled down to making improvements to the hotel. She even began to feel pleased that she had left Billy to his own peculiar pleasures, for he seemed very happy and it pleased her to see him so. He occasionally spent a night on stand-by down in the lifeboat hut and drank and played darts with his pals in the bar at other times. He still went out fishing in his own boat and on these occasions, would come home in the early hours of the morning. Sue would listen to him thumping across the room in his heavy boots, his frame coming into the bedroom looked so burly in his dark blue sweater and smelling, as he drew near of fish and the fresh salt of the sea. Sue would always sit up in bed and hold out her arms to him.

"Now Sue," Billy would laugh, "pack it up."

But Sue would nestle close and kiss his rough whiskery face. "Come on, Billy, get your things off," she would whisper enticingly. "Sue wants to make love to you." And in spite of Billy's protests, she would have her own way. Their two strong bodies locked together making passionate love in the early dawn. Then afterwards, Sue would lie contentedly in his arms, smoothing her hands over his perfect body. "Oh, Billy, my love, I could never lose you now; it would kill me," she would whisper.

In December there was snow on the cliff tops and the thatched Dorset cottages looked very picturesque with their roofs snow-capped and their gardens covered in a blanket of virginal white.

"This is the first white Christmas I have ever seen here," remarked Gladys as they decorated the hall and rooms with Christmas garlands and wreathed the pictures on the wall with holly.

"Put a big bunch of mistletoe out in the hall, Gladys," Sue told her. "I've been lucky, really," Sue said. "We've got some guests coming for Christmas—Americans who have a family in the village but they're sleeping here. I think I'll have a Christmas Eve party. Billy would like that, and he could invite all his sea-going pals."

Gladys could not help having gloomy thoughts. "It will be just our luck if that bleeding Freddie turns up."

It was as if a dark shadow crossed Sue's path. She scowled. "Oh, shut up, Gladys! Don't remind me. I just hope that we've seen the last of him. Now, hand me that paperchain . . ."

The next morning, wearing navy blue slacks and bright blue jumper, Sue took a brisk walk down to the harbour to look at the little boats now all covered with snow. Large gannets, uttering shrill cries, perched on top of the masts, as the boats rocked gently from side to side at their moorings. These were holiday boats which would not be back in action until the spring.

Noticing that the door of the small fisherman's church was open, and acting on some impulse, Sue walked inside. It was cold inside but smelled of pine wood because the altar was decorated for Christmas with huge pine branches taken from the woods. It was not at all like her own church, yet she suddenly had a weak-kneed feeling that frightened her. She sat on the edge of the polished pew but she did not pray; she had forgotten how to. But the peace and serenity that pervaded the building soothed her. Looking up, she noticed the board of remembrance on the wall, containing the long list of sailors' names and the ships that they had gone down with. Alongside that was a big brass plaque commemorating the very first East Bay lifeboat that had been lost with all aboard her. Sadness crept over her—imagine, twenty men from a small place like this. How terrible. There must have been so many widows, so many orphans. She gazed about her. A shaft of pale wintry sunshine glanced through the stained-glass window which depicted Christ walking on the water. The vivid blue, greens and golds of the glass entranced her. "Oh, dear God . . ." The words came from her lips involuntarily, and almost unconsciously, she began to pray. "Do not let that terrible sea get my Billy," she whispered. When she left the church, her cheeks were wet with tears. She did feel a little depressed but she also had a sort of inner peace. She went and sat on the sea wall for a while, to listen to the relentless waves pounding the shore.

Gladys had come down to meet her, well wrapped up in heavy coat, scarf, gloves and big woolly hat. She looked just like a little gnome. "I've brought you a coat, Sue," she said. "Fancy going out like that! You're perishing with the cold."

"I'm not cold," insisted Sue. "In fact, I'm quite warm inside."

The Christmas Eve party went with a bang. All the locals turned up in a very festive mood, and all the staff joined in. Sue gave free drinks after time and served a good supper of turkey sandwiches, mince pies and the usual traditional fare.

The American family were most impressed by all the celebrations. They let themselves go and danced and sang "Knees up Mother Brown".

"Who is this Mother Brown?" the wife frequently asked, but no one seemed to know or care.

The snow continued to fall, deep white and silent, and for a while, the roaring sea abated. At midnight the party goers gathered outside on the terrace and threw snowballs at each other, singing "Good King Wenceslas" around the lamp posts.

At last, everyone went rolling home singing in inebriated harmony, "By the light of the silvery moon", and Sue was able to relax at last. Putting her long legs up over the arm of the chair, she sipped her last drink.

Billy was quite flaked out and fast asleep on the settee. After she had watched him for a few minutes, Sue went over and smoothed back his unruly hair. She kissed his brow and covered him with a rug. Gladys had long gone to bed and the whole place seemed full of memories as the dawn light came across the sea. This had been the best Christmas Eve she could ever remember. Last year old Claud had still been alive but he was never one to entertain and before that, well, she had been in Soho where she had worked half the night. She shuddered and tried not to think about it. But the bad memories still persisted, pushing aside the good ones, so she kept thinking about how the men were very drunk and then often violent and little Gladys had fought with them and pinched their money. It all seemed so unspeakable to her now. She could not bear to think about any of those days in Soho and she knew that it was because if Billy ever found out, he would never forgive her.

The sea seemed to get rough once more, and the howling of the wind was tremendous as the tide came in. Sue shivered a little and kissed Billy once more. "Happy Christmas, darling," she whispered. "May we be together for the rest of our lives. I'll ask for nothing more." Then, as tiredness overcame her, she went off to bed.

On Christmas morning a strong north wind had risen and sleet viciously lashed at the window panes. She turned restlessly in her sleep as Billy's big hand thumped her on the shoulder.

"What is it?" she mumbled sleepily.

"Hear that?" he asked. "It's distress rockets being fired out in the bay. There's a ship in trouble. I'm off down to the lifeboat shed—I might be needed." He was sitting on the bed struggling into his big woolly sweater and pulling on his long boots.

"Oh, Billy," murmured Sue in protest, "you can't go out in this weather."

"Don't be daft, Sue. Wake up! It means I might get a bit of action. So long." He kissed the top of her head and strode out. Moments later she heard the front door bang shut, and she managed to rouse herself enough to sit up and listen to the roaring sea and the strange swishing sound of the rockets going up. Then she flopped back and snuggled down under the blankets. There was not much point in her getting up; she would not be needed.

At ten o'clock Gladys woke her by bringing in a tray of tea. "Mean to say you slept through all that excitement?" she cried.

"What excitement?" Sue was still half asleep.

"Been a ship on the rocks. Six men been rescued—all foreigners," said Gladys.

Then Sue remembered Billy. "Where's Billy?" she cried, with a touch of panic in her voice.

"Need you ask?" sneered Gladys in disgust. "Downstairs getting drunk, of course. Thinks he's a bleeding hero."

Sue jumped out of bed. Dressing hurriedly, she was downstairs like a shot. Although it was so early in the morning and the bar not yet officially opened, it was full. Everyone was talking at once, and oilskins dripped all over the carpet. Behind the bar, Billy was serving drinks hand over fist.

259

His red face wore an ecstatic expression and in a booming voice he called out to his mates and recounted to others the story of the six men being rescued from their sinking ship.

The ship had been a Dutch tramp steamer that had been swept onto those vicious rocks by the heavy storm. Four of the crew had been taken to the hospital in town. The remainder of the crew, the captain and first mate were in the bar. They were big, whiskery men who looked very jaded and depressed.

Billy gave them free drinks and they seemed to cheer up a little. Sue noticed that in the lap of one young man sat a big ginger cat. She rubbed the top of its damp head and the cat purred in satisfaction. "How did you manage to rescue the cat?" she asked.

"We couldn't leave the poor sod on board," replied Billy, explaining how he and one of the crew had scrambled up to the crow's nest to get the cat. Everyone laughed and talked. It was a good start to Christmas Day.

"So, now we've got a cat," said Sue, delighted, picking up the ginger bundle and cuddling him to her.

The captain and his mate stayed for Christmas dinner and afterwards Billy took them into town to visit their pals in the hospital. All this was carried on with great enthusiasm by Billy; he was having a great time. Sue was very pleased for him and even her anxiety about Freddie began to wane.

"Billy has settled down so nicely here," Sue said to Gladys.

But Gladys screwed up her mouth and muttered, "Well, he's got it made, ain't he?" She still had very little affection for Billy and was eaten up inside with jealousy of him.

On Boxing Day it had stopped snowing at last but the sea was still like a raging tornado. The bravest of the locals went up on the cliffs to look at the tramp steamer breaking up on the rocks. Among these was Billy who, because of his big hangover, went up with the American couple to get a breath of fresh air.

Sue could see the small knot of people standing in the cold as she looked out of the window.

"They want a bloody job," said Gladys. "Must be freezing out there."

Sue agreed. "Well, you know Billy, he can't stay away from the sea for long."

As Billy stood on the cliff top, a small bedraggled figure in a long mackintosh and a large cloth cap edged up close to him. "Hallo, 'ow are yer, mate?" a thin voice piped out.

Looking down, Billy recognized Freddie the Sly. "Well, I'll be blowed," he exclaimed. "What hole did you crawl out of?"

"Well, that's nice," whined Freddie. "What a way to greet an old pal."

"Sorry, cock," said Billy giving him a thump

on the back. "But you sodded off without a word. Where did you go?"

"Only went up to London. Had a bit of business up there but the coppers pulled me in because I'd not reported. I was only on parole so they done me and made me finish me time. I just got out."

"Oh, you poor sod," said Billy sympathetically. "What about a drink, then?"

To Billy's astonishment, instead of jumping at this suggestion, Freddie sidled furtively away from him a little and said, "Not now, mate," and looked quickly from side to side like some trapped animal.

"Come on," declared Billy. "Let's go up to the hotel and see Sue."

At this remark Freddie behaved even more oddly. He hunched his shoulders and turned away. "No," he said, "she won't want me up there. I'll see you tonight when it's a bit dark."

"Now, what have you been up to, you sly sod?" growled Billy.

"Nuffink," said Freddie, shaking his head. "Just got a little business to do, somefing what might interest you. I'll meet yer six o'clock by the boathouse." And after these enigmatic remarks, Freddie slid off into the mist.

Billy strode back to the hotel wondering what Freddie was up to. "Can't trust him," he muttered to himself. "I ain't going to get involved in nothing shady, not now that I've settled down here."

So when Billy returned home to lunch he did not mention Freddie to Sue, knowing that she would start to nag him. Sue was in a lazy, languid mood and after lunch she sat with her feet up on the settee reading a love story in a woman's magazine. The log fire blazed brightly, their new ginger cat lay in front on the sheepskin rug. Bowls of Christmas fare were strewn about the sideboard—oranges, apples, nuts and tasty mince pies.

The warm, cosy atmosphere made Billy feel nostalgic. "Looks nice in here," he said. "This room's got a nice warm feeling. I feel like I used to when I got home to me muvver after a long spell in the nick."

Sue looked up from her book and shook her head. "Now don't start thinking about your old lady just because it's Christmas," she said.

Billy grinned. "She'd laugh her head off if she could see me now," he said. "Never had a day out of London in all her long life, and never wanted to neither."

Billy's stomach was full after their big lunch and he was soon dozing peacefully in the deep armchair by the fire. And Sue, unaware that her fate was in the balance, continued to read her magazine.

At five-thirty, Billy was woken by Gladys who grudgingly handed him a mug of tea. He yawned and stretched, drank his tea and then got up. "I might take a walk down to the beach," he said casually. "Won't be long, Sue." Pulling a big woollen cap over his ears and then his sou'wester and oilskins, he went off into the cold air to meet Freddie.

"I'll bung Freddie a tenner," he told himself as he walked down the hill. "Need to get rid of the sod. Don't want him hanging about down here."

Sleet was falling again, driven by a heavy wind. He saw Freddie huddled next to Billy's boathouse which nestled under the cliff. Billy had built it earlier in the year to protect his boat, the *Saucy Sue*, from the winter tides and heavy gales. "Come in, mate," Billy said, unlocking the wooden doors, "there's a bottle of rum in the locker."

"Bleedin' rotten weather," whined Freddie, as Billy lit the hurricane lamp. "Dunno how you stick it down 'ere."

"It's great," said Billy, pouring the rum into two enamel mugs he had pulled down from the cupboard. "You'll never get me back in London."

Freddie swallowed the rum very quickly and the two men sat on a plank beside the boat.

"Well," said Billy, "what's all this you are going to talk to me about? If it's dodgy, I don't want to know. I am going straight down here."

"No, it's nuffink like that," muttered Freddie.

"I just wanted yer to read this." Putting his hand into his pocket he pulled out a letter that was addressed to Sue.

Billy stared at it suspiciously. "It's addressed to Sue," he said. "What are you doing with Sue's letter? You pinched it, didn't you, you sly bugger?"

"Read it!" snivelled Freddie. "Read the bleeding thing, then you might have something to get mad about."

With a puzzled frown on his face, Billy opened up the letter. It was just one page long and written in a big printed hand. In very plain language, the writer of the letter thanked Sue for a hectic and enjoyable weekend and suggested that they did it more often. As he read through this, Billy's face first went white and then scarlet. With a snarl, he screwed up the letter and threw it on the floor. "Dirty rotten sod, you are," he said to Freddie, "prying into other people's business."

"She was on the game in Soho an' was a bloody old tomcat," sneered Freddie, standing up for himself. "And I got more letters to prove it."

Billy was on him in a flash. Swiftly, Freddie tried to wriggle away from Billy's grasp but Billy had grabbed his tie and pulled it tight. Freddie's eyes seemed nearly to pop out of his head as Billy half strangled him.

"You blackmailing bastard!" he shouted, shaking Freddie about like a captured rat.

"Where are the letters? By Christ, I'll do for you if you try to upset Sue and me."

"All right, all right, I only wanted a stake," gasped Freddie. "Let go and I'll give them to you."

Billy let go and Freddie dropped to the floor gasping for breath. The moment he got to his feet, he tried to run for the door, but Billy's big arm barred his way.

"I'm yer mate!" wailed Freddie. "I thought yer ought ter know. That's how she came down here with that kinky old bastard who left her the hotel. Just give me a hundred quid and I'll part up with the rest of the letters. I've got them at me lodgings."

Billy had grabbed the bottle of rum and was drinking from the bottle. His face was red and angry-looking and his eyes had a murderous glint in them. "I'll make you eat those words, you git," he hissed. "Come on, we'll go up and talk with Sue. I'm going to get the bloody truth, I can assure you." He pulled open the door and Freddie quickly pulled away from him with a jerk and fled out into the night. "Come back here, you blackmailing cow son!" roared Billy out into the dark night but only the crashing of the waves and the whistling of the wind were his answers. Freddie had disappeared.

With a grunt, Billy sat down and finished the bottle of rum. There was a deep frown on his face and the drunker he became, the more the veins on his forehead bulged. Almost purple with rage, he got up, kicked the wall and banged his fist against the door. Then he stumbled out into the night and ran all the way back to the hotel.

Sue was in the kitchen making some coffee. After all the festivities they had decided to give the staff a night off, so there was no bar that night. Suddenly Billy dashed in from outside, rushed across the room and grabbed her by the throat. Pushing her viciously against the wall, he held her tight and glared at her with his wild, drunken eyes.

Sue was stunned. "Billy, Billy, whatever's wrong?" she gasped.

"Tell me that you are not a whore," he growled, "and that I've not been living off your immoral earnings. What sort of a ponce am I, for Christ's sake? Now, tell me about the flat in Soho when I was in the nick. I want the truth, Sue, or I swear it's the last word you'll ever utter." To show her what he meant, he squeezed her neck with brutal strength.

"Let go, Billy!" The pain was excruciating. Sue tried to push his hands away but he was much too strong and she felt weak with fear. Freddie had obviously been in contact with him.

Billy then loosened his grip and Sue put her arms about his neck. "Oh Billy, Billy," she cried. "It's your Sue. Don't hurt me," she begged.

"Talk then," he said, swinging off to the other

side of the room and pouring himself a mug of coffee.

"I suppose you've seen Freddie the Sly," said Sue dolefully.

"Yes, I bloody well have," returned Billy, "and I read a filthy letter addressed to you. He says he's got lots more that he wants paying for."

Sue felt as though her heart had almost stopped beating. Her worst fears had been realized. How was she to get out of this? Billy certainly meant what he said about killing her. "It's not true, Billy," she whispered. "Or only some of it is."

"Bloody hell!" swore Billy, slamming down his mug on the table. "So I *did* marry a whore, and God only knows who you have mucked about with." He seemed to pull himself up to twice his normal height and rushed at her again. He took a swipe at her and missed. Picking up his mug, he hurled it at the wall with such violence that it crashed into the shelf which was neatly stacked with glasses. There was a loud crack and the glasses flew in all directions. As a large piece of glass hit Sue in her face, she screamed and instinctively brought up her hands to protect her eyes. Blood poured through her fingers all over her clothes and on to the tiled floor.

Billy looked in horror at the sight of Sue bleeding, then he dashed to her, crying, "Oh Sue! Sue!" He was too late to stop her falling to the floor as she fainted, and he groaned in anguish when he saw the huge gash on her face which ran from her eye to her mouth. Overwrought and panic-stricken, he pulled her tightly into his arms. "Gladys! Gladys!" he yelled.

But Gladys was already there, having been listening to the rumpus from outside. Rushing forward, she pushed Billy away and held a clean white towel to the terrible wound. "Go and get the doctor," she whispered between sobs, "unless you want her to bleed to death."

Without a word, Billy rushed to the telephone.

20

The Cruel Sea

THE next day, an atmosphere of gloom hung over the hotel as the news spread that the missus had had an accident. It seemed she had tripped on a rug carrying a big glass in her hand and had cut her face very badly. It had happened the night before.

Sue was a very popular employer and everyone sent their condolences and flowers. Now she lay upstairs in bed, heavily sedated after the village doctor had stitched up her face. Beside her Gladys sat with her eyes red from weeping.

"It's a deep wound," the doctor had told Gladys. "She really ought to go to the hospital but she's losing so much blood, I'd better do the stitching here."

While Sue was in bed upstairs, Billy served in the bar downstairs. He had been completely devastated by what had happened, and kept crying like a baby. Now he just filled himself with drink. It never occurred to anyone that Billy might have been responsible for his wife's injury. Everyone knew that Sue and Billy were a devoted couple, and nobody knew, except Gladys.

Gladys had cleaned up the mess in the kitchen

before the doctor had arrived, for she knew that Sue would not want anybody to know what really happened. She was glad to do that for Sue but she hated Billy more than ever and stared at him malevolently whenever he crept into Sue's bedroom to kneel beside the bed. "Oh, Sue," he would weep, "I'm so sorry."

Over and over again Gladys would listen to Billy's deep, racking sobs and miserable apologies, and she sighed disapprovingly when Sue on one occasion reached out her hand to him and whispered sleepily "Don't worry, darling, Sue has forgiven you."

And on another occasion, Gladys had snarled at him, "Sling yer bloody hook and leave her alone. Ain't you done enough damage?"

Late that night, Billy staggered out of the bedroom, ran downstairs and went out into the dark night. "I'll find him," he muttered to himself. "I'll get the bastard." He lurched along the beach, fighting the fierce wind until at last, exhausted, he reached the little boathouse and slept all night there.

Early the next morning he set off on his quest for Freddie once more. Going down into the village, he asked his friends down at the harbour. "Has anyone seen a stranger in a long mackintosh?" But he had no luck there. Shaking his head, Billy went on through the village to the town, searching in all the sleazy bars and lodgings, and looking in the hotel registers. Still there was no trace of Freddie. He had completely disappeared.

At the end of the long day, Billy returned home to Sue and sat beside her bed. She seemed more alert and he tried to persuade her to take some nourishment and to cheer her up.

"It hurts me to smile," she said. "I hope I'm not going to have a big scar on my face."

"I'll never forgive myself for hurting you, Sue," Billy said gently. "I don't care about anything else any more."

"It's not all your fault, darling," said Sue. "It's that swine Freddie."

"I swear I'll get him," vowed Billy. "He won't ever bother you again once I've finished with him."

Sue shook her head but winced at the pain. "No, Billy," she said, "let's forget about him. You and I are happy here. We've learned our lesson the hard way. Let's live and love each other—that is all I ask."

Unable to hold back his emotion, Billy put his big unruly head down on the bed and wept like a child.

For a week or ten days peace was restored, and the East Bay Hotel business carried on as before even though Sue was still recovering in bed and Billy spent most of his time at her side. The staff had volunteered to do extra work to keep things running smoothly for the time being.

Gladys continued to sit in the corner of the bedroom, crocheting a long scarf and casting evil looks in Billy's direction as if he were likely to attack Sue again. She would never forget or forgive what he had done.

The day the dressings on Sue's wound were to be removed, the doctor took Gladys aside. "She's going to have a very nasty scar on her face and it's not going to be very pleasant," he said. "When I remove the bandages, I don't want you to react in any way. It's going to be a great shock to her so it's best for us to be as calm as possible."

Gladys nodded in agreement and was glad that Billy was absent. He had gone out fishing that morning.

When the doctor removed the dressing and Gladys saw the beautiful face of her mistress so badly disfigured, she wanted to cry out. Instead, she looked away.

"How does it look, Gladys?" Sue asked anxiously.

"It's fine," replied Gladys turning back. "Can hardly see it." But the bright red angry scar went from Sue's eye to her lip and made her mouth appear distorted.

"Let me see," said Sue. "Hand me the mirror." She reached out towards the hand mirror on the dressing table.

The doctor coughed nervously. "Now, Mrs. Rafferty," he said, "remember that it's going to get better and better with time. It looks a bit red now but the colour will gradually fade until it's quite pale." He picked up the mirror to hand it to her but hesitated again. "And of course, if necessary we can later talk about cosmetic surgery —they can do marvellous things nowadays . . .'"

Instead of allaying Sue's fears as the doctor had hoped, his words only alerted her. "Hand me that mirror!" she shouted. "Let me see!"

The screams that came from Sue's throat as she looked at herself in the mirror rang throughout the hotel. Over and over again she screamed, holding her hands to her face in horror, screaming as if she would never stop.

As the doctor stood immobile and speechless, Gladys gave him a great shove out of the room and rushed to Sue's bedside.

"Oh God! Oh God!" sobbed Sue. "Have you seen my face? It's horrible, it's dreadful. Oh, Gladys, why didn't you warn me?"

But Gladys just cuddled her tight. "It'll be all right, dear," she said reassuringly. "The scar has not healed yet. You'll be as right as rain."

Sue was quite hysterical by now and continued to scream.

Moments later, Billy, who had just returned from fishing, came dashing upstairs to find out what was wrong. He was shocked to find that his sweet, gentle Sue had disappeared, and in her place was a screeching cursing virago who hurled angry, bitter words at him.

"You bastard!" she yelled. "Get out! Get out

of here and don't come near me!" She picked up the breakfast tray and hurled it at him across the room. "Get out! Don't come in here!" she yelled hysterically. "Just look what you've done to me!"

Billy held out his arms to her, and tried to plead with her. But Sue began to hurl everything in sight at him; toilet brushes and pillows flew across the room until finally, with an earsplitting wail, she threw herself back on the bed and continued to scream loudly, kicking her legs in the air.

"Go and get the doctor!" Gladys said to Billy. "Get out of here! You're only upsetting her more with your presence."

As white as death, Billy ran down the road to catch the doctor whom he had passed on his way in, and then he went down to the harbour wall where he sat dejectedly looking out to sea.

An old man puffing his pipe joined him and made a number of comments about the weather but Billy was so down in the dumps that he hardly heard a word he said.

"Heard you was looking for that Cockney git who used to hang about here," remarked the old man.

This Billy did hear. He raised his head and looked at the old man.

"Yesterday," the old man continued, "I took a trip round the cove to Medport and I think I saw him there. There's some sort of hostel in the town there. Lots of slimy ex-convicts staying there. Supposed to be rehabilitating them, they say. Bloody cheek if you asks me, all us tax payers' money down the drain."

Billy leaped off the wall. "Are you sure?" he asked, alert and ready to go. "How do I get to Medport?"

"Well, I sailed me boat o'er there. Wanted to get some repairs done to 'er. I came back by train. But if you go in the boat, it's a long haul and very rocky, it be. You have to know the tides."

"Right!" said Billy determinedly. "I think I'll make it. The tide's full now. Give us the bearings, and I'll go pull out me boat."

"I shouldn't go alone if I was you," warned the old man. "The sea's fair choppy, there's a storm not far out."

But Billy was not put off by these words and soon he had the *Saucy Sue* out of the boathouse and on the runway. The old fellow gave him a hand to push her out.

With a final wave, Billy sailed away into the mist, heading for the shore on the other side of the bay. His raging thoughts were focused on one thing: vengeance on Freddie.

It was evening by the time he arrived at Medport. The harbour lights were winking and the waves rocked his boat and drove it quickly inshore. Billy was cold and hungry but he did not care. All he wanted was to find Freddie. Once he had anchored his boat in the small harbour, he trudged along the pebble beach towards the lights

276

of the town. Medport was a fair-sized town with rows of seaside bungalows, caravan parks and a long winding main street with bars and other tourist attractions. At the bus depot he asked an old man sweeping the floor about the re-habilitation centre. The man stopped sweeping and glared at him suspiciously but then pointed to the end of the street.

Billy soon found the place. It was a large Victorian house standing apart from the other houses in the street. A dim lantern hung in the porch and just inside, in the lobby, several young men were lounging about.

"Anyone seen Freddie Hicks?" asked Billy boldly. No one answered. The young men just surveyed him in stony silence. Having been inside himself, Billy knew the drill. He took out a packet of cigarettes and offered them around. The men accepted eagerly. Then as they lit up, Billy held the match quite close to the face of one long thin lad and muttered, "It's all right, I'm his mate. We done a bit of bird together."

The man's narrow eyes flickered, and he took a long drag on the cigarette. Then, slowly, he looked over the road towards a sleazy bar where music was drifting out into the street.

Not a word needed to be said. "Thanks, mate," said Billy.

As Billy entered the bar, the bright lights dazzled him for a moment, but it only took a few seconds for his eyes to adjust. He spotted Freddie

277

over in a remote corner playing shove ha'penny with another man. Freddie's sandy lank hair hung over his eyes and, judging by his obviously deep concentration, he had a good wager on this old rural game.

Billy bought himself a pint of beer and slowly edged his way over to Freddie's corner. He was very careful not to let Freddie see him first, for he knew that the crafty blighter would spring like a rat from a trap if he did.

Eventually Billy stood beside him. "Hullo, pal," he murmured.

Freddie turned swiftly, tensed up as if to run, but Billy grabbed him by the elbow in a hard, brutal grip.

"Don't start nuffink in 'ere," whispered Freddie. "I ain't supposed to be in 'ere."

"Right, then!" said Billy. "Let's go outside. I only came to settle up that unfinished business, so there's no need to get the wind up, mate."

Hearing this, Freddie relaxed. Sweeping his long hair back off his forehead, he said, "Come on then, let's go."

As they walked up the main street, Billy said, "I don't bear any grudge, Freddie, and I'm quite willing to give you fifty quid for those other letters."

Freddie's little eyes gleamed. "I won't tattle, mate." He gesticulated with his hands in his plausible manner. "But you can see how I'm placed, on the bleedin' rocks, stuck in that old gloomy 'ostel. I ain't even got the price of a packet of fags in me pocket."

Billy handed him a packet of Players. "Come down to the harbour," he said. "I came over in me boat. We can talk there."

"You've got a lot of bottle," grinned Freddie, "sailing round in weather like this. Just wait a tick, I've got the letters in me suitcase at the 'ostel. Yer got the money with yer?" he asked anxiously.

Billy opened his wallet so that Freddie could see it was well stuffed with notes. "Right, mate," said Freddie. "Won't be long." He sidled off like a fox.

As Billy lounged against a brick wall waiting for Freddie's return, Freddie crept up to the hostel dormitory, and pulled the pile of letters from his suitcase. Then he slipped out into the overgrown garden at the back and dug under a bush to find his old friend, the sharp stiletto knife. It was well-wrapped up and well hidden. No weapons like that were allowed in the hostel. "Just in case," he muttered to himself pushing the blade down the inside of his boot. Then, with a satisfied smile on his face, he went to meet Billy.

The two men walked together down to the harbour to the *Saucy Sue*. The boat rocked and rolled at her moorings as the heavy swell of the sea tossed her around.

"Bit dangerous, ain't it?" said Freddie, hesitating on the ladder from the shore.

Billy gave him a quick shove. "Get aboard, yeller belly," he said. His voice had suddenly become much harder.

Without further argument, Freddie jumped aboard and went into the small cabin.

Billy watched him disappear into the cabin, and then quickly unhitched the mooring rope. As he jumped down on to the deck, his heavy figure caused the small boat to leave the harbour wall.

"Some booze in there," said Billy pointing to a small locker.

Freddie went eagerly forward to grab a bottle of rum. Through the porthole, Billy watched the harbour receding fast, then he sat on the bunk to survey Freddie, with a wry hard gleam in his eyes.

Freddie took several long swigs from the bottle. He held it out to Billy. "'ere yer are mate," he said.

Billy shook his head. "Well, got the letters?" he asked.

"Yes, mate, 'ere they are," said Freddie diving into his pocket with one hand and holding on to the bottle with the other. The next moment, the boat lurched and he staggered and fell over. "Cor blimey!" he exclaimed. "The boat's adrift."

But Billy just picked up the bottle, replaced its cap and put it back in the locker. Reaching over, he grabbed the packet of letters from Freddie's grasp.

"Christ!" muttered Freddie, struggling to rise, "the bloody boat's moving out to sea."

"I know," said Billy quietly.

"'Ow am I goin' to get back?" yelled Freddie. "I 'ave to be in by 'alf past nine."

"Don't worry so much, son," said Billy counting out fifty pounds. He placed it on the bunk. "Here's your blood money. Count it, son!" He turned and went outside to start up the outboard motor. The *Saucy Sue* rocked and rode high on the waves. She was now out in the stormy bay and was heading for the open sea.

Freddie grabbed the money but dropped it again, scattering the notes everywhere. As the boat rocked precariously, he fell down again and banged his head on the floor. "For Christ's sake, Billy," he hollered. "Get this bleedin' boat back to the 'arbour. It's murder out there."

Billy stood by the motor as the huge waves crashed over the sides. Deaf to Freddie's pleas, he forced the little boat further and further out to sea, bravely mounting the great Atlantic rollers, occasionally laughing at Freddie's cries for help.

Freddie crawled out of the cabin and held on to the mast, gasping for breath. "Turn around, you barmy bugger!" he cried.

Billy laughed cruelly. "Why? Are you afraid to die? Too bad," he continued, "because tonight you will, one way or another, you evil scum. I nearly killed my Sue because of you." But his words were lost in the wailing of the wind.

Freddie prepared to attack and pulled the knife from his boot. Then he flung himself at Billy, who let go of the wheel and struggled with him in an effort to loosen Freddie's hold on the knife. But with a sudden thrust, the knife entered his side. Billy let out a howl of pain.

"You asked for it," screamed Freddie. "You bastard! Now tell me how to get this boat back to Medport."

Although in pain, Billy's strength had not gone. Reaching out with his great arm, he grabbed Freddie's long hair and cracked his head on the deck. Freddie immediately collapsed and lay limp and bedraggled in the hold, motionless as the waves washed over him.

Still holding his wounded side, Billy valiantly tried to reach the wheel, which was spinning around, to tie it in position for the duration of the storm. But as he staggered towards it, a huge wave that looked like a galloping white horse, swept over him and picked him up as if he were a rag doll. Carrying him high on its foaming crest, it roared off again into the great Atlantic, taking Billy with it.

In the morning when the storm had dropped and the tide had receded, the *Saucy Sue* was found stuck fast on some jagged rocks. Freddie's dead body was quickly found.

Later that day, the local radio station reported that a small motor boat had hit the rocks in the storm, and an unidentified body had been found inside. Gladys heard this and, knowing that Billy had not returned home the night before, guessed immediately what had happened. "Silly fool," she muttered to herself, "I knew he'd do it in the end." She went upstairs and sat beside Sue who was sleeping peacefully. The doctor had sedated her to control her hysteria.

At midday Sue awoke and sat up. Gladys fed her with hot chicken soup as she would a child. Sue asked what time Billy had come in. "I was having such a terrible dream about him," she said. "He was hanging on to something and crying for help and his cries were drowned out by the sound of that hymn, 'Rock of Ages'. I was unkind to him, wasn't I, Gladys?"

"I suppose so," muttered Gladys.

"After all," continued Sue, "it was an accident. He never did it deliberately, did he?"

Two little tears fell out of Gladys' eyes into the soup bowl. "Oh well, I'd better get on," she said, getting up and hurrying out of the room. Her heart was almost breaking at the thought of Sue's great sorrow to come.

Downstairs, the police inspector and the coast guard captain had already arrived to see Sue. Gladys' heart sank. The traumatic moment had come. But according to the police, it was not Billy in the boat at all. The lifeboat captain had apparently identified the man in the boat as Freddie Hicks, an old pal of Billy's. It had, however, definitely been the *Saucy Sue* that had been wrecked in the storm. Everyone was in a quandary about whether to break the news to Sue or wait for Billy, or his body, to turn up.

"By six o'clock the air patrol will hand in their report," the police inspector informed Gladys. "They are at the moment searching the area for signs of a body, so I think we might as well hang on for a bit longer."

Later that afternoon, Sue got up and dressed and sat looking out of the window with a very pensive expression on her pale face. A chiffon scarf was wound around her head and draped over her face at one side to cover the scar. She called Gladys. "Has Billy come home yet?" she asked. "I haven't heard him at all and it sounds very quiet downstairs."

Gladys murmured and muttered but did not give any clear answer. But she watched in horror as Sue then suddenly reached over and turned on the radio. It was already too late to do anything; the voice of the announcer came over the air very clearly: "A search has been going on all day off the coast of Devon for a missing yachtsman. A small boat was wrecked on the rocks in last night's storm. One man was found dead on board but an air sea rescue is still searching for another man who, it is understood, owned the boat."

Sue stood in shock. "Billy!" she called, "it's Billy! Oh Gladys, why did you keep this from me?"

Her little companion rushed to her and put her

arms about Sue's waist, hugging her gently as she always did. "Sue, Sue don't panic, dear. It was Freddie the Sly they found in the boat. Billy might yet turn up."

Sue sat down again and turned to look out of the window again. "My Billy's gone," she said calmly. "The terrible cruel sea has taken him from me."

The winter sun floated on the horizon like a huge orange ball and the grey, now calm sea washed quietly over the rocks. Sue sat very still and quiet just staring out across the water.

And that was how she stayed for many days. Many people came up to her room to offer their condolences but she never seemed to notice any of them. She just sat watching the sea with her big dark eyes in a bewildered manner. And not one tear did she shed.

Down in the bar the locals wept for her and the extrovert Cockney, Billy, who had been their host and companion.

"I wonder what he was doing so far out in the bay," one of them said, "in a bad storm, too."

Old John, who usually sat down on the harbour wall, sucked his pipe. "Saw him, I did. Helped him get the *Saucy Sue* out. He was looking for that fellow what got drowned. I told Billy that I'd seen this fellow in Medport, but I warned him. 'Don't go alone,' I sez, 'dangerous tides out there.' But he went just the same."

Upstairs, at last, Gladys had persuaded Sue to undress and get into bed. But Sue seemed to be in a trance. All she would say, as Gladys tucked her in, was "It's all my fault, Gladys, God has punished me for my sins."

Spring had come at last and the daffodils were once again in bloom in the garden of the hotel. Clumps of golden blooms that Sue had planted grew under the trees and along the path the primroses and tiny crocuses declared their beautiful presence. This year Sue had no eyes for previously beloved flowers. Still she sat upstairs in her bedroom just staring out of the window with a chiffon scarf round her head and face, or standing alone on the shore.

Billy's body had never been recovered. For a while, Sue had hoped that, having settled his score with Freddie, Billy had disappeared back into the underworld of his youth, but in her innermost heart, she knew that he was gone forever. That cruel sea which he had loved so much had gobbled him up like some enormous monster. And she had finally known this to be true when a memorial service had been given for Billy in the little fisherman's church and his name had been added to the remembrance board in gold ink. She knew for certain then that her big, robust Billy was no more.

Sue had taken to going on her own to the shore every day and would sit beside the breakwater out of the wind and watch the water, always waiting and watching for that grey stormy sea to return her lover to her arms.

When she did this, Gladys would keep an eye on her and go down and persuade her to come home. "Come on, Sue, you've had enough for one day. It's blowing up cold."

Sue showed no interest at all in the hotel which she just left in charge of the staff. They were very distressed about her state of mind and felt that their lovely alert Sue seemed to have left them with her Billy.

"Ought to do something about her," advised Bess. "She's going to lose her wits if she mopes about much longer. Can't you get her to take a holiday?" she asked Gladys. "We'll carry on here till she's better."

Gladys thought it was a good idea but when she broached the subject to Sue, there was no response. Sue just stared at her in a scornful manner and said nothing. So Gladys knew not to pursue it.

One morning, however, Gladys was amazed to find Sue sitting at her desk in the office writing a letter. Gladys did not comment but Sue turned from the desk and said, "If anything happens to me, this hotel is all yours. Then you'll have an inheritance to last you for your lifetime. I'm writing to the lawyer in London to get it legalized. There are also those Maritime Holdings shares that I have.

I've put them in there." She pointed to a drawer in her desk.

Immediately little Gladys was like an angry bantam hen. Glaring furiously, she strutted up and down the room. "For Gawd's sake, Sue," she said, "give over. I don't want yer bleedin' money. All I ask is for you to pull yourself together and let us leave this bloody gloomy cold place and go back to where we belong."

Sue just drooped her head and said, "Don't get awkward, Gladys, where would we go?"

"Back to London!" cried Gladys vehemently. "I never did like it here and you ain't the same person. We was close friends when we was up in London." Gladys started to weep.

Sue cuddled her. "Well, dear, you can go if you want, if you're really unhappy here."

"Sue," sobbed Gladys, "I couldn't get along without you, now, let's get home."

Sue shook her head. "I can't leave, Billy," she said. "It's no good, I've tried hard but he calls me all the time. Whether I'm asleep or awake, he's out there calling to me."

Gladys threw up her arms in despair. "Oh, my Gawd! Whatever am I going to do with you?"

"Go and make a cup of tea, Gladys," said Sue. "I'm going to take a short walk."

"But it's getting dark," cried Gladys.

Sue did not answer. She got up, put a dark-blue chiffon scarf around her head and pulled on her raincoat. Then she gave Gladys a kiss on the top of her grizzled head. "I'll expect a nice cup of hot tea when I get back. You stay and make it, there's a good girl." In a slow, majestic way she took a quick look round the room where she had spent her happiest days with Billy then calmly went out into the cool spring air.

It was dusk. The birds twittered as they settled in their nests and a sweet scent of blossom from the May trees was in the air. Sue was oblivious to it all. With a vacant expression on her face, she glanced around her garden and then slowly went off towards the cliff top. There she stood a slim dark shadow, watching the tide cover the rocks below. "Billy," she whispered, "are you there?"

A gannet gave a shrill cry and the waves battered the cliff.

"I'm coming to you, my Billy, I can't live without you, darling."

A dark mist began to rise and Sue wavered on the edge of the cliff. "Billy! Billy, darling," she pleaded, "give me the courage to jump." Then, bending her body forward, she took a final step towards the edge. But as she did so, two strong arms grabbed her from behind. "Sue! Sue! You mustn't! I thought you were my friend? How could you think of deserting me?" Some kind of telepathic sense had told Gladys to follow Sue outside, and now the two women stood there, poised on the edge of the cliff, mistress and servant clinging to each other like frightened children.

Sue stared down at the funny wizened face as Gladys' words rang in her ears.

"Sue, Sue, it's me, Gladys." Gladys' stubby fingers gripped her tight. "I know you've lost your Billy," she said earnestly. "And I'm sorry, because I hate to see you so unhappy. But you haven't lost everything, Sue. You've still got me, you've still got me to look after you and love you. You can't end it all just like that and leave me. You know I love you, Sue, and," she added as tears appeared in her eyes, "I thought you loved me, too."

For the past weeks Sue had been shut off from the rest of the world, thinking only of Billy who was no longer with her. But gradually now, seeing the tears pouring down Gladys' imploring face, the words began to penetrate the barrier that had detached her for so long, and a strange sensation seemed to travel from Gladys' strong hold across to her own body.

Slowly Sue began to hear again the crashing of the waves against the rocks below and see the muted colours of the sea grasses around them. She smelled the salt in the air and heard the rustle of the wind in her hair. And there before her was Gladys, her friend, who, with utter devotion and love had brought her back in touch with the world. With a little cry of relief, she hugged her tight. "You're right, Gladys," she murmured, "I've been nothing but selfish. You are my friend and I could never leave you. I've promised you that before, and I'm sorry for all this . . . Billy's gone and I have to accept that."

Gladys was leading her away from the cliff towards the hotel. "I'll stop complaining about being here, Sue," she said. "I promise I'll stop pining for London. I understand that you would want to stay down here where you were so happy with your Billy."

There was silence for a few minutes while Sue was deep in thought. Finally she spoke. "No, Gladys," she said. "We're going back to London. Being down here will only remind me constantly of Billy. We have to live in the present, not the past. You have never been happy here and we had some good times in the city. No, I'm going to sell up and buy a comfortable flat in London." She touched the scar on her face. "I don't know if I'll ever work again, looking like this, but I could have plastic surgery, as the doctor said. I don't have to decide now. We'll just take it one step at a time."

And so the two women walked back to the hotel with their arms linked—a tall, willowy figure next to a short, squat shape. Both had resigned and calm looks on their faces as they took their slow, deliberate steps away from the wild, murderous sea towards a fresh start and a new life together. And both knew that despite all their tragedies and losses in the past, so long as they had each other, the future ahead was bright for them . . .

THE END

Other titles in the
Charnwood Library Series:

Other titles in the
Charnwood Library Series:

The Man from St. Petersburg	*Ken Follett*
Triple	*Ken Follett*
No Time for Tears	*Cynthia Freeman*
Blake's Reach	*Catherine Gaskin*
I Know My Love	*Catherine Gaskin*
Sara Dane	*Catherine Gaskin*
The Cardinal Sins	*Andrew M. Greeley*
Wheels	*Arthur Hailey*
Threat	*Richard Jessup*
Ice!	*Tristan Jones*
The Incredible Voyage	*Tristan Jones*
Firestarter	*Stephen King*
Follow the Drum	*James Leasor*
Mario's Vineyard	*Michael Legat*
The Chancellor Manuscript	*Robert Ludlum*
The Matlock Paper	*Robert Ludlum*
The Osterman Weekend	*Robert Ludlum*
The Rhinemann Exchange	*Robert Ludlum*
The Scarlatti Inheritance	*Robert Ludlum*
Rogue Diamond	*James Broom Lynne*
An Indecent Obsession	*Colleen McCullough*
The Hidden Target	*Helen MacInnes*
Cattleman	*R. S. Porteous*
The Mahdi	*A. J. Quinnell*
Man on Fire	*A. J. Quinnell*
Never Leave Me	*Harold Robbins*
Never Love a Stranger	*Harold Robbins*
79 Park Avenue	*Harold Robbins*

Other titles in the
Charnwood Library Series:

Other titles in the Charnwood Library Series: